MIDNIGHT BREW
THE SEQUEL TO VAMP CITY

BY C.D. BROWN

This novel is dedicated to
the memory of my aunt
Elyse Derbes, the closest I
ever had to a Rosalinda.

Prologue

Another Friday night arrived and Aida Menendez had no plans. Again. Her mother hadn't confined her to the house exactly, but she had said unless she knew where Aida would be at all times that she wouldn't be allowed out. And any time after dark, Aida had to be where Mama could see her. This policy had reduced the number of Aida's close friends to zero because no one wanted to deal with her mom's shit. Aida felt constrained being housebound, very unfair to a 19 year old, but she couldn't work up the courage to defy her mother.

Her brothers had. As soon as the evening meal was over, they disappeared until well after midnight. They jumped in their cars, these wild Frankenstein monsters of hydraulics, stereo equipment, and rims so shiny they created rainbows, and then rumbled through the streets of Boyle Heights, cruising for any action: races, drinks, and all the bad _chicas_ whose mothers didn't control their every move.

When Aida complained, she got the hard matriarchal line. Mama would say in Spanish, "Boys are nothing but animals. Why would you want to spend any time with them?"

She would answer in English, a language her mother could understand but not speak. "How would I even know? I meet nice boys at school all the time, but they get afraid when I talk about your rules."

Mama would first snort then laugh. "If they can't stand up to me, then they aren't husband material." Then her face would soften even though Aida felt patronized. "You are a delicate flower. My only daughter. You need to be protected from all that nastiness until you find a good man."

Usually, Aida stopped the argument there. No doubt her composition professor at Cerritos College would call Mama's logic circular, but Mama also didn't like Aida going to school.

"You should be working, bringing in money. This school costs too much." Just another part of Mama's strategy to box in her girl until Mama felt ready to release her. But Aida's mind was expanding and this little trap wouldn't stay closed for long.

So she went to her room and her only solace: the Internet. She started with the social media sites: Instagram and Snapchat. When she saw what Selena Gomez had worn to a movie premiere, a bright yellow tube-topped minidress that clung to her form and exposed a good four inches of cleavage, Aida jumped over to YouTube to see any video footage from the event. Selena's shoes were bright white with six-inch heels, the star goose stepping like all females who faced a red carpet with tall shoes and tight dresses.

Aida thought Selena was a bit extra but wondered if she could pull off that outfit. Their builds were quite similar, although Aida's bust was smaller and her butt bigger. Aida knew she'd look super hot in that get up, but then the usual thought appeared: Mama would never allow that.

After the Entertainment Tonight video ended, Aida saw a make-up tutorial in the "Watch Next" column where the presenter was copying a look Selena had worn a few months over. With nothing else to do, Aida clicked on it.

The design was cute: eyeliner horns that were lighter than the heavy hand most young girls had, a mix in the eye shadow to give it a sunset color, and an eyelash curler technique that really separated each hair. But the peppy Latina in the video, only a few years older than Aida, made Aida's mind race. She pictured this bubbly kid out in Hollywood or Downtown L.A., walking into any club she wanted, draped with hot men, and drinking rainbow-colored cocktails from martini glasses. In other words, Aida saw her having fun.

Something snapped inside Aida. She dug out her make-up kits from under the bed and sat in front of her table, three offset mirrors ready for her to paint up. She was expected to look nice for Sunday mass, but that was the only time she put on even a little coloring. She just wanted to see her face look as good as that girl on the screen. Just once and right now. As she brushed, painted, and curled, she felt transformed, a butterfly finally pushing its way out the cocoon. As she started working on her lashes, she heard music, that bumpy, driving *Norteño*. She recognized the band—Los Tucanes de Tijuana. Her brothers loved to pump their music through the car's subwoofer to emphasize the big polka beat. Lots of kids loved this new take on the old music, especially in L.A. where everyone outside the neighborhood tried to tamp down Mexican culture.

She went to the window to discover the music's source: the creepy house up the block was having the party. Even though they were Mexican like everybody else, they were shunned. Mama would never speak of them without spitting as if they were devils. Her brothers had once tried to talk to the girl who owned it because she was hot, but she wouldn't even talk back. Something about her was weird because Aida was sure she had seen the same woman growing up and she never seemed to change. But the few times Aida had caught sight of her, she could see the power radiating off her. Not only was she beautiful, she was definitely a badass.

Aida finished her lashes and looked in the mirror. While this was way more than she'd ever done, she felt good, maybe even empowered, by the beautiful woman staring back at her. As she heard a volcano of laughs from the party, she made up her mind. She was sneaking out. The rest of the neighbors may hate these people, but Aida would bet that badass woman would like her. She could be just the thing to get herself released from Mama's wing.

She looked in her closet: nothing as nice as that Selena dress. Seeing the boring array of Sunday dresses and plain Jane hoodies nearly killed her spirit, but she rallied. No one dresses up these days. She just had to be hood appropriate. She pulled her nice jeans over her boxers and layered her newest flannel over her sleeveless white tee. Since she still had her toenails polished from last Sunday, she slipped on her Birkenstocks. With one last breath, she carefully pushed up on her window, climbing out slowly. Even though it was only a first-floor drop, the sandals clopped when they hit the driveway, but that didn't stir anyone. She pulled the band from her hair, letting it flow to its full length, and strode across the street with a determination she'd never felt before.

But that determination waned as she approached the driveway fence. It was aluminum but woven through with those strands so no one could see through. The music was really loud as she paused. She quailed, deciding to make sure it was a full party before entering. The house next door belonged to her father's friend Josue who collected old, junky cars. Skirting between the fence and a 1977 blue Cadillac more rusted than painted, she got up on her toes but stayed under the shadow of a small palm tree.

As she peered into the backyard, she got a good look at her neighbor. The woman was lanky, showing off her long legs and tight butt in very tiny denim shorts but stayed tough with a weathered biker-style leather jacket. Her hair was so dark that it must have been dyed, especially dark since the white woman she talked to had hair the color of the moon. This white lady was also dressed down, outfit nearly exactly as Aida. This gave the younger woman some confidence. She was going to fit in after all.

She walked to the end of the fence, stopping to fluff her hair once more. As she prepared to round out into the street, she heard a bunch of cars pull up. Scared again, she squatted down and titled her head out.

Four black Escalades rumbled at the corner. They all stopped at the same time and a bunch of black men streamed out of the SUVs, lining themselves up along the house's porch. She held her breath when she saw a few of them scale the outside as easy as if they had a ladder. What the hell was this?

In under thirty seconds, the party went from bumping to a brawl. Aida couldn't figure why neither side used guns, but she knew she had to get back to her house. She'd heard shrieks which sounded like death cries of at least ten people. Why did her first break-out attempt come with a drive-by? She wiped at her tears, her hands now bright with eyeshadow. She knew she had to act, so she dashed out to the end of the driveway. She gasped when she saw one of the black men guarding the front door. He stared her down, then sprinted straight at her. Were his eyes somehow red?

Aida knew she couldn't get across the street, so she bolted to the Cadillac. Josue never locked them, figuring no one would be stealing these heaps. She made it into the back seat, pushing down each lock as fast as she could. As she got the driver's front pushed down, the man slammed his fists on the back door opposite her. How had he gotten here so fast? She screamed, hoping that someone close would hear. Her voice was overwhelmed by a fluctuating sound. She knew it well like everyone in Los Angeles: police choppers. She was safe or so she thought.

The man looked up and smiled. The helicopters didn't bother him at all. He continued to beat his fist against the window. Cracks webbed their way around the points of his impact. In a few more punches, she thought he might break through.

And then he smiled wider, a predatorial look. His teeth were so bright and long. She had a weird realization: those were fangs. Were these people all vampires?

That thought crushed her screaming. As something cracked in her brain, she could only whimper. Dying at some gangsta's hand was one thing. But the undead? Her mind's eye blinkered as he reached back for his final crash through the window. But something else took over her vision, a blinding light bright as the sun. The copter hovered over them, spotlighting her attacker. She took one final look at him, his fist raised but his face drooping. In that quick second, he became a pillar of ash in the form of a human, something like Lot's wife who Aida remembered from Bible study. As fast as it formed, it dropped away, a mound of dust and pile of clothes scattered quickly by the chopper's beating blades. And with that, she slipped into the blackness.

Josue found Aida the next morning. He tried to talk to her, but despite her open eyes, she couldn't communicate. Josue called 911 then sprinted across the street. Aida's father got her to sit up, but no words penetrated Aida's brain. As the ambulance arrived and they strapped her in the back, Mama wailed in the middle of the street. "I raised her better than this. I swear to the Mother of God, I raised her better than this!"

Part One: Reborn in Fire

Chapter One

"New idea: travel agency for the supernatural." Sophia Fontanelle looked out the back door of the apartment she'd rented for the week. Even though the San Francisco neighborhood was called Noe Valley, this place was up high and she could see all the way to downtown, the night sky and a few blinking stars framing this hilly city. She cradled her cellphone between ear and shoulder as she closed the door. "Getting here was such hell. We need people to accommodate for that."

"First of all, there's already a system in place. They're called thralls. Vampires love holding that shit over your head." Pamela Garland's laugh, deeply cynical to Sophia's ears, hopefully helped process the lingering pain of the death of her lifelong partner Jim. That she, a former thrall, now held power over many undead as CEO of VampAmp, a L.A. tech company which specialized in vampire-centric apps and social media, might also be a balm. "Secondly, since I know you're anti-thrall—"

"Aren't you?"

"Of course, dear. But that's beside the point. The real point is that the Internet destroyed travel agencies. Airplanes, hotels, Air B&B, rental cars—it's all do it yourself now."

"The things you learn when you break out of your bubble."

"That should have been popped a long time ago. Anyway, when's the meeting?"

"In a couple of hours. I'm going to stroll among the living for a bit since I've never been here." Sophia ran her hands through her hair, wishing she could stare into a mirror to get her look right. Ah, well. Vanity was a good exchange for eternal life.

"Oh, the parties we used to have." Pamela wasn't old, mid 60s although she looked much younger, but the life was well lived. "Jim said I missed all the good things in the '60s, but the '80s? You'd laugh at punk rock Pam with her green hair and bondage gear."

"I'm sure if there were pictures of farm girl Sophie, you'd react the same way."

"Yeah. But I hear San Fran's changed. It might be hard getting a group together there." Pamela's voice had a slight waver. Sophie rarely heard doubt from her, even only for a second.

"We'll see. Let me go. I'm ready to experience a walking town again."

As she walked to Church Street to descend to the Mission District, she reflected on her trip north. No one could drive her, not even her boyfriend Jeremiah. Since his turning from werepossum to vampire, he'd been spending much of his time in the VampAmp office where he worked as a community manager for the online boards. He blogged about his transition and bridged the two communities, although he mostly had an audience of werewolves since lycanthropes like his former self were rare. According to Pamela, the number of registered werewolves had tripled since he started. And while he could work remotely, they were doing a major redesign and needed all hands in the office.

It was fine with Sophia. She needed a little time away and really wanted to connect the Bay Area vamps with their Southern Cal counterparts so she could continue the mission of David Hennessey, her sire and the one to espouse the end of hunting humans. Maybe one day she could get vampires to stop being predators and start being accepted by the world, an impossible task maybe but surely a noble one.

But when she started planning this trip, so many little things got in the way. She could fly, but those giant deathtraps they called airplanes scared the hell out of her. Jeremiah teased that she could fly herself as a bat, but that only got him pinches. So she had to take the train from downtown L.A., but the sunlight margins were thin. She ended up paying an extra 100 dollars to take the Pacific route instead of the inland so she could get to the rental as quickly as possible. She'd arranged an early pick up of keys, but still, she found herself dragging her bags uphill blocks from the apartment with less than a half hour until sunlight. When she got upstairs, she saw the main bedroom faced the street, twelve-foot windows with wispy curtains dominating the wall. She ran all around the apartment, hearing the phrase "tons of light" bursting from a real estate agent's mouth. She had to sleep in the bathtub with the curtain closed to make sure no sun slipped in.

But that was last night. Earlier she went to the corner store and bought black construction paper and taped it over the small windows in the second bedroom. And now she was out in the street, the cool night and moist air tingling her skin.

The hilly angle of 24th Street flattened out at Valencia, one of the main strips in this section of town, and Sophia could see the shining neon signs stretching out to her left. At midnight on Friday, this street was still full of action. She had asked Montana, the woman vampire who set up the meeting, if any places were friendly to their kind and had gotten a few names. As she cruised the streets, her predator senses kicked in. So many couples arm in arm passed by, followed by packs of young men and woman, both on the prowl. The pheromones were thick here as bar after bar pulsed with rock music and drunk young'uns. She'd gone a few blocks down when she saw what she was looking for: Radio Habana.

Small, maybe 400 square feet, the bar had a dusty feeling to it like drinking in a thrift shop. But almost every seat was taken with leather jacketed twentysomethings sipping on bright green margaritas and a few more lingered in the doorway puffing on vapes. She saw one stool open at the end of the bar and slipped in using her vampire quickness so no one else would get the spot. Bass-heavy reggae pumped out of a '90s era CD jukebox. She looked around at the wall full of black and white pictures, all hung asymmetrically and barely fitting into their allotted space. Over the door transom, a mask that looked like the evil queen in Snow White sat in the middle of a spider web, eight legs attached at odd points. A G.I. Joe doll sat entwined near her, waiting for the evil to strike. So much art hung in odd places that it overwhelmed Sophia. She waited until the bartender, a middle-aged Mexican man in a sparkling white *guayabera* shirt, pointed her way.

"I hear you have a *sangria especial.*"

The man nodded, a sly smile streaking across his face. Did he give her a slight bow? Sophia wasn't sure, but he disappeared into a curtained-off room and returned with a short glass full of ruby liquid, a few limes floating on top. Sophia sipped and her trained palate knew exactly what it was: pig blood. It wasn't the highest quality, but that little squeeze of citrus took it to a better level.

She saw the bartender look up then shift over to the sound system. He muted the jukebox and turned up a CD player in front of the bottles. At that moment, a six-foot four *senorita* dressed in the full Spanish regalia swept into the room. The magenta dress clung tightly to hip and chest, spanning out in white and pink layered ruffles at the knee and forearm. The headdress was all black, four large pins with webbing in between and holding a lace veil that Sophia could tell was old. The woman popped open her peacock-bedecked fan as the new music swelled, a syrupy *bolero* older than anyone in the room—Sophia excepted—and sang along. Her voice contained great power, each note of the ballad smeared thick with pathos.

Sophia could tell this was a trans woman. She had seen many drag performers, going as far back as her Storyville days, but this was different. No lip-syncing. The singer was belting it out with a pure voice when the notes called for it, but vibrato when some extra soul was necessary. When the song wrapped up with sweltering crescendo, the bar exploded with applause.

The performer moved over to the bar where the bartender handed her a basket which she held out to the patrons on her left. When she looked at Sophia and then down at the vampire's drink, she stopped.

"I normally don't break character, but are you Sophia?" Her voice was soft and accentless.

"Yes."

"I'm Montana."

"Oh my! You were great!"

"Thank you. Look, let me get my tips quickly. Meet me down the street at the Latin America Club in twenty minutes."

"Sure."

Montana resumed her haughty diva demeanor, waving her fan and bowing at each tip. She collected the cash at the bar and stuffed it into a purse. She pointed down the street, nodded and smiled at Sophia, then swept out with as much drama as her entrance.

Sophia finished her drink, paid, then stepped out the door. This new bar where Montana directed her was closer to 24th Street, but she took her time, scoping out the scene. This wasn't exactly New Orleans, but it had the same raw energy of a walking district. The people were out for fun, shifting between the many venues.

The Latin American Club was a typical American dive bar, an open room with a pool table and booths by the windows. But the feeling was very San Francisco: psychedelic and gothic art in ornate frames, the Mexican string of flags across the transom, and young people in various leather clothing drinking pints of beer. Sophia sat in a booth, looking around until Montana came out of the bathroom. Sophia saw the hair was all natural, falling in long, dark ringlets around her shoulders, but now she wore a Mexican cowboy shirt in maroon and gold, indigo boot cut jeans with pointy brown leather boots. Sophia stood and Montana enveloped her in a hug.

"Welcome, my dear. I hope our town is treating you okay."

They sat in the booth.

"I'm only just venturing out, but this strip seems fun."

"Here and Mission Street have a great vibe. I usually stick around here because it's easier to perform. I can make my bread without having to get in a car."

"I'm still dealing with the whole car thing."

"In L.A.? Honey! All that racetrack makes me too nervous. I prefer boots on the ground. Speaking of which ..." Montana stood. "The meeting's just down the street. We have a connect with the community college, so it's in there."

"Great. I hope everyone is enthused."

As they stepped outside, Montana put a hand on Sophia's shoulder. "I think your ideas are amazing. But I must warn you, things here are different." Montana brought her clasped hands to her lips. "Not bad, but different. Just be prepared."

Sophia was confused, but she hoped her vampire reform movement was universal. Maybe she could find ways to adjust to the problems.

Six months after they found her passed out in the back of the Caddy and three days before her twentieth birthday, Aida stirred in her hospital bed. After a week at USC Medical Center, she was moved to Rancho Los Amigos, a care facility for coma patients. The doctors refused to call it anything else since her brain and body were functioning, but her consciousness wasn't alert. The doctor, a Japanese woman who looked only a few years older than Aida, told Mr. and Mrs. Menendez she'd never seen anything like it.

"There's no trauma." She stopped, looking to be more specific. "There's no physical trauma. Nobody hit her or anything like that. It's like she fainted and never woke up."

So Mama started going in earlier to work so she could spend her afternoons looking over Aida. The hospital was close to home, but this nursing home was in Downey, another half hour east on the interstate. The city was famous—some might say infamous—as the Mexican Beverly Hills, where nicer houses with wider lots were the reward for those who'd finally made it out of poorer spots like Boyle Heights or Compton.

"That was the only way any of us would ever get to Downey," Raphael, the oldest brother, joked at the table later that week. Mama slapped him hard on the back of the head, but the other two brothers laughed. When she pulled her *chancla* off her right foot, threatening to spank all of them, they scattered but didn't stop laughing.

Thus began long afternoons of sitting next to Aida and watching *telenovellas* until it was time to go home and cook dinner. But on the day she stirred, Mama cried.

She looked like she was fighting, twitching right and left like she was tied up or something. Then her arms spasmed and she slapped the bed. Her head lifted off the pillow, but she banged down three, four times. Mama's joy had turned to fear as she yelled down the hall for the doctor on duty.

Doctor Heng, a second generation Cambodian American in his first job post residency, had taken an interest in the young Latina. A coma so unusual right out of school had kept him monitoring the case, even when little had happened for months. He kept her on a heart monitor only because they didn't know what else to do. When he entered the room, he was glad that equipment was hooked up because now Aida's pulse was racing.

Mrs. Menendez screamed in Spanish, Heng catching "God" and "Jesus" within her frantic outbursts. He called out to the nurse who brought in the crash kit just in case Aida's heart stopped. He was about to inject her to calm the twitching when she sat straight up. She inhaled sharply as if she had been drowning and just surfaced. When Aida was fully awake, Mama engulfed her in a bear hug.

"Mama!" Aida's first words had anger within them. The mother let her go and Aida stretched herself out. Dr. Heng knew she would need some physical therapy; that long in bed would certainly lead to muscle atrophy. As the young woman's shoulders and joints popped and cracked with new movement, her breath slowed and she finally realized where she was. Now she embraced her mother. "It's okay, Mama. I'm back now. I'm back."

Over the next week, Aida continued to surprise Dr. Heng. She was very strong and in need of no therapy. It's like her time away had been fewer than one night or had been a grand vacation. He wasn't sure which.

A few days later, he decided to roll her to the front door himself, something he never did for patients. This girl was so extraordinary, but she wouldn't say a word about what she experienced. He knew this was his last chance to get an answer

He asked, "I know you're leaving, but did you see anything when you were down? Was there dreaming? Or just blackness?"

"Dr. Heng," she said, a sarcastic edge in her voice, "Believe me when I say this. It was the best time of my life."

They reached the center's exit and Aida popped out of the chair and into her mother's car. As they disappeared up the street, he made a note to himself to check back in with her later. The whole experience was too wild. It needed to be documented somewhere.

The first thing Aida saw after she blacked out in the back of the Caddy was roses, a thick hedge with emerald leaves, thorny stems, and ruby flowers surrounding her with no clear exit. This trap was circular, yet she felt the need to move. Approaching the hedge worked: it split and formed a path for her to follow.

While the hedge had almost glowing colors, the air seemed white: not light, not dark, not nothing, just devoid of anything except illumination. Aida paused and looked down. She wore a green dress strapped so her shoulders were bare with a skirt hanging just below her knee. She was barefoot, but the dirt path didn't bother her naked soles. In fact, it felt soft and velvety. She followed the hedge path, too tall for her to see over. After a few minutes of walking, she emerged at a circular hub where many of these paths converged, too many to count without serious effort. A Ston pyramid, three times the size of her house, stood on a short, grassy hill. Carved into the lower blocks were pictures of roses with snakes as stems. From what she could tell, it looked Aztec although her family had never traveled to those sites. While Aztec culture had been important to many of her high school teachers, her parents were too Catholic to care about such ancient symbols.

An open arch on what she thought of as the north side let her inside the structure. She entered to see the walls were thin compared to the size of the structure. The inside was wide open with only a giant statue in the middle, the pedestal taller than Aida herself. As she wound around to see the face of the statue, Aida fell to her knees. The giant figure before her looked just like the Virgin of Guadalupe, the omnipresent saint found pictured in almost every Mexican household. Reflexively, Aida began praying Hail Marys with her eyes closed. But a voice in her head stopped her and she lifted her head to look the statue in the eyes.

"Little one, no need to pray to the European gods. You have followed the plants to the roots and now is the time to re-center yourself."

Aida noticed many things different about this statue and the one Mama prayed to in the little cubby hole in her bedroom. First of all, her skin was much darker, looking less Spanish and more like those Mexicans who had deep Indian heritage. Aida could now perceive the rose bushes at the foot of the statue, these not stone but alive. Finally, the goddess' robe was a deep red, almost burgundy. Normally, the Virgin was seen in white and green or at least pale clothes. This red undercut the whole virginal picture.

Aida tried to find her voice. Coughing dryly, she spoke. "Who are you?"

"I'm known by many names: Coatlaxopeuh sometimes but mostly as the Earth Mother, Tonantzin." The voice pulled Aida closer, alluring and sympathetic at the same time.

"Why am I here?"

"It's been a long time since anyone has visited this realm. I did not pull you here, but your spirit may have. My followers are few."

"You were replaced, I guess. Mexicans think you're Mary, Mother of God."

"It was a fine disguise for a while, but I have felt my power wane. There's little but a few sparks in the waking world. You may not know why, but I welcome you. Together we shall find the reason." Somehow, the stone looked directly into Aida's gaze. "I am known for new beginnings. Your journey will bear out your power." Aida flushed at the words. Her journey? Her power? Every feeling that had ever kept her down released itself, leaving her unencumbered for the first time since she was a baby.

In this liminal space, Aida had no idea of time. She had no day of chores and nights of sleeping, only instruction and practice. Tonantzin pointed her to the corn seeds, telling Aida where to plant them. The vast field that stretched to the horizon soon saw sprouts. As they grew, Aida's consciousness filled the plants, seeing the way energy pushes up the stalks and into the grain. In each part of the process, she was shown the rivers life creates and how Tonantzin was the source.

As the stalks produced their cobs and then withered, Aida penetrated the process of death and its return to the river, visions of the oroboros and life's greater cycles. From there, Tonantzin instructed her about the balance of four, the sacred number. The directions and the winds originated within all of us, centering our being and imbuing the middle point with its power. And that power was strong. Crossroads and other waypoints held immense energy.

But the next quartet was important for her Earthly journey. The four elements—air, fire, water, and earth—each held magic. The believer could tap into their energy as a source for spells. The practitioner needed to hone their connection, but it was there for anyone focused enough to draw out the enchantment.

After these revelations, she talked with Tonantzin. "Mother, why has my world forgotten all of your knowledge?"

"Our existences have always been separated by a veil. In earlier days, when the Earth was integral with humanity, it was thinner. Our connection was direct: the power and the growth connected to the work. But while the severing was slow, it's almost complete. But remember our lessons: all return to the source. You may be one who can change the direction."

"Are there others in my world who know your secrets?"

"My wisdom is like the stars. It's infinite but perceived in small points. Even when you depart here, your own knowledge will be greatly inadequate." Aida couldn't contain her disappointment, for the statue smiled upon her. "You are still young. The path is wide and extends in many directions. You will pick the right one for you and narrow your life until your need for me will be minimal. But it will take some time."

"When will I be ready to return?" Even after all this work, Aida still felt incomplete.

"One test remains, my daughter."

This sounded ominous, but Aida had moved through this world effortlessly. Hopefully, this test wouldn't be too hard.

Chapter Two

Montana said they had some time, so she suggested they walk down to Mission Street. The vibe shifted from Valencia, going from hipness to Mexican quite quickly. While the same type of people roamed the street, the businesses changed. Many more restaurants, groceries, knick knack shops, all with bilingual signs. As they approached from 24th Street, Sophia saw a huge line outside a small restaurant.

"What's that?"

Montana smiled. "Oh, I miss that place. El Farolito. The Lighthouse. It's the place to go at the end of the night."

"Mexican food?"

"Yeah. San Francisco style. It's all about the burritos. Fat like this." Montana widened her hands to the length of a football. "But that's all gone in my undeath."

"Did you grow up here?" They had turned to head down Mission, the numbers on the street signs decreasing.

"Oh, I wish. I'm from Lost Hills. Sounds romantic, doesn't it?" Montana chuckled wistfully. "But really, it's just like Bakersfield. I wasn't very happy there."

"I'm from a small place, too. Doesn't really have a name, just a spot on the bayou."

"So you know. I got here at a good time, the early '80s. Found my way to The Castro and the small-town boy had his eyes opened wide."

"When were you turned?"

"Which one?" Montana gave a knowing laugh, but Sophia felt caught. "Oh, just messing with you. Vampire came first. He was old, probably turned in the 1920s or so. He loved putting together a harem of young men. I was to be the protector because all the others were little things. Served him right."

"What?"

"He was a user and an abuser. Together, we put him down." Montana hung her head. "I know that's probably against some larger code—"

"You don't have to justify it. Hell, I know a few I'd like to ash."

"Ha! Sure. But I never talk about it. You're easy to talk to."

"Makes my work easier."

They passed a line of Latino boys, maybe seventeen, eighteen at most. One of them whistled and called out to Sophia, "You need a man not a *maricon*."

Sophia whipped around. "You ain't talking to me." It should have been a question, but her old Cajun accent made it a statement.

"Hell, yeah, I am." The boy wore a black hoodie over his head. He pulled it down to reveal a sneer surrounded by a wispy mustache. "You should come with us and we'll show you what."

Sophia stood shoulder to elbow with Montana and looked at the gang. Seven in total.

"It ain't worth it," Montana said.

"I think it might be." Sophia stepped away from the taller vampire. "Whatcha got, little boy?"

"Lots of this!" The boy laughed and pulled on his crotch. His friends took swigs from the 40-ounce beers.

In one quick motion, Sophia sped over and knocked the bottles out of their hands. They crashed and fizzed, the golden liquid puddling on the ground. Before he could react, Sophia had the leader by the throat.

"Mama didn't teach you manners, kids?" She flashed her fangs and the boy paled. She let him go and they scurried off into the night. Sophia turned to Montana.

"Feel better?" Montana looked weary.

"A little."

"I know you wanted to help, but it never ends." They started walking again. Montana took a left and headed back to Valencia. "And they'll be back at it tomorrow with somebody who can't defend themselves."

Sophia would have blushed, but her nature wouldn't let her. Still, her stomach hurt from the shame. "I don't know what to say."

Montana smiled and hugged Sophia. "Being a vampire is tough. We have so much aggression, but we still need to exist in society. It's just like when I transitioned. At first, drag was the thing, so it was man by day and Montana at night. But about fifteen years ago, I don't know. Attitudes shifted. Being a woman full time just felt right. Now Manuel is gone. Really and legally. I adjust to my new needs, but others can't understand."

"You chose the right name, boo, 'cause you look like a mountain."

"Oh, you got it!" Montana smiled. "I figured I was Mexican, but that means you have some native in you. It's probably Aztec or something, but it felt right. Speaking of Aztec—"

They turned back onto Valencia to see the two-story facade of City College, a giant, circular Aztec calendar at least fifty feet in diameter hanging on the front. They entered and went through the usual antiseptic school hall until they found the classroom. Ten vamps stood around, talking and sipping from Dixie cups.

Sophia approached a thin man, head shaved and wearing a motorcycle jacket. "I see the deer blood made it. How is it?"

"Oh, it's great." He smiled, undercutting the badass biker look. "Milton." He held out his hand and Sophia shook it.

"Shall we?" Sophia walked to the circle of chairs and all took their seats. They were an eclectic mix: a hippie woman in a flowing dress who even wore a headband, a couple who wore matching cardigan sweaters, a thin black man wearing a bow tie whose every stitch was sharply pressed, and a long-haired man who had been turned later in life but still looked like he was holding out for the Motley Crue reunion. Montana kissed the bow tied man on the cheek and sat next to him.

Montana stood. "Sophia asked me to bring all of you together, the leaders of the vampire community, so I'll turn it over to her."

She started into her usual spiel: keeping to animal blood, connecting through meetings, and trying to keep the animal instincts at bay. Something was off, however. She stopped to talk it out.

"I know this isn't L.A. So tell me what doesn't apply here."

"Look, we like the overall message." Milton had leaned in to talk. "But the big problem we have is we don't have VampAmp money here." The nodding of heads created a wave of new enthusiasm.

The hippie woman, Zahira, spoke, her voice that whimsical tune of the '60s. "I've been here for so long. I thought things would only get better. But the bread these children are throwing around. I'm losing my place."

More agreement vibrated through the group. Montana focused

on Sophia. "That walk we just took? That used to be cheap places for working class people, mostly Mexican but plenty of others. Now, these techies are paying ten grand before they even move in. You know how hard it is for us to have jobs and make money. We just can't stay anymore."

Milton leaned back. "I've lived off the grid many times. You know, find an old industrial place, black out the windows, squat until they find you. Did it for decades. But those places aren't there anymore. This little finger of space is gone, man. And so we're gone, too."

"What are you doing?" Sophia wished she had been taking notes.

"We have enough to grab some land out in Stockton. We can raise a few head of cattle, some chickens, enough to sustain some people. We have a few like Jonathan—" He pointed to the bow-tied man. "He's got some tech skills and sets us up with side gigs. But a big plan like yours? Unite everybody? Online, sure. But this city has spoken and we aren't welcome."

"He's talking about poor people. Not vampires." Jonathan spoke through his thin lips. "I know this kind of gentrification is affecting you too, Sophia. But L.A. has space and we don't."

"It's enough to make a vamp want to hunt." Montana stood up and bared her fangs. But the group laughed, Jonathan playfully swatting her elbow. "I joke, but it's such a weird feeling. Together we could reduce the population by half in a matter of weeks. But we're the powerless ones."

Sophia nodded. "Let's find a little power through convergence. When we all work together, we can find the solutions."

They closed their eyes. This strange talent had been discovered by her sire, this ability to harmonize deeper than any living human. They hummed until they found the shared note, the grip of each hand tighter and tighter as the wave rose. As it reached its top and the windows started vibrating, they released the singing. Zafira started giggling.

"Man, I miss getting high so much. That's as close as I come."

As the meeting broke up, Sophia got all of them to agree to sign up for VampAmp communities and to organize their groups, a small step but something positive she could do. She felt they may have been patronizing her because of her power the vampire world, but once they got into it, she hoped the quality of the service would shine through.

The rest wandered off, leaving her and Montana out in front of the school.

Sophia said, "What now?"

"The bars are closed. I think we should both head home." Montana sighed. "You make sense, but this city doesn't. I don't know. We're all on the verge of losing what we love, but we can't let go yet. It hurts."

Sophia embraced her. "I know. I had to do the same thing, but it was quick. This is more of a slow-motion torture."

Montana zipped up her jacket. "I'm going home to listen to my *boleros*. They make me sad and happy at the same time, y'know?"

"I do." She watched as Montana walked away, the marine layer fog starting to descend to street level. Her mind was too small for their problems. She hoped that someone down in L.A. could bring something to them. Anything to make this life better because while they may be getting kicked out, the population wasn't going anywhere.

One test, the voice had told her. Aida looked to the pyramid, but nothing happened there. She turned her gaze to the surrounding greenery.

The hedges parted to reveal a cave opening, a small tube barely wide enough for Aida, but Tonantzin directed the young girl toward the maw.

Bending over and crawling in, she felt the dirt scratch her knees. She had to keep shrinking herself so the rocky ceiling wouldn't do the same to her back. She scooted further and further, unsure she was getting anywhere, when the tunnel opened into a natural cavern. Light glowed from the bottom of a pool of water, giving the room a blue tint. As she stirred the surface, the light also undulated, making her feel underwater. She washed her face and knees, wondering if she should strip off her dress to clean that off. She decided against it, not wanting to feel damp for an extended period.

As she studied the pool, she caught sight of some flittering around the edges where rocky outcroppings threw shadows onto the wall. She peered closely to see tiny cave fish, albino and probably blind, dart from the side. The little creatures each did so: stillness followed by a burst of speed. Aida reached into the pool to scoop one up, but whenever her hands neared, they would squirm away, dodging her grasp.

She stood and examined the cavern: dead end. No exit except to crawl back through the tunnel. She returned to the pool where the mysterious light originated. She reached again for a fish, this time seizing one. She brought her hands together in a pool and held the fish close in order to examine it. The closer she brought the fish, the more unsteady she felt, until she lost her balance and fell into the pool.

As soon as she splashed, she felt herself transform. She had little sight, only being able to tell brightness from dark, but she felt part of a pack. Had she transformed into one of these fish? She couldn't tell, but she knew they were traveling down: deeper into the water and toward the light source. The rushing was intense. She could feel her whole body vibrating at the thought of reaching the light, that somehow this would also change her. Closer, closer, closer ...

She could swim no more. The light source was gelatinous, but a membrane kept her from continuing. She glided along the surface, looking for some way to meld with it. She could feel the warmth emanating from it and wanted it to encapsulate her, to so fully engulf her as to be subsumed by its mass. Finally, a fold revealed a way in and she slid her wiggling body into it. She and the light were now one: no separation, no consciousness, nothing but pure, ego-less existence.

What had once been down became up. The mass rose from some deeper place but gained density within its ascent. The heavier she became, the more her light dissipated. No longer a pure existence, now she formed into a shape, her shape, and crawled forward as Aida reformed. She emerged from another pool with the same form, the same dress, and the same feelings as Aida but all had been scrubbed and cleaned. This new girl exited the water with a reshaped understanding.

She thought back to the Botticelli painting of Venus being born on the shore. She had studied it so many nights when she wondered about herself and her own journey in life. And now she could feel that same excitement of becoming.

She was in another cave, but this one was far more alive with fungi clinging to the wall, the air's humidity heavy in her breath, and a light around the corner. She turned to see a wide opening filled with bursting sunlight.

I have been reborn, she thought. *The cave is my mother. Tonantzin is my mother. My mother is my mother?*

It was all so confusing, so Aida paused. Something drew her outside, but she thought about resisting. *Maybe this is the test*, she thought. She looked over her shoulder to see there was no going back. She strode out of the cave mouth, ready for the next step.

Here was a primal place, a forest overgrown and fecund. The cave had been underground, but this new world held no limits. She could see peaks on the horizon, but also trails that led down dark, twisty paths. She felt overwhelmed, paralyzed by choice. Where should she go when could go anywhere?

The branches of a brambly bush shuddered in front of her. From the thick green came a doe, sleek from nose to tail with heavy spotting along its flanks. Aida was scared, but the animal showed no fear, approaching her and looking directly into her face.

"Greetings!" The deer looked to be smiling.

"Who are you?"

"I'm here to help."

"Okay, but what does that mean?"

"We need to start on a path. You can't stay here forever now, can you?"

"Can't I?"

"Even that would be choosing a path, although quite short."

Aida looked around her. "Where should I go?"

"Wherever you want." The deer looked at the many paths in all four directions. "I'll ask you a question. What are you drawn to?"

Aida had never considered this. A vision of the beach, Santa Monica beach, that place where the city ends and can go no further. "I'd like to go to the water."

"Follow me."

They took a winding path through a forest. This area was tropical, the air heavy and the flowers big and blooming. Hibiscus, jasmine, ginger, even birds of paradise blossomed from small bushes. Few trees towered above, left behind on alternate routes.

The doe took the lead, slowing down whenever Aida wanted to stop and take in the vistas. She could see they were descending with a wide bay at the end of the trail.

Aida found herself imitating the loping gate of her guide. The deer didn't walk so much as strut, comfortable with each step. But the doe was also hyper-aware, freezing at the sounds from the interior of the forest. Aida recognized herself in the animal but also felt constrained here. She felt this too, confidence within her boundaries but never ready to engage something new. Had she always been so modest, so vulnerable with others? Certainly, that was true of Mama. Her home was comfortable but also a jail of sorts. On the other hand, the one time she stepped out, she ended up on some supernatural quest.

She could still see the face of the vampire right before he was destroyed. The anger on his predatory face didn't take her own humanity into any regard. But what would a deer do when faced with such hostility? The same that her mind had done: run.

The forest opened on a wide sandy beach. The water stretched out past the horizon, but on her right were more forests, including tall pine trees. But in the middle of this bay, still very wide, was an island with a mountain in the middle. In fact, it looked like the mountain *was* the island. Something stirred Aida's heart.

"How do I get there?"

"You must swim. And what's more, I can't follow you."

"That's fine. You will be here when I get back, right?"

"Back?" The deer said it like the whole concept was foreign. But it stayed on the beach as Aida entered the water.

The waves were gentle and the water warm, but the swim took a very long time. But something inside Aida shifted. Instead of getting tired as she approached the island, she strengthened, each stroke building her muscle. Since time stood still in this world, daylight remained as she walked upon the island's beach.

The island was measurably bigger than her initial estimate, but only one path extended from where she landed. Giant palm fronds framed the sandy track while no trees grew. Still, she couldn't see over the plants and felt she shouldn't get off track just yet. As she reached the base of the mountain, she could see how bare it was compared to its bottom portion. It stretched up high, maybe 500 feet. Giant boulders lay along the bottom, but a smaller fissure garnered her attention. She touched the mountain's side and felt it hot, burning and hard to handle. But she could feel the draw within it. Summoning as much energy as she could, she grasped the fissure with both hands and pulled it open to reveal a curtain of red-hot liquid behind it. Lava?

Yes, she now felt the volcanic energy pulsating through the

stones. She took a few steps back, put her hands over her eyes, then plunged into the fiery river.

Almost too much to bear, the heat sizzled her skin but didn't melt her body. She had felt the connection with the deer, but this was much deeper. Now she felt alive with the upward force. She could see nothing but lava, but she felt the eruption as she approached the rim. And just when she was about to be blown out the top of the crater, she heard herself breathe.

Breathing, breathing, breathing ...

Then a catch.

And she sat up to see her mother staring into her eyes.

All the way home and through days of rest, she pondered what her comatose visions meant. But one thing was sure, the volcano had replaced the deer.

Sophia got off the train to Los Angeles with all the other after dark travelers. The hodgepodge of "children of the night" goth types, tattooed rockers, and a few regular schmoes who could only do this midnight run looked relieved that the ride was over. The arrival time was 2 a.m., easier than the trip up and plenty of time to make it from Union Station to Silver Lake.

She strode through the art deco building, feeling more comfortable in the old-fashioned wood swoops and arches than in the modern glass buildings, but she was still older than the place by forty years. She rolled her bag into the main hall, forty-foot ceilings arching over her and shining parquet floors in square patterns. When she got to the end of the runway, Jeremiah waited with a smile on his face.

But he was different, a whole new look since she'd left for San Francisco. His hair was slicked into a tall cock's comb with hair buzzed short on the sides, his jeans were new and retained their indigo deepness, and he wore a leather biker jacket with a buckle at the waist. She must have looked surprised because he twirled when she approached.

"You like it?" Jeremiah's sideways smile could never change, however.

She stood back to assess. His normal dress was like hers: flannels and white t-shirts, broken-in jeans with random holes, sneakers. This new look was something else. She flashed back to her dead ex

Chip and his obsession with *guayabera* shirts and spectator shoes. "You look...slick." She meant it, too, but wasn't sure if she liked it.

"I went shopping with Maisie. She thought you might dig it." Jeremiah had been hanging out a lot with his VampAmp co-workers, so it was no surprise they might influence him. But Maisie was—what did she call it? Normcore? Something about dressing in the most functional way. That's what Sophia thought she was doing, but even her look was too stylish.

"Let's talk about it on the way home."

Sophia had made the call three months previously. The trip to the Valley was too far for her and her carless ways, so Jeremiah packed up and moved over the hill. Most of the business end of her non-profit was run out of VampAmp, so they turned the old office into a living room, but kept the conference room set up for meetings. The Los Angeles chapter of the Vampire Rehab and Gourmet Society now had four locations: the original in Silver Lake, one in Orange County, a regular meet at VampAmp in Venice Beach, and the newest one in Hollywood which catered to lycanthropes and was made up mostly of Jeremiah's old wolfpack. They followed a different set of rules but still pledged to control themselves and stop any human killing.

As Jeremiah drove through Chinatown, the neon colors of all the signs glowing through the windows, Sophia gave him a closer look. "I could get used to this."

"Maisie said I looked like a lost logger. Guess I'm a city boy now."

"Here's the question: does it feel like your clothes reflect what's inside of you or is it a costume?"

"That's a damn good question. I don't know the answer just yet." Jeremiah looked like he was pondering something seriously, but Sophia wanted his attention now.

"Good thing you have a few decades to decide." She snuggled up under his arm despite the split seats. As she avoided the gear shift, he pulled her close.

"Missed you," she said.

"You, too."

She could feel him shifting in the uncomfortable position, so she pulled back into her seat. He gave her a quick glance. "So?"

"Yeah. It was weird. They all like our ideals, but they can't really act on them. The money hustle is breaking up the community."

"That's happening here, too."

"It is?" Was Sophia that out of touch? She had been lucky with money. She might have to rethink her whole existence.

"Check the boards. You mostly see people who had established careers when they were turned. Since we all stopped killing, we need things to do. Jobs are hard, money's tight, and the rent is due."

"Is that why you didn't fight us moving in together?"

"I mean, partly. We just have to make enough to pay the small bills. We got to start thinking about these things 'cause a homeless vamp these days is a dead one."

She had to ponder many things now. Her movement was one of peace, but it meant being more human. And with that came a return to the normal kind of life with all the problems of house and home. Was she wrong? Was this going to destroy vampires instead of saving them? It was all too heavy for one night.

They made it back to the ZLVG Center in thirty minutes and slunk upstairs. They had a few hits of blood from the fridge and went upstairs together. Newly energized, Jeremiah welcomed Sophia back to their shared bed. Since becoming a vampire, their sex had changed. He used to be more playful, laughing and tickling, but now he was more aggressive. Not frightening because Sophia would never allow that, but his needs became about intensity instead of wooly softness. She liked the change sometimes, but then also missed the old days. Still, it was better that he was here with her instead of sent to the afterlife. She chose to turn him that fateful night instead of letting him die. She would never regret that decision.

She could see something was troubling him when they were done. He looked like a newly reined horse.

"It's been a bit, yeah? But I'm still getting used to this new skin," Jeremiah said.

"You've changed. I see it. Are you mad about it?"

"I don't know. Sometimes." He sat up, his bare chest now snowy with white hair. "It's just so different. My body, my mind, my eyes. The old world seems so black and white and now all I can see is color. It's overwhelming."

"It would have been different if you were a wolf. Possums aren't predators. And that's what you are now. You're a predator. This body is meant to hunt and kill. Search and destroy. It's why we had such a hard time getting people into rehab. To even admit that your new life is the problem? That's hard."

"Finally! Something makes sense. I thought I was going crazy."

"In a sense, you are. Before, you could eat, drink, and exist. You met your needs with relative ease. But now it's different. There's a reason we call it blood lust. It's the exact same drive that's pushing your sexuality now."

He looked ashamed, unable to meet her gaze. "It's so hard now."

"That's what she said." The joke landed flat, but Jeremiah still smiled. The attempt was to lighten the mood, but she saw he need-ed the serious side just now.

"Even with the blood, it's far more difficult. I have to push and push to feel anything. Like when we're out and I'm taking in rooms, that's far easier in this form. But sex is always just beyond my grasp. Like I'm wrapped up in four condoms." He stroked her hair. "I mean, you should know. It takes you forever to come."

"It does?" She did the math in her head. She'd been having vam-pire sex for over 100 years, so maybe she didn't notice anymore. What a human feels during sex or at any other time? That had been wiped from her memory. "I guess so."

"But now it's both of us. I... I need to get used to it."

She snuggled close to him. What hadn't changed was the strength of his hugs, an emotional blanket for her.

"So the woman I met in San Francisco is trans. We had a small conversation about it, but something she said feels like something you should hear. The old Jeremiah won't ever come back. You've come out of your cocoon all fresh and new—"

"A butterfly or a moth?"

"Now he's got jokes." She rubbed his chest just above the breast-bone. "Regardless, you're different. So maybe when you wear these new clothes, you try this new haircut, maybe this does fit you. The new you. The one who isn't mortal anymore."

"Not even alive, right?"

"Exactly. Transition, resurrection, rejuvenation. Call it whatever you want, but we can't act like things are the same."

"You want to know how it feels?" Sophia nodded. "I go back to waking up and you giving me the blood needed to save my life. My skin felt like it was on fire, the top layer burning off to reveal a new, tougher hide underneath. What's that bird, the reborn one?"

"A phoenix?"

"Yeah. Like that. My ashes made the new me. The vampire me." Jeremiah's stare was blank now. What he said needed processing by both of them. She looked him in the eyes and could now see the struggle. "I know, Sophia. I know." His eyes closed and he slid down, both of them feeling the day approaching and the deathly sleep coming. "I don't think this will be easy. For either of us."

"You will be tested, love. But like any change, it's inevitable. Just like day follows night." She blacked out then, knowing no dreams would follow.

Chapter Three

When she got home from the hospital, Aida started planning. In the car, she decided to make a case for staying out of the world for some time, five or six months. She was sure Mama would definitely embrace that thought, her girl kept away from all the bad things that made her sick in the first place.

During her convalescence, she would read up on the Aztecs, magic, spellcasting, anything she could use to further her rebirth. The sun hung low at the end of this day and the red fingers surrounding it reminded her of roses, of Tonantzin, the inner glow present in everything the goddess touched. She felt peaceful, but something nagged at the back of her neck.

Vampiros. While she walked in the sun, those evil creatures were dominating the night. And all in her neighborhood.

They pulled into the driveway before the sun went down, so Aida felt safer. Rushing out of the car, her mother ran to help Aida out of the front seat and hovered behind her as she walked inside. This could present a problem. Aida had factored helicopter mom into short-term plans only. Hopefully, Mama would fuss over her for about a week and then go back to her normal routine.

Before she stepped inside, she took one last look at the vampire house. While the rest of the neighborhood wasn't cheery, this place looked extra shrouded: the large oak shading it, the curtains in every window, and the tightly-sealed backyard. Why had she never noticed how secrecy enveloped it?

The first thing she did was take a shower. Sure, the nurses must have been cleaning her, but she wanted to scrub the experience from her skin. Instead of using her normally tepid water, Aida jammed the hot water all the way open. Maybe she wanted to recreate the lava of her dreams or maybe she was jumpstarting her new life, whatever. The scalding liquid renewed her spirit while stripping any residual gunk from her naked skin. She had a rosy glow when she stepped out and toweled off.

After dressing and wrapping her long hair, she went to the front room. Mama and Papa waited for her, no brothers anywhere.

"Where are the boys?"

Papa sat on his leather recliner. He sat up and cleared his throat. "We asked them to go out for a bit. You know how rowdy they get."

"We wanted you to have some quiet for tonight." Mama's chair was stiff backed, so she put her bare feet on a short ottoman. "Come sit, *mija*."

Aida got nervous. Whenever her mother was gentle with her, she knew something rough was coming. But she sat on the sofa, pulling a throw pillow on her lap.

Papa went first. "You know we don't want to upset you—"

"You already are!" Mama rarely scolded her husband, but he looked like he didn't want to say what he needed to.

Mama took over. "Your brothers aren't here because they don't live here anymore. The night after your...your accident, they decided to fight our neighbor because they heard about the riot at their house."

"Oh, no." Aida had visions of the beatdown they must have received.

"I raised my sons better," Papa said. "But they thought they were defending you. Juan, like you, ended up in the hospital, broken ribs and a dislocated knee. We called the cops after, but they did nothing."

"Didn't you tell Juan they're vampires?"

Both of her parents recoiled at the world.

"Where did you hear that?" Mama whispered, her tone harsh.

"I saw one right before I passed out."

"You don't know what you're talking about!" Mama now leaned forward. "Your mind was in a fever or something."

"But—"

"Shh! I won't hear it." Mama leaned back. "Anyway, your brothers are in our new house in Riverside."

"What?" Aida wanted to jump. Riverside was far away, at least an hour and a half east and on the edge of the desert. It was hot and miserable, and full of hot and miserable people. Why would anyone move there?

"Things are changing, Aida." Her father looked into his lap, either unwilling or unable to meet her gaze. "And they're changing fast. Half the block put their houses on the market."

"And we can get so much more than what we paid." Mama almost looked excited. "The new place is bigger and there's not so many criminals around."

That's not what I heard, thought Aida, but she left it alone. "So we're letting those people across the street push us out of our own neighborhood?"

"No. But it was the last straw." Papa stood. "I'm sorry to throw all this at you at once, but we only have a few weeks." Papa went into the kitchen and Aida could here the fizzy pop of a beer can.

"You wouldn't believe who bought the house, *mija*. White people!"

"Are you serious?"

"Yes. They said they couldn't afford anything in Los Feliz, so they crossed the river. So many of the houses on the market are selling to them."

"But what about the neighborhood? Our heritage? Y'know, Mariachi Square and all the history?"

"Oh, people are angry. They broke the window of this new coffee house. And they stormed into some gallery."

Papa stuck his head in. "The crazy *gabacho* who runs the place is selling paintings for $25,000! Took me fourteen years of working to make that in a year!"

"Anyway, you'll have to pack your things. Take about a week, rest, sleep well. But we are leaving." Mama came over to Aida, wrapping her arms around her daughter. "My joy, I know you think this is bad news, but we'll make a new history. A better one. We'll all be happier away from here."

As Aida turned to go to her room, her mother called out. "Oh, your *Tia* Rosalinda has moved back to Los Angeles. She wanted to see you."

But Aida's thoughts weren't with her mother or *tia* or anybody else. They were concentrated on how she was going to exact her revenge on the monsters next door before she moved away.

Readjusting to life in Los Angeles had been difficult for Rosalinda Suarez. She'd gotten used to the slower pace of San Francisco, having everything she needed right in the few blocks of her neighborhood and no greater burdens like cars, insurance, and gas. But the shift had happened, not the tectonic movement she thought it would be but a slow erosion that left her stranded.

She'd lived for over 50 years in the Haight-Ashbury neighborhood, having moved there right in the middle of the hippie times. She'd seen the turnover from hippie paradise to heroin hell, but the smaller changes were the ones that nagged her, like the famous corner that gave the neighborhood it name no longer had the Psychedelic Shop or the Diggers. No, that corner had a Gap for all your yuppie clothing needs.

She took solace that Golden Gate Park remained untouched. Every dawn, she would take her mat to the wide lawn and do sun salutations, then take an hour to wander the forests. She could see fleeting animals every now and again, but the people kept them hidden. Every few weeks, she caught the spots and white tails of deer, but soon they flitted away from her.

Then the changes shifted from micro-aggressions to major upheaval. First, the building which held her business, psychic card reading, was sold. The new landlords threw her out immediately, knowing they could quadruple her rent overnight. For the next six months, she conducted her sessions in her home. But then her landlord there, the grandson of her original one, found out and used that fact to get her evicted. She knew that rent would also be raised by many thousands.

He came over on a Sunday to serve her the papers. He looked like many of the tech boys who were flooding the neighborhood—flannel shirt, jeans, Timberland boots. But he set her background senses off, his aura so dark and oily like the demons she'd seen on the edge of society.

"You'd do this to a seventy-five-year-old lady, huh?"

He scoffed. "You broke the lease. I have the right."

"Your grandfather's not around to stop you. He would have, y'know. And your dad would have asked for a few more dollars of rent. But you? Put me out on the street?"

"You act like you deserve to live here." He waved at the hallway of the four plex. "This is mine now. It's time for you to scuttle off to some retirement home and let the new people enjoy San Francisco."

She peered harder into his aura, smiling as his life revealed itself. "You act tough, eh? But you go home alone. Home to no one.

Why? You think it's bad luck, but you just show off your rot. Until you look into yourself and do some serious work, your life will be covered in black. You will make your money and it will bring no happiness. Your only company will be the glow of your computer screen."

She could tell she'd only pricked him minorly, nothing but a mosquito bite.

He threw the papers at her feet. "You're outta here, lady. Good fucking riddance."

She had ten days, but she did little packing. Her life had followed this pattern. Something going wrong meant something else would come along to replace it. It had been that way with jobs, men, friends. The tide was rushing out, but it would return and be high once again. In two days, she got the call.

Her mother had died. It shook her, but they had never been close. Her mother was too traditional. Losing her *abuela* thirty years ago, now that had been bad. But her mother was 96 and on her last days. Her brother was the one who gave her the nuggets of news.

"She left the house to both of us. Now if we can sell it—"

"Pablo, I'm getting kicked out of my place. I need a place to live."

Pablo laughed. "What are you gonna do? Move back to Boyle Heights?" He laughed. Many times at Thanksgiving and Christmas, Rosalinda had said she'd die in the Bay Area. But the Mother Goddess laughed when you made plans.

"I don't want you to lose the money. But give me six months to get settled. After that, I'll find a place and you'll get your share."

Pablo hemmed. Again, he'd taken such a traditional path, working first as a gardener before putting together his own construction company. He had said many times he thought she was *loco*, living alone in the dangerous city. But in the end, family still meant everything to him. He let out a breath. "Fine." He chuckled. "You ain't never gonna believe how much we're gonna get for this house."

And it was true. After a few months, she found a small one bedroom in Glassel Park—although she liked to call it Frogtown, the weird alternative name for the neighborhood—and rented stalls at the weekly farmer's markets to read cards. When a white couple with a newborn bought the house, they paid nearly $600,000. Pablo laughed as they left the closing.

"I hope you can live on this."

"I'll find a way. I always do."

He promised to keep closer in touch, but she knew they may only talk once a month at most. She hoped the rest of the family—nieces, nephews, grandnieces and nephews—might spend some more time with her.

With the new cash, she could rent a tiny storefront in Eagle Rock, just up the street from her new place, and set up for other, later hours. Pablo even helped her build the place out, including the bright neon "Psychic Readings" sign in the window.

Something had told her to stay open a little longer, for some time into the night, in case some who lived by dark might want to come. And so a few weeks later, when the pale woman with the dark features rang her bell, she realized exactly what the Universe had been planning for her.

The girl—was she more than twenty?—looked wary as she walked in, probably because the place was sparse. Other than a small bathroom and a personal space, the front was a 400 square foot rectangle. Rosalinda had painted the walls deep purple with the right wall having a built-in cabinet filled with candles, essential oils, and incense for sale. On the left was a giant poster of *loteria* cards, the names of each spelled out in Spanish.

The young woman laughed when she saw them. "*Loteria*? My parents used to play that. They called it the Mexican Bingo."

Rosalinda smiled. "It has other uses. I find the visions from it connect with the other worlds better than Tarot."

"You're weird." She said it with a smile, but when she sat, Rosalinda could feel the real energy of this person.

"And you are much different than you portray. Older, but maybe not wiser." Rosalinda shuffled her cards. "What's your name, *niña de la noche*?"

"Tamar." She rested her hands on the table between them. "Maybe you are as advertised."

"The number of charlatans in this business outweighs the true psychics, but yes, I do have talents. Why are you here, Tamar?"

"Why don't you guess?"

This happened with every third or fourth customer, so Rosalinda was used to it. "I can do it in three cards." She dealt three down from her deck, then flipped the first one: the ladder. She read the quote, "Ascend me step by step, don't try and skip." She looked at

Tamar to gauge her reaction to the card. "You're dealing with a loss and you have no idea how to do it. Mostly because you've never had to. Tell me, where are you in the process?"

"I don't know. He died violently. I'm still mad they killed him."

"Anger, eh? So still early. Do you have someone you can talk to about it?"

"Yeah. But she's got too much to do."

"I have a feeling she'll listen. Now for the next card: the bottle. Tool of the drunk. You have a liquid addiction."

"We all do."

"We?" Rosalinda felt defensiveness. Tamar had opened up just a little, but the picture was becoming clearer.

"I'm working on that. My…addiction."

"With the same person you can talk to?"

Tamar nodded, but her attention was elsewhere. She snapped back after a few seconds. "Okay, so I believe you."

"Hold on. I was going to do this anyway." Rosalinda flipped the last card: the heron. Rosalinda smiled while she quoted, "On the other side of the river, I have my sand bank where sits my darling short one with the beak of a dark heron."

"The fuck does that mean?"

"It could mean many things. You keep what's private private. Or you value those things which are useful. But think about it. The heron stands above the flow of the water, plucking its prey without any notice."

"You can see all that, huh."

"I see what you are, but I don't see the evil usually associated with it." Rosalinda gathered up the cards. "I see great hope within you. But that's all about the now. You want to see the future, *sí*?"

"Yeah." The word came draped in contemplation. Without a second thought, Rosalinda dealt out three more cards.

The first one was the cello, a strange card. Rosalinda read the saying, "Growing, it reached for heaven and since it was not a violin, it had to be a cello." Tamar looked confused by the card, but Rosalinda felt the meaning deep inside. "Let me make a guess: this other world you live in? There are few like you. Like us, I should say."

"There's a few. But no, it's mostly Anglos. It took them a long time to take me seriously."

"They always do. You will be misunderstood by most. But look, you have to be what you are. People listen to symphonies for the violins, but without the cello is the music as sweet? You'll have to make your mark as you, not as something else."

"They have this office thing, like in Venice Beach. And every time I go there, I get weird looks. They still don't know what to do with me." Tamar studied the card. "It looks kinda like those big bass guitars in a *mariachi*."

"Now you're getting it. Next." Rosalinda revealed the shrimp. "Poor little *camaron*. The shrimp that slumbers is taken by the tide. Where are you from?"

"Boyle Heights."

"Ah, me too. At least I grew up there. Many, many changes."

"Not for the best."

"Exactly, stay awake. But..." Rosalinda struggled with a detail, unclear in her head. "There's other changes. Don't ignore the obvious when something is right upon you."

Tamar shrugged, so Rosalinda flipped the final card: the heart.

"*Amor*?" Tamar's face was immediately building walls.

"I don't think so. The saying goes, 'Do not miss me, sweetheart. I'll be back by bus.' When I put all this together, I see you protecting everything: your heart, your home, *su familia, sí*?" Tamar nodded. "You will be finding trouble where you least expect it, something close. But the way to solve it comes from within. And whatever it is that you may lose will come back." Rosalinda shook her head. "You have me in a strange place. Things are unclear. They are for me, at least. Hopefully, you will see."

Tamar smiled, not unfriendly but generally disappointed. She stood. "I'll talk to my friend. About the ladder."

"That's good." Tamar handed over a crisp hundred for the reading and walked into the night. For no particular reason, Rosalinda turned over one last card: the moon. The streetlamp of lovers, according to the cars.

Rosalinda wasn't sure of much after this reading, but she was sure at least one fact: her involvement in Tamar's story was only beginning.

With moving day getting closer and closer, Aida grew more impatient. She could feel her anger constantly, a rumble in her stomach she couldn't control. Food held no flavor and any task took so much concentration that she gave up long before they were finished. Her mother scolded her, saying she would have to throw away anything that wasn't packed. But Aida didn't care. Leaving wasn't the problem; those damn vamps were.

On Monday one week before the move, she finally had some time to herself. Papa had gone to work and Mama wanted to go to the new house. She asked Aida to go, but the daughter said she had packing to do. This gave Mama some hope, but also Aida gained some alone time. And that meant action.

She dressed for combat: Doc Marten boots, heavy jeans, and a leather jacket she took from her brother when it got too small for him. Over the last few weeks, she collected vampire hunter gear: stakes from Home Depot which she shaved into sharpness, a vial of holy water which she "liberated" from church, her father's ancient Zippo lighter and spare fuel, and a handful of peeled garlic cloves. She didn't know if the latter would be effective, but the books all said so. Piling them into her school backpack, she hitched her pants and walked outside into the mid-morning sun.

She scanned the block to make sure none of the neighbors would stop her to talk. She didn't want to lose nerve or have them distract her. The rumble in her stomach turned into a boil as she crossed the street.

As she approached the porch, she saw a man sitting there, smoking a cigarette and listening to *Norteño* at a low volume. Heavy and in his late 60s, he wore an old *guayabera* shirt open over a tank top, shorts, and flip flops. In other words, he looked like one of her great uncles, not some evil monster. Still, this was the house. The man smiled and nodded as she approached, but he looked shocked when she stopped.

"You know who I am?" Aida could barely contain herself.

"Of course! I've seen you grow from a baby to the beautiful woman before me." His tone was pleasant, but Aida could tell he knew something was wrong. "Now I don't know your name..."

"Aida."

"Like the opera?"

"I don't—"

"Such a tragic story. A slave girl in ancient Egypt must choose between the man she loves and the love of her home, Ethiopia. See, the princess loves the same man as the slave—"

"Mister, I don't care."

"Maybe you should. It's about choosing your destiny. Finding what drives your life. Many important questions a young woman has to face."

"Do you know what happened to me six months ago?" Aida had her fill of his ramblings.

"I do. That was unfortunate. But you look healthy now."

"I know who's in that house."

The man sighed, an expression so world weary it nearly diffused Aida's anger. "We have done our best to keep ourselves away from you. That night? One of the worst things that has ever happened to us."

"You keep saying us, but I see you in sunlight."

"I serve my sister. I'm human like you. But I'm still part of her cabal and sometimes things turn nasty. And yes, somehow you were caught in it. I apologize, sincerely and from the depths of my heart. But we don't mean harm. Not now or into the future."

"What about my brothers?"

The man laughed. "That was also unfortunate. Tamar doesn't take to boys trying to intimidate her. Like you, she was born in fire." Aida must have reacted because the man nodded. "Oh, yes, I can see that. There's a spark within you beyond normal people. I hope you pursue that. But I will be clear: stay away from this house. I know you're moving, so let it be. I take one thing seriously: *mi familia*. You keep on your side and I'll stay on mine. *Comprendes*?"

"Fine." Aida turned to walk up the street, away from her house. Buying time was key now.

"*Bueno*. I hope you like your new house."

Aida went to the end of the block and out of sight. She waited a few minutes, then peered around to see if he'd left the porch. He was stamping out the cigarette when she looked. Pulling back, she waited another minute before trying again. Now he was gone. She needed to find a way in.

She approached the house from the side. Like most of the houses in this block, the vampire lair was a Craftsman, probably built in the 1920s or '30s. This one was two stories with a second story window facing the street. Aida felt the front was too open to climb up there, so she skirted the chain link fence to head to the backyard.

But she saw the man puttering around, picking up dishes and

dusting all the front surfaces. He was in the front of the house still, so she set her back to the wall, crouched down, and waited. She heard him whistling along with the radio. When it faded, she stood up. He had moved to the back.

Using the fence, which was only a foot from the outer wall, she climbed up. These old windows had thick wooden frames, making the holds easy. Soon, she was balanced on top of the lower frame and reaching up to the higher one. She started to feel weak, the long time of rest doing nothing for her muscle tone, but she also felt a surge of energy to go along with her increasing tension. She was doing it! Finally, someone would stand up for all the people around here.

Pulling up on the second window, she got her stomach on the sill and raised her right leg. She got purchase on the outcropping and soon was on her knees in front of the panes. From here, she could tell how thick the curtains were. This must be where the vamps stayed during the day. She pushed up on the window, but it was locked.

Aida pulled her backpack forward, laying it across her chest. Slowly so as not to fall, she worked one of the stakes out of the bag. She ran the sharp end along the corner of one of the panes, this window having four set into a wooden crossbar. She could scrape away some sealant, so the edge was more or less clear. She stabbed into that edge, chipping the glass. In three more thrusts, she'd cleared a hole about an inch wide. Sticking the pointed end into the opening, she wedged it back, breaking off two pieces of glass. She carefully pulled them out and put them in the backpack's front pocket. One more pull and she had enough room to reach in and unlock the window. She hoped the leather jacket would keep her from getting cut and the tough cowhide did its job.

She flipped the lock, just a metal slide along the top of the window, and opened it. Leaning forward, she slowly lowered her hands to the floor and walked herself forward until only her feet were outside. She'd pulled the curtain forward, so she didn't want to go too far. With a quick bounce, she contracted her legs and rolled to a seated position underneath the covering. Moving slowly, she stood and inched into the room.

The room wasn't huge, maybe enough for a couple of queen beds, but a series of privacy screens formed a maze within. She looked around each one: they were all hiding coffins. Portraits hung on the screens and none was the tough female she'd seen so long ago, so she went toward the back. There was a coffin all alone. Apparently, even a boss vampire got their own room.

She had multiple pictures hanging here, one from long ago. The '80s maybe? She had that feathered hair and a silver satin jacket. So even though she looked like she was in her twenties, she was close to Mama and Papa's age. It didn't matter. Aida had a job to do.

She lifted the top of the casket. The woman laid there, surrounded by the velvet lining. She didn't look peaceful; no, she just looked dead. And Aida would make that state permanent.

Lifting the stake, she aimed for the heart. But as she went to drive it into the vampire's chest, the right side of her face exploded and she felt herself thrown to the floor. She rubbed the side of her head and saw her hand covered in blood. She looked up at the old man standing over her holding a bloody claw hammer.

"See, the alarms they make now send alerts to your phone."

She pushed back to try to get away from him, but she didn't have enough strength to get up. He got close. She tried to kick him in the nuts, but he batted her foot away. He knelt right on her chest, the pain sharp.

"I said walk away. But you don't listen. Now I have to make you disappear."

She saw the head of the hammer rushing toward her, but blackness came before any pain.

When she woke up, she heard a loud wind rushing around her. Her feet and hands were bound and her mouth was gagged. She got her bearings, realizing she was in a car trunk. She figured he was driving her somewhere far out where no one would find her. The desert, maybe? Hell, there were parts of industrial downtown which could do the trick, but she figured he'd be thorough. Her head throbbed and soon she passed out again.

She was awakened by a violent thrust, the car braking quickly and her rolling into the back seat. She laid there for a long time, the heat building up until she was covered in sweat. Finally, the trunk opened, the light bright and blistering. He'd chosen the desert. He leaned in but not close enough for her to kick.

"Almost done, kid. Let's get you ready."

Aida's head pulsed with her heartbeat. The pain overwhelmed any other sense. When he grabbed her, she tried to struggle, but nothing came of it. She knew it: she was near the end.

He lifted her easily out of the trunk, his strength sneaky for an older man. He sat her on the edge of the back bumper. He backed up. "Come on."

She stood and he pushed her forward. Her feet were still tied and she struggled to stay standing. She looked around: dirt road, desert floor. Nothing for miles. Not only was it over, but no one would ever find her. Twenty feet from the car, he'd dug a hole and he pushed her to the edge. She looked in to see a plain wooden coffin at the bottom.

"Every good thrall has a few spares. This will keep the coyotes from digging you up."

Turning her around, he pushed her back and she fell square into the box. She felt her shoulder dislocate, but the pain of everything else was too much. Hopefully, it would ease soon.

The man placed the lid but only hammered a few times. She figured he was tired and the wood was doing most of the work. The whoosh-whoosh-whoosh of dirt piling up followed quickly.

Her mind was set, but her body rebelled. A primal scream, unheeded by her consciousness, pierced the new darkness. Five more followed until her lungs gave out, then she hyperventilated. In a few minutes, all was soft and the black seeped through her. She felt her soul slipping away and would fight it no more.

But darkness didn't last. Burning waves passed through her body and she tensed hard, like electric shocks rolled across her body. She saw something in her mind's eye: the volcano. She felt like she was on the far beach, back where she'd left the deer. The island vibrated, rumbled, and shot hot lava into the air in four big explosions. Ash filled the sky and fell onto her skin. She rubbed it and rubbed it, trying to clean off her arms.

But it wasn't ash anymore. No, it was dirt. She looked around and up: the coffin had split and light flowed in. She pushed out and the top opened, a bit more dirt falling on her face. She sat up to see something miraculous: a jagged line, like one of the fault lines she'd seen in science class, had split the earth around her coffin. She stood: no pain. Her hair was caked with blood, but the wound had closed. The headache was gone and, she could barely believe this part, she felt great.

She had been born for the third time, once more in the fire. The man had meant to kill her, but he had cracked open her last shell. She could feel the power pulsating below the surface, the heavy energy of nearby faults waiting for their chance to release. She was not a girl anymore; age didn't matter when connected so close to the earth.

She thought about her mother and father, the brothers who'd fought to defend her. She would have to let them mourn. She had progressed beyond them and now she needed to surround herself with others, those who could manipulate this magic all around her.

And that vampire back in Boyle Heights? She would be the first to suffer. Her mission was clear: rid the world of these abominations. The volcano demanded it.

Part Two: A Gathering of the Left

Chapter Four

Being resurrected in the desert turned out to be much easier than finding an acceptable place to live in Los Angeles.

For two months, Aida lived on the streets, joining the nearly 60,000 homeless people in and around the city. She found the camp villages along Fourth and Fifth Street near Main downtown to be too intimidating. Row upon row of grizzled people too near an absolute breakdown cut into her heart, but she still needed a level of comfort, so she started with the shelters. Mission Los Angeles was big, but it came with a heavy Christian message. The Midnight Mission was better and for two weeks, she made sure to get there before sundown in order to get a bed. But then the staff there started bugging her about getting into a placement program. She was sure that dead people didn't qualify.

She also had to rebuild her wardrobe. She only had the clothes she was buried in and while the jacket was nice, she needed other things. Combing through the free sections at the shelters, she grabbed anything black. She'd already started calling herself Black Rose to anyone who talked to her, which were either often-ignored older people or other young homeless, men and women alike, trying to get laid. She did her best to hang with the old heads because they knew the best ways to manage: which shelters were best, the food schedule of each charitable organization, and where to go during the day to avoid harassment.

The best place for her was the downtown library. She still didn't get a card on the off chance her parents were still looking for her, but the section for religion and occult books was large enough for a new topic each day. She used the free Internet to see what she should be studying, then searched up those books. Wicca, Alistair Crowley and the Golden Dawn, Tarot, Principia Discordia, all these ideas bubbled in her mind's cauldron. In her wanderings, she found a Zen garden accessible to the public in Little Tokyo. Deep in a building that served as a cultural center, she would walk there after reading, usually about three in the afternoon, and meditate, trying to fuse all her new knowledge with the powers she felt within herself. The garden had three short tiers with a waterfall in the middle. She would concentrate on the babbling water and soon visions of water flowing through all living things—blood, sap, lava—would overwhelm her unconsciousness. But the power she felt had no focus. She needed someone's help.

However, she needed friends. After a few weeks, she figured out a few street cliques. Most were punks, heads shaved and what little hair remaining dyed, with leather jackets and cut up jeans. She shadowed one set of white kids while circling 7th&Fig, an outdoor mall in a big bowl below street level with a high-end food court and a few clothing places like Zara's and Macy's. She hid in a corner while watching them go up and down the open-air escalator and hit up everyone for spare change. Finally, a security guard with a hefty belt line asked them to leave. She followed as they went down the tunnel to the parking lot. As she stood near the entrance, she saw them drive by, all piled into a Honda Pilot. They were obviously not her people.

That night she decided to skip the shelter. She was restless, even after walking all day, and after realizing it was a Saturday, she figured more action might be out in the street. She went to Pershing Square, the small green space where the Metro Red Line dropped off many who headed downtown. She looked at the poles around there, finally finding a flier for some gallery right off Skid Row. It started in two hours, so she started walking.

When she got there, a crowd of around 50 was mulling outside. The building was a former warehouse, made of stacked brick and three stories tall. Large casement windows opened to the street, but they were closed to the brisk night air. Inside, the walls were brick also and rose eighteen feet above her, but the gallery owner had set old hooks as hangers. Some paintings hung there while others were installations on the floor or put on stands. She perused the hall, giving each piece her attention.

Since she was surrounded by people around her age—from late teens to early 30s—she assumed the artists were young, too. She could tell this much: kids were fucking angry. This art wasn't subtle. Instead of impressionist or surrealist imagery, these paintings were blunt. Text reading "Black Lives Matter" and "Destroy the Rich" and "Socialism Now!" sat next to paintings of black and brown people in chains, being whipped or beat up. The police were also a subject, the L.A. badges traded for swastikas and other fascist looks. Aida had never been political, but maybe because she'd been in her protective bubble for so long. She'd heard her brothers say this and that about cops only to be scolded by Mama. In college, when other students wrote about their own issues, she didn't have half their anger. But something was brewing with her generation, a sleepy volcano ready to blow.

The inside got more crowded and stuffy, so Aida stepped outside. As she passed the doorway, she heard someone say, "Nice jacket." She turned to see a black woman about her age, head shaved bald and lips colored purple. She had ripped jeans and the exact same jacket as Aida who smiled.

"Stole it from my brother."

"Killer." The woman nodded her approval. She put a cigarette in her mouth and bent over to light it, Aida catching sight of a tattoo on the back of her neck. She wasn't sure, so she asked, "Is that a pentagram?"

The woman rubbed the back of her neck. "Yeah." She laughed. "I'm a devil," making her hands into claws and sticking out her tongue.

Aida laughed and introduced herself as Black Rose. "Tamala. But people call me Spex."

"Why?"

"'Cause I'm a black punk like Poly Styrene." Aida must have looked confused, because Spex said, "X-Ray Spex? Badass British punk band?" Aida shook her head, so Spex said, "You listen to punk at all?"

"No."

"Girl! You are in luck. Mike Watt's playing tonight."

"I don't—"

"Don't say it. You're already hurting my heart. He's from Pedro—" She pronounced it with a long e like most L.A. natives. "He was in The Minutemen, one of the best ever. Anyway, we're schooling you tonight. You can't wear no jacket like that and not get a little punk."

At that moment, they heard the buzzing of guitar amps turning on. Spex grabbed Aida's hand. "Come on!"

She pulled Aida to the front where an older man in overalls and a t-shirt tuned up a bass guitar. His face held a grizzly beard and his hair was thinning on top, but Aida saw Spex couldn't take his eyes off him. All of the band were older men dressed in flannels and jeans. Aida realized this music had been around a long time. Maybe you could rock past 50.

Watt nodded at his compatriots and let loose on his bass. The music wasn't what Aida pictured punk to be, nothing like Blink-182 or Thirty Seconds to Mars. This was stop and start, fast and slow, and Watt sang like a fisherman who'd just returned to port, his voice scratchy and phlegmy but filled with old soul. But whatever this was, she got it. Spex bumped her as the music got fast, not going full slam dance but making sure the music was digging in. Then during a heavy and fast run, she caught the wave. All of the trapped tension let loose and she shook like a wild woman. She felt her eyes widen as she looked at Spex, yelling while she shoved her new companion. At first, Spex looked angry, but she then inhaled all of Aida's energy and the two gripped each others' hands and pogo-ed to the beat, yelling all the time.

"There you go," Spex said at a slower point. "You got it now?"

"Yeah. This! This is magic! This is the magic I need."

Spex stopped her bouncing and stepped away a few paces. "You saying what I think you're saying?"

Aida shrugged but paused. "Yes. I think you know."

Spex pointed outside and started walking. Aida followed. When she caught up, Aida could see Spex was serious.

Spex whispered, "So, you know about the pentagram?"

Aida felt part of a conspiracy. "I've been studying about a month. That and some other stuff."

"I...I've been dabbling. A few years, but not serious yet." Spex shook her head. "Shit, I never tell anyone this stuff. But you?"

"Yeah?"

"I don't know. There's...something? Damn." Spex looked away, her hand on the back of her neck.

"I've had a few experiences. It's why I'm on the street. But..."

"Yeah?"

Aida pulled close. "I need help. For the magic stuff. And you?"

"Yeah." Spex looked around. "I do. Let's...let's figure this out after Watt."

"Sure." But Aida stopped her new friend. "I have an idea of who to talk to. It puts me at risk, but I think I know."

It had been some time since Sophia had been down to Venice, down to the VampAmp offices. She'd been giving Jeremiah some space, mostly because the center was fine living for one person but a little cramped for two. At least they didn't need a real kitchen.

When she returned from San Francisco, she immediately had a meeting with Pamela to figure out if there were any ways to help those NorCal vamps keep their homes. Sophia sat in Pamela's office, glass paneled so that all could see in but sound proofed for her privacy.

Pamela's eyes were still on her computer. "Haven't you seen the homeless here in L.A.? We're all overmatched."

Sophia gathered her thoughts. "You never lived under a vampire council. I hate the system, totally bucked against it, but when you have that structure, everybody has a stake—so to speak."

"Don't scare the youngsters." Pamela sipped green juice from a bottle. Her face was unlined despite her age and her short cut hair made her look even more ageless. She had to work hard as a living person when all her employees would be young forever. "Anyway, that kind of set-up takes decades to build. What was his name, Dragos? He had a whole century to build up equity, establish a passive income, get credit. You can't just wave the magic wand here."

"I know. But something can be done. Does VampAmp do any charitable stuff?"

"Outside of you?" Pamela smiled, but Sophia felt the jab. "Yes. Some." She looked flustered. "We could always do more, I guess."

"Give me a little time to work up a proposal. Maybe Sandy could help."

"I'll be open, but I can't guarantee anything."

Sophia left VampAmp with a purpose, but all of her ideas seemed woefully short. She called Sandy, the vampire lawyer who ran the rehab program in Orange County, and made her promise to come up to L.A. one Saturday night to brainstorm. Sandy showed up with a Yeti cup full of blood.

Sandy laughed when Sophia first pitched her. "You wanted to just save Angelino vampires a while ago, babe. Now all of California? What's next? The whole country? Worldwide?"

"I've got time. Centuries, in fact."

"Like the rest of the world will still be here. Regardless..." Sandy faded out, a concerned look on her face. "Yeah, this would be a good thing to do."

"What's going on there?" Sophia rarely saw Sandy lose her cynical edge.

"Nothing. I just think of all that time and I still have no one to share it with."

"I thought you were looking." Sophia waved her phone. "That app thingy."

"You might have guessed, but I'm a picky bitch." Sandy took out her phone. "You want to see the action happening here?"

She opened the app and pressed a button to see available male vamps. They fed hand-drawn pictures—photos being impossible— one at a time, but instead of swiping, you pressed a button that said "Bite" for yes and "Stake" for no. The first one had a lantern jaw which Sophia thought was charming. "He's not bad."

"I've seen his type. He's not a vamp. He's a wanna-be thrall and I'm supposed to be the sugar vamp."

The next one had that dark gothic look. Even Sophia laughed. "How about Dracula here?"

"I need someone turned at least ten years ago. Not a squab like this." Sandy paused. "No offense to Jeremiah."

"That's okay. I like tender young flesh."

On Sophia's third try, the guy had a round face cut into a real photo of someone wearing a Star Wars t-shirt. Sophia held up the picture.

Sandy laughed. "Lives in the basement. I bet his mom is his thrall."

"Yep. You're a picky bitch." Sophia handed Sandy her phone. "You paying for this?"

"To my undying shame, yes."

That clicked with Sophia. "How much?"

"It's a $35 registration fee, then $4.99 a month."

"And it's all processed through VampAmp's servers?"

"Look at you getting all techie, babe. Yeah."

"Now we're making pumpkins."

Sandy guffawed at the expression. "What the hell is that about?"

"Damn. I just reached back to Reconstruction." Sophia laughed. "Seriously, we have the making of something here. VampAmp is connecting everybody out there, right?"

"Yeah. They even have some European and Asian sites going."

"This is what I'm talking about. We all need little things. The ones in San Francisco said they were making a farm. Perhaps that blood could be considered gourmet somewhere. So, and I'm just throwing stuff out, what if someone in New York can't get good pig blood, so they pay the ones on the farm a monthly stipend for a shipment."

Sandy started rattling her laptop. "Wait a sec. Yeah." She showed Sophia a website about micro loans. "Five dollars in Los Angeles won't get you a cup of coffee, but it will buy a couple of goats in Africa."

The ideas flowed rapidly, but soon Sandy had to go to avoid the dawn. For the next few nights, they phoned each other while Sandy constructed spreadsheets and text files. After two weeks of hashing out details, they brought it to Pamela.

"What do you want VampAmp to do?" Pamela looked genuinely interested.

Sandy took the lead here. "Since we're talking about microloans, this will need infrastructure, payment processing, all that. Mainly it needs computer power."

"I think this is workable." Pamela looked genuinely impressed. "I'll get the team on it."

And so, after three months of work, Sophia went to the offices to see how it was all coming together. Pamela sat her down at a computer and led her through the main site, some of the functionality, and ended with, "And we already have a few clients using the open beta version. Including your friends on the farm upstate."

"This is great."

"It's far from finished, but once again, the sheriff is looking out for everybody." Pamela embraced Sophia. "David would be proud."

"He would." Sophia stood, but Pamela stopped her.

"I think we have something else to show you."

Pamela led Sophia to the bullpen where Jeremiah waited for them. Next to him were his two new besties Maisie and Horton, young vamps with the millennial vibe of slouch hats, chunky jeans, and sweaters. They had been heading the tech team at VampAmp since Sophia first found out about the business.

Jeremiah pointed at a seat in front of a workstation. "Sit." As she looked at the screen, she saw a screen with a green grid on it.

Maisie came up behind her. "This might freak you out a bit, but you'll like the end result." She wrapped a white mask around Sophia's face, velcroing it together in the back. She felt gel inserts pressing against contours of her cheeks and a wire hanging from the right side.

Pamela laughed. "*Eyes Without A Face*."

"Isn't it more *Vanilla Sky*?" Maisie said.

Pamela waved off the young one. "Regardless, everyone who does this looks like a burn victim during the process."

Maisie pulled on the plug, maybe putting it into the wall or the computer, Sophia couldn't tell. Soon, the gel warmed and spread. She could feel it filling out the mask. "Now look."

Sophia looked at the computer. The outlines of a head appeared on the grid, slowly filling in until a face appeared. It was cartoony, but Sophia saw herself in that screen.

"Oh, shit!"

Pamela said, "This is the next step from those initial face scanning experiments."

Maisie typed on the keyboard between Sophia and the screen. "Let me save it for you. Hold still."

The program captured a still shot. The avatar looked like Sophia felt: huge smiley face. Horton began typing next to her, but Sophia reached out for Jeremiah, pulling his hip to her shoulder.

"Oh, boo. You don't know."

"I do." He gripped her shoulder. "And damn if it ain't like you."

"How close?"

Horton pulled a sheet of paper off the laser printer. "This close."

She looked at the printout. They'd taken her old Storyville portrait, the one where that crazy photographer Bellocq scratched out her face ages ago, and superimposed this new shot on it. She couldn't cry, but she felt the same emotion.

She put her face in her hand and let it all pour out. "I mean...I can't even." So many thoughts ran through her head. All those years of hiding because she didn't know what she looked like. Her uniform wardrobe because she wanted to be as plain as possible. She remembered putting on silky underwear for the New Orleans clients in the 1890s and hoping she was as sexy as she looked. She quivered with all of the contrasting emotions.

Jeremiah must have bent over because he was squeezing her tight. She opened her arms and enveloped him, putting her head on his shoulder. She kept repeating, "I ain't never..." over and over as the small group smiled.

Pamela whistled behind her. "Can I say, nice rack! I hope my boobs look that good when I'm over a hundred."

"They look even better now," Jeremiah said, which earned him a swat on the back of his head. "It's true!"

Sophia took off the mask and stood. "Y'all do great things every day." She slurred her words, but he didn't care. "I'm just happy to see them."

"This will be revolutionary," said Pamela. "It will make everyone more personable."

"Sandy will be happy. She'll know what the vamps on the dating app really look like." Sophia pulled up her phone to see her picture in the text messages.

"Oh, Sophia, there's something else." Horton was pulling down another printout. "We've had some people going through the Caballero's house. There's a huge archive in there. It's close to you, so I thought you might want to check it out."

"Yeah, for sure." She looked at the address: below I-10, but not far. If they went as far back as she thought, there must be something in there she would need to know.

In Eagle Rock, the clock hadn't reached 9 pm yet, but Rosalinda was ready to call it a night. She still hadn't bought a car—probably wouldn't—and felt these ride shares were great but an easy way to waste money. So she thought she'd get an early start on her 30-minute walk and lock up the place.

She'd been doing okay, not breaking even just yet, but enough that she'd had some return customers. The Mexicans of her age loved the *loteria* cards, but some of the white people she'd seen were disappointed she wasn't reading Tarot. Even though the readings were effective, she decided to buy the traditional deck. Why alienate customers when she was just starting out? She could try and convert them later. And while her readings weren't as strong, she dipped into her natural theatricality to sell her visions. That worked just as well as anything in this Hollywood-obsessed town.

As she locked the door, she heard some scrabbling behind her, setting off her internal alarm. She hadn't been as scared in San Francisco, but this town was much bigger and filled with people who spent all their time in cars, hiding themselves from their neighbors. They were just as apt to shiv you as buy you a drink.

As she set herself for danger, she heard a small voice in the dark. "*Tia?*"

"What? Who's there?"

At first, she thought the vision in front of her was a ghost. She'd seen enough of them over the years who needed help moving to the beyond. But tonight was different because the young woman who stepped out of the shadows was real. The young woman rushed up and embraced her.

"Oh, Aida! Everyone thinks you're dead. You never cease to surprise."

Rosalinda noticed a young black woman with her grandniece, both dressed in that shabby punk rock way. This friend had fully embraced it, with band names scrawled in white on her leather jacket. Aida wasn't as committed, but the girl looked filthy. Rosalinda figured both had been living on the streets.

The black woman held out her hand. "Spex."

"Rosalinda." She turned and re-opened the door. "Let's talk inside. You both look beat." As they all came in, Rosalinda asked if they wanted something to drink.

Spex said, "I'd love a beer."

"Sorry, dear. But I have a multitude of teas." Rosalinda set an electric kettle and joined the youngsters sitting at the table.

Aida avoided meeting her great aunt's eyes. "You can't tell my family anything. I've moved on from that life."

"Come." Rosalinda extended her hand and Aida walked over, kneeling before her aunt. Rosalinda lifted the young woman's head with her left hand and studied her face. "You don't lie. You've been through a lot in the last year, but I can see past the outward changes. Your aura has completely shifted since the last time I saw you. It almost burns my hand with all the fiery reds."

"I knew you were the right one to see."

Rosalinda flashed her eyes to Spex. "Aida, how much does she know?"

Spex laughed. "We only met last night, but damn."

"Spex knows one thing you know and one that you don't." Aida shuffled back to her seat.

"Well?"

Rosalinda had known about the coma, but Aida added the final detail she hadn't known, the vampire dying in front of her. "That's interesting. A vampire woman came to see me a few weeks back. Quite troubled, that one. Not far from how you look."

Spex laughed and slapped her knee. "Dude, your aunt is badass."

"More than you can know." But Rosalinda smiled. "At least right now. Now what don't I know?"

Aida filled in her ride to the desert. This story cut deep into Rosalinda's chest. How was she not there to help this little one who she cherished so much? But it explained the aura, the alien look in her eyes, the whole transformation of body language. While they weren't blood related, she knew her niece had access to the same river of magic she'd been dipping in since the late '60s. But how will she handle it? Rosalinda would love to rein her in, but she couldn't be sure Aida would let her.

"You have many roads before you, Aida. But what do you want? How can you serve the magic within you?"

"Spex and I were talking about this last night and today. We have many things for the future, but for now? We want to destroy the vampires."

Rosalinda laughed. "Really? Just that easy?"

"They've caused me pain. They must be doing it to others."

The kettle clicked and Rosalinda stood. "I won't deny that. But every living thing has a place in the universe. We may not be able to see it right away, but from afar, you can see the great mosaic." She returned to the table with three cups.

"But they aren't alive." Spex snickered at Aida's retort.

"Don't be pedantic. Magic won't fill a closed mind." Rosalinda poured out the water. They each picked their flavor from her small wicker basket and steeped the tea. "Let's not argue right now. Let me read the cards."

She handed the deck to Aida who shuffled the cards and turned to Spex. "We used to play this for candy."

Spex looked amused. "I've seen these but never knew what was going on."

"It's usually a game," Rosalinda said. "But somehow my vision is centered by them."

Retrieving the cards, she drew the first one: the deer. Aida's breath caught.

"Jumping, it goes searching, but it doesn't see anything." Rosalinda felt her niece's apprehension. "What is it?"

Aida described her vision of the deer leading her through the primal forest. She made sure to include that she left the deer behind for the volcano.

"Because our history is ill defined, you were born both under the deer sign and the volcano." Rosalinda paused to make sure she was being exact. "That's why you saw those visions in your...vacation from reality. You may embrace the volcano for its power, but the deer is still a major part of you. This fight will continue for the foreseeable future."

Rosalinda drew the next card: Death.

"Cool!" Spex's smile showed her bright teeth. But Aida wasn't as excited.

"I've done some reading, *tia*. Yes, Death means death. But in Tarot, it can mean transitions."

"And in our culture, it's just the next phase. A place to spend time with your family." Rosalinda smirked. "I'm putting it off for as long as I can."

"What do you see?" Aida looked cautious.

"This one is fairly obvious. You were dead. Are dead to your mother and father. And you have made a pledge to hunt those who are already dead. Look at the card."

Aida read the inscription at the bottom: "Death, thin and lanky." Aida shrugged. "So?"

"It means people don't get nourishment from death. It leaves them starving. This path you choose will not be satisfying."

"I don't see that. I see death as healthy."

"Not for the dead." Rosalinda saw her comment cut Aida, but the young woman was making some serious choices. She may be dead to the rest of the family, but Rosalinda would rather her stay alive.

"Let's do the last card." The draw brought out El Mundo: The World. "The world is a great ball and we are a great mob."

Spex looked confused, so Aida said, "It's a pun in Spanish. *Bola* and *bolon*. But I still don't see any meaning."

"It means you should have some perspective." Rosalinda took a drink. "I would understand if you wanted revenge against the man who harmed you. But to kill all vampires? You don't know all of them. They contain multitudes. As do we Mexicans. As do the many descendants of Africa." Spex nodded at the point. "The world is bigger than you can imagine it. You want it to be small. There's always more than expected."

Aida stood. "Thank you, *Tia* Rosalinda."

She turned to go, but Spex stopped her, saying, "Wait. We wanted—"

Aida stopped. Rosalinda could tell the reading had upset her, but she still had needs. Aida asked, "Where can I learn more about magic?"

"Unfortunately, I had to sell most of my books when I left San Francisco. Here's a few." She went to the back and grabbed some essential texts. Aida had read one, but her eyes lit up at the titles. Rosalinda then said, "I've heard USC has a few collections you might want to see." As she handed the books to Aida, Rosalinda put a fifty-dollar bill on top. "It's not much—"

Aida embraced her aunt. "Thanks."

"This comes with one requirement. You come here once a month and share your progress. You may not always like what I have to say, but I must see which choices you're making."

Aida nodded, leaving with Spex quickly. Rosalinda cleared the dishes and shut out the lights. The darkness will try and take Aida and the young woman would probably not fight it. But Rosalinda would, even if she had to sacrifice herself.

Chapter Five

As she and Jeremiah were driving home from Venice after seeing the facial construction technology, Sophia couldn't take her eyes off the picture of her computer-generated face superimposed on her Storyville body. She felt it was some sort of latent narcissism that cut close to the actual mythology, her staring into the pool at her own face and unable to look away. Jeremiah's laughter shook her from her reverie.

"Now you know how I feel."

"Shut up." She elbowed his right arm. "I won't lie and say I'm not pretty. But this isn't about attractiveness. It's...I don't know. Nostalgia? Maybe. Some vanity, for sure."

"I know. It's something new," Jeremiah said. "Just like when you moved here and every little thing was a big deal. You didn't change much for a hundred years, then pow! New things make your head twirl."

"I guess you gotta point." She looked up at the freeway signs. "Did we already pass the 10? Why are we at the 105?"

"Look at you finally figuring out L.A." Jeremiah laughed. "Pow! We're going somewhere new. It's a surprise."

"You're full of 'em tonight." She was a little angry, but she decided to go with it.

"I hope you like it because Maisie, Horton, and I have been working real hard on this."

They drove further south than Sophia had ever been, following the 405 all the way to Long Beach where Jeremiah finally exited the freeway. They drove through the downtown section, past the aquarium and the huge old ocean liner The Queen Mary, following the ocean until they turned up Alamitos Boulevard, a street at an odd angle instead of the grid down here. He pulled up after three blocks outside of a two-story building. The top story was flush with the street, while the bottom had large wooden columns supporting the upper floor. It had the vague look of plantation style and the sign hanging looked like a mermaid from the front of an old sailing ship. A sign in the window said, "Opening Soon."

"We have normal human partners who wanted to open a pirate themed bar. The front room is called 'The Deadman's Chest.' C'mon, take a look."

They crossed the street, empty and abandoned this early in the morning. Jeremiah unlocked the front door as Sophia crossed the street. His wide grin looked like the boy of old, not the new, predatory version. He held the door and Sophia entered.

As soon as she stepped in, she felt a weird rush. This place looked exactly like the hold of an old ship, complete with portholes, curved wooden walls, hanging lanterns, and lots of rope and nets. But it wasn't all realistic, as niches and alcoves held obvious fakery, like stuffed parrots, a mannequin dressed in full Long John Silver wear, and a plastic giant squid entangled in hemp on the roof. They continued to the back room which held a full polished wooden bar and a small stage to complement the tables and chairs.

"This is crazy." Sophia wasn't sure this was her kind of place, but it was fun.

"One of the humans is a set designer for Hollywood shows. He has all these connects for the props and stuff. He and another guy did a lot of original woodwork, too."

"The bar's magnificent."

"It's weird. I think he bought it in Louisiana and shipped it here."

She looked closer. It very well could be cypress, that weird tree that thrives in the swamps. She knew cutting them down was illegal now, so if it was authentic, it would be original and old. Maybe as old as her. Regardless, the investment was worth it because it elevated the space.

Sophia was confused. "Are you really expecting vamps to hang out with humans?"

"Oh, no. Here's the best part." He led her to the back, near the restrooms. On the wall were two stacked barrels with a keypad next to them. Jeremiah tapped some buttons and the barrels opened with a clack. "Magnetic lock," he said and proceeded up the hidden staircase. As he got to the top, he held out his arm like a game show host. "Welcome to Vampirates!"

Where the bottom bar looked like below decks, this place looked more like the captain's quarters. The whole top floor was open and each set of tables along the walls—five in all—had a velvet curtain for privacy. The rest of the place had puffy oxblood leather chairs, solid wood tables, and a small dance floor. On the front wall was a stage riser with railings and a giant ship's wheel and the full bar sat opposite it in the back. All of the windows were bricked over so no sunlight could enter.

Jeremiah took her to the bar. "We'll have bottled blood mostly, but we'll also have rotating taps for those who want something special."

"It looks like you really thought this through. But I have one question: why Long Beach?"

"This is also something I wanted to talk about. Sit." They reclined into two of the chairs, Sophia noting they were very comfortable. "We looked in Venice because that's what they know. The money was just too much. Everything from Malibu to LAX was too far out of our price range. But that's happening to a lot of people, vamps including. With the prices going up, certain pockets are getting an influx. Long Beach has cool architecture, an established downtown, a beachy attitude—"

"And plenty of poor people."

"Don't you think I know that? Shit, I'm making more than I ever thought I would, but there's plenty people doing worse. I know our coming will mean their going, but I don't know what else to do." Jeremiah shifted in his seat. "We ain't alone. Half the VampAmp users are moving here or San Pedro. They're all thrilled to have a dedicated space for them."

"I'm worried about that drive. How far is it back to Silver Lake?"

"'Bout 25 miles."

"You're gonna want to do that every night?"

Jeremiah sat up, looking like he'd prepared what he said next. "Do you know how much you'd make if you sold the center?"

Sophia's stomach dropped. This wasn't what she expected at all. "No. A lot, I guess."

"Everything around there is listed close to or over a million."

"Dollars?"

Jeremiah laughed. "Yes. It ain't the prettiest thing in the world, so I'm thinking it would be less, like maybe 800-900 or so. A house in Long Beach would be half that and we could live high on what's left over."

"Okay, two things. Where would I hold meetings?"

"We talked it over. You could take over VampAmp's or you could use Vampirates until you found a better set up."

"Then there goes the extra money. But the other thing is, y'know, I like Silver Lake."

Jeremiah nodded in agreement. "It's one of the best neighborhoods in the city. But we live on a crowded street. And that place ain't a house. It's an office building with amenities. Didn't you yourself talk about the apartment you had back home? With the garden?"

"Courtyard, but yeah. I didn't own it, but it was nice having a little outdoor space." Sophia stood and walked to the bar. "This is too much, boo. You gotta give me time."

Jeremiah slinked behind her, embracing her from behind. "We have time, but..."

Sophia leaned back into him. "But what?"

"The prices are gonna shoot up here."

"But so will Silver Lake. I'm thinking there will always be a discrepancy."

"No, you're right." Jeremiah turned her around. "I didn't think you'd dive into this. But... I got plans. I want you to be a part of them."

As they kissed, Sophia could see the first cracks in their relationship, a simple chink which could widen easily. She was flushed with too many emotions right now. He needed to let her sink into this easily if his plans were going to pan out.

They went downstairs, finally, as the hours were getting short.

"When are you planning on opening?"

"Halloween is always too much, so we thought we'd launch on Solstice just to make sure we've built up the buzz."

Sophia always loved Solstice parties, so much darkness and so much time awake. Hopefully by then, three months down the line, she'll have some sort of decision.

While it took the Aida and Spex a few weeks before they could get there, when they finally made it to USC, they were both surprised by this expansive campus. They had spent some time trying to wrangle up a squat but found nothing that didn't feel dangerous.

They spent all their time together, mostly as protection, but they also discussed their magic plans.

They made two goals. First, they would assemble a circle to expand their studies but also gain help in the anti-vampire quest. Next, they would find a place for their gatherings, hopefully somewhere Aida and Spex could sleep. A coven community really appealed to them as life on the street was wearing them out.

Spex even confessed, "If this doesn't work out, I'll move back to Compton. It sucks, but maybe Moms has a place for you, too."

"Let's consider that the safety net. Once we have a place, we can get a side hustle to keep it together."

USC was on the southern side of town, Spex jokingly calling it "the north part of South Central." She talked about how the neighborhood kids back in Compton all dreamed of going there. "You see all this USC gear everywhere: sweatshirts, pants, hats. Since the Raiders left, it's like they're the pro football team."

They got off the Expo Line at the stop between the campus and Los Angeles Coliseum. Crossing the street, they entered the university's gate, thick brick columns with thinner wrought iron poles between them. From there, the main street, pedestrian only, opened up. Big enough to include a median, it stretched from Exposition Boulevard to 32nd Street, the full width of the campus. As they walked, the October heat, always more oppressive than summer, radiated off the beige concrete, making both of their leather jackets unnecessary. As they looked around, they saw all of the female students wearing a version of the same thing: tank tops, athletic tights, and running shoes. As the crowds passed them by, Aida said, "Guess we didn't get the memo."

"Seriously. Are they going to class or the gym?"

As they reached the crossroads where the two campus landmarks stood—Tommy Trojan, the giant bronze statue of an ancient warrior, and the Shumway Fountain, two tiered and shooting over twenty feet in the air—they saw a few different looking people. But they were more the hipster types, always in flannel shirts and wearing cotton skullcaps. While checking out the students was part of the mission, the real goal lay in the Doheny Library.

Standing at the end of a small park intersected by a six-way crosswalk, this library was older than most of the buildings. The front steps lead to heavy doors which were propped open. Aida felt it might take the two of them to wrench back a sealed one. Aida had written down where to find the Encyclopedia of the Occult, just a short right turn from the front desk in a room full of academic journals. In the back right were the heavy volumes. They each picked out a few interesting topics, grabbed four books and took them to two overstuffed chairs facing each other with a small reading table between them.

The reading was dry but informative. Both took notes on what to read next. After an hour, Aida felt thirsty, so she left the room to find a water fountain. As she stood after drinking, she saw another woman staring at her. Thin and even shorter than Aida, she wore a cotton flower print dress—older, but not vintage; more thrift store style—and worn Birkenstocks. Her dark hair was a tangle that fell to the right but also down her forehead and over her circular granny glasses.

"I, like, never do this." Her voice had that tone where everything sounded like a question. "But the books you're reading? I've never seen other students using them."

"I'll tell you a secret. We aren't students. I mean, not at USC."

"Oh. Cool." She seemed nervous about that fact, but she still held out her hand. "Lisette."

"Black Rose."

This also got her to draw back, but Lisette pressed on. "Are you a practitioner?"

Aida nodded. "My friend and I are doing some... real cool stuff. But we're looking to—" She looked over her shoulder to see they were mostly alone. Still, she whispered, "Form a circle."

"I have a few friends into the same thing. Hey, let's get some tea. Or coffee, maybe."

Aida had spent all her on-hand cash on the Metro TAP card. "Yeah, we're pretty broke."

Lisette brightened. "I can pay. No problem."

She took them to the coffee shop in the library building on the other end of the building. A courtyard offered metal tables and chairs as well as some seating under a brick breezeway.

"They sure like their brick here," Spex said as they waited for Lisette. In a few minutes, Lisette brought a coffee for Spex and two chai teas—one for Aida and one for herself.

Lisette sat. "So between the books and Spex's tattoo, I picked up on your studies."

"Damn." Spex rubbed the back of her neck. "This thing is like a billboard, yo."

They had found a place in the furthest corner, away from the scattered few drinking and studying. Lisette leaned forward, still not wanting to project. "We have a little subset of our women's studies group—"

"Hold up." Spex looked confused. "You can just study about women's issues?"

"Sure. It's been around at least until from '70s."

"And they give you a job for that?"

Lisette looked serious. "What job I get doesn't concern me. I want to be defined by other actions and beliefs. Capitalism is a tool of the patriarchy. I'll leave that to the unenlightened."

"Now you're speaking my language." Spex nodded deeply. "A little old-fashioned anarchy."

"Well, I'm more of a socialist, but I think we all want some collapse of the system."

Aida laughed. "My college classes were, like, how to write a thesis statement and algebra. I didn't learn any of this."

"As much as we're getting from USC, it's still somewhat hindering. This is essentially a conservative campus with pockets of really neat ideas." Lisette giggled. "It's a bit nerdy, but the people I'm finding here who get it? They really get it."

They chatted about their home lives for a bit. Lisette was from Seattle and was happy for the L.A. weather. She'd found some insights in high school, like Taoism and Zen, but she found more power in her own European Jewish background. She dug into kabbalah, but that was hard to penetrate, so she found more practical magic books which led her to Wicca. "I like that you can use anything within it as long as you invest the power."

"Like her aunt." Spex nodded at Aida.

Aida sipped her chai, a little too hot for the time of year. "Yeah. She reads futures using *loteria* cards."

After Aida explained the game, Lisette looked impressed. "Exactly. How cool!"

After a promise to take her to her aunt sometime, Aida pushed further. "Here's the real problem. Our families don't want us. We've both been on the street for months now."

Lisette looked concerned but not put off. "One of our group lives in Orange County. She's dying to get a place near campus." She paused. "Not to be fascist or anything, but if she gets the place, can you guys cover half the rent?"

Aida focused. This was serious for her and she wanted Lisette to understand. "We will work our asses off. Just give us the opportunity."

Lisette looked away. "I think you'll have to prove yourself first. I want to trust you, but it's not my money."

Aida reached out and took Lisette's hands. "All I've ever wanted was the freedom to be my best. If we put together a circle, we can empower each other." She felt some fire enter her eyes. "This power will be beyond whatever you can imagine."

Lisette looked shocked, but that quickly turned to desire. "Whoa." But she shook her head. "Still, we'll need to do at least one ceremony together before any commitments."

Spex nodded. "I get it. Shit's tough, but so are we. I promise what we show you will be exactly what you're looking for."

With that, they headed out as Lisette needed to get to class. While walking back to the Metro stop, Aida laughed.

"What?" Spex smiled but also looked uncertain.

"How am I gonna get a job? I'm dead."

"Shit." Spex elbowed her in the ribs. "We'll figure that out. But I'm no slacker. I'll do whatever. You, *chica*? All you gotta do is bring the magic."

Two days after touring Vampirates, Sophia phoned Horton's friend Roxanne about touring The Caballero's house and maybe getting a peak at the archives. She sounded excited to meet Sophia, so they set an appointment for a Thursday evening when they both knew they'd have some time to wade in the records.

Apparently, the exact location of The Caballero's house had been a secret before his death. Pamela had never been there, nor had any of the Black and Whites. The Caballero had kept companionship with a thrall who had piles of papers stacked for a few decades, but Lucretia had kept her mouth shut until his passing. So when the Uber dropped Sophia off in a grand Spanish-style mansion, called a villa in the local parlance, in the West Adams area, she was shocked. The neighborhood was below I-10, closer to USC and

South L.A. than to Hollywood, and the house was surrounded by rows of apartment buildings. If anyone cared to drive through this neighborhood, which most of the glittery party animals in town wouldn't, the house would stick out.

The brick fence looked as if it had been patched a few times, as the beige didn't match in places, but the yard was much bigger than anything around it. Taking up almost a third of the block, the green lawn had brown spots, seen everywhere due to the recent drought conditions.

As Sophia walked through the gate, a young-looking woman dressed like a 1940s secretary—pencil skirt to the knee, button up blouse with puffy shoulders, and a rolled-up hairstyle like Lucille Ball on her TV show—opened the door to her. She identified herself as Roxanne.

Sophia said, "Pardon, but are you older? Like the Black and Whites?"

"Oh, heavens, no. I'm only 35. I just love these fashions. I troll all the Goodwills and consignment shops for authentic clothes. I even have a few thralls out there shopping for me."

"I remember them coming and going. Never could get my hair to stay put like that."

"It isn't easy." Roxanne pointed into the house. "Please, come in."

Sophia found the front was its own form of fence since the door opened onto a veranda. She remembered those Creole cottages back home which hid all the architectural elements from plain view. They all had courtyards and balconies, but only for the residents to enjoy. Roxanne took her into the inner sanctum to a room lined with metal file cabinets. She thought it must have once been the master bedroom because the room was large enough to hold 30 of these boxes.

"From what we can gather, The Caballero stayed in the basement." Roxanne laughed. "I know what you're thinking and, yes, he added it in the mid-20th century."

"I would hate to see what an 1850s basement would be like in Los Angeles."

"Seriously. Oh, you're from New Orleans, right? What are the basements like there?"

"Swimming pools." When Roxanne looked confused, Sophia said, "You dig six, seven feet, you hit water. Not a basement in the whole city."

"Wow." Roxanne went to a small desk which was neat, but it still had stacks of papers on its corners. From the desk, she grabbed a leather-bound book. "So, here's what I got so far. I've been doing my best to index the major sections. I've been able to identify the following from his filing system: personal anecdotes and stories, lists of all the cabals—some not around anymore—with detailed lists of members, and what he thought were inherent threats to vampires."

"May I?" Sophia thought that last section might be interesting since the only threats she had seen—other than those New Orleans werewolves—were other vampires. She combed through the list, reading it aloud. "Lycanthropes? Sure, although my boyfriend used to be one."

"Oh, I've met Jeremiah. I'm really looking forward to the opening of Vampirates."

"So is he." Sophia's eyes continued down the list. "Zombies? I'm still not convinced they exist. 'Various Monsters?'"

"Those delve into Mexican folklore although he was convinced there would be threats."

"Good to know. And what is a *bruja*?" She pronounced it *broo-jah*.

Roxanne corrected her. "*Broo-hah*. Witches."

"Oh really?" Sophia scanned her mind. "I've known a few Voodoo priests, but I haven't met an actual witch."

"This is actually very interesting." Roxanne seemed to have the location memorized as she walked directly to a cabinet and pulled out two files. "Here it's cross-filed under autobiography and threats." She handed the manila folder to Sophia.

"Do I need gloves or something?"

"No, he had these notes typed up, so the paper isn't archival. But you can read it over there." She pointed to a line of three wooden desks, all empty.

Sophia took the file and began paging through it. The beginning was a wild story of some witch who became obsessed with The Caballero in 1830, a few years after Spain had surrendered California to Mexico. According to this story, she had known The Caballero as a young boy and was shocked when she saw he hadn't aged. She figured he had been turned and decided he needed to be killed because, as the text said, "His everlasting soul had been surrendered and the body was now a vessel for evil."

She tried many spells to entrap him, but he eluded her. By 1835, she had convinced a young priest to follow her, but when she revealed the spells used in trying to capture The Caballero, the padre turned on her and had her hung. The Caballero then got access to her house so he could study her works before the church representatives destroyed the whole thing. He collected everything he could and brought it back to his villa.

Sophia then read what he saw as necessary for fighting witches. First, all of their power is supernatural.

The text read, "They talk a great deal of nature and the derivations of magical energy as if it were natural phisicks (sic) which all the philosophers are keen to discuss. But no, outside of ley lines, I can find no source but those beyond the veil."

He later wrote because they had connected to a higher entity, the best way to counteract a spell was by cutting off that source. He suggested circles of power, gathered energy, or, when all else failed, the vampire should tap into their own supernatural sources. Sophia laughed when she saw that, Roxanne coming over to see what caught her attention.

"I've seen some religion hook in vamps," Sophia said. "But magic? I've never seen one of our kind doing that."

"Excuse me, but didn't you say something about Voodoo? I thought you were a practitioner."

Sophia laughed. All vampire societies were small, everyone knew everyone else's business. "I have a... I hate to call him a friend because he's threatened to kill me more than once. But I did see him connect to his higher power." Sophia cocked her head, something nagging at the edge of her consciousness. "I mean, I did bleed him, so maybe there's a bit of Voodoo in me."

"Man, my life seems so boring compared to yours."

"My girl, I've had decades where nothing happened. Like the '50s? Soooo boring. You'll have all of those experiences later. It's one of the best parts of being like us."

Sophia skimmed the rest of the book but didn't see any other points of interest. She looked back at the files, knowing many nights would be needed to understand the overall vision. She looked up at the clock and saw it was closing in on 2 am. She walked the folder back to Roxanne.

"I'm going to head out, but can I come back later?"

Roxanne nodded vigorously. "Seriously? You're the first to come here other than perfunctory hellos with VampAmp. Somebody has to use this info, right?"

"I should know it," Sophia said, "but I hope I don't have to use it."

Chapter Six

Lisette didn't waste any time setting up Aida and Spex's trial run. She invited the two to meet her other Wiccan friends and run a ceremony in her dorm room.

"My roommate is in a sorority. At this point, she only spends a few weeknights here." She gave them the entrance directions for her building via text. They were going to run an Esbat, or full moon ceremony, since that was the closest worshipful day to their first meeting. Before they went, Spex wanted to discuss what they were doing.

"I mean, this is a Goddess ceremony. Who would we be invoking?"

"I haven't done any sacrifices for Tonantzin since my rebirth. Would you be open to that?"

"Sure."

In preparation for the meeting, they went to Santee Alley, an open-air bazaar on the eastern side of downtown. They walked past stalls filled with sparkly but cheap *quinceanera* dresses, cowboy shirts with fanciful inlays, boots of all skins, and CD shops until they found what they were looking for: a small *botanica* stocked with foot-high statues of Our Lady of Guadalupe. They negotiated the price down to five bucks and then returned to the mission where they'd been staying. They pulled paints from the arts supplies set aside for the homeless children, darkening the statue's face and hands until it resembled the deity Aida saw in her vision. They made sure to put her into a bag right away so no one would get angry at a perceived heresy. Spex went through her backpack to see that her supplies—ritual knife, salt bag, crystals—were all intact. With her thumbs up, the two departed for the university.

They came in the front gate on Jefferson this time, then followed to the left through a small quad which led to a library. A thin and shallow fountain with waterfall feature sat outside the dorm tower, stretching close to 20 yeards. They were supposed to show ID at the front desk, but the bored looking undergrad wearing a Greek-lettered sweatshirt waved them in from behind the front desk.

As they rode the elevator up, Spex looked despondent. "Dammit, I really wanted this life."

"Shit ain't fair, for sure. I got some community college, but that was me going to class then straight home. This would've been fun."

"All I know is if these chicks hook us up, then we won't have to worry. We'll get all this plus some."

They fist bumped and the elevator doors opened. The hall to Lisette's room was an antiseptic white broken up with colorful banners. Some were school rah-rah propaganda, others were advertising clubs and activities, but mostly the doors were the expression of choice. Lisette's had the Greek letters of her roommate, but nothing to identify her beliefs.

They knocked and entered. Small as rooms go, this space was totally utilitarian: two beds on metal racks, two wooden desks with chairs, and a window out on the quad. The roommate's side was decorated with posters of Drake and Justin Beiber, but Lisette's side was blank.

With Lisette was an Asian woman taller than both Aida and Spex. She wore mid-calf combat boots, a short red plaid skirt, and a Fields of Nephilim t-shirt. But the main difference between her punk look and Spex's? Her stuff was clean. Mall punk. Aida hoped Spex wouldn't reject her out of hand.

She introduced herself as Mina. "I'm the one looking to move."

Aida went over to Lisette while Spex and Mina started chatting.

"You really keep yourself hid." She looked past the bed to see the only personal item out: a picture of her and what looked to be her parents under the reading lamp and next to a stack of books.

"Plenty of people already think I'm weird. Why confirm it?"

Aida looked around the room. "Are we waiting on someone?"

"I'm supposed to text Gilly when you got here, so..." As Lisette typed into her phone, she approached the closet. Putting her device away, she pulled open two floor length doors. Inside were all her clothes, but a hidden cubby hole was filled with candles, herbs in bags, and a folded up black velvet cloth. She pulled these and other ritual supplies out and put them on her bed. "We're not supposed to have candles. Fire hazard, they say. But fuck them."

A knock sounded on the door and Lisette opened it to a woman with very curly blonde locks falling just past her neck. She had pale skin accented by the very black dress she wore: long, blooming sleeves with a mid-thigh skirt. She hugged Lisette.

"Omigod, omigod, omigod! We're finally doing it!" She hugged Mina, then bowed deeply to Aida and Spex. "I'm Gillian but everyone calls me Gilly. So glad to be in this august company! May we rattle the pillars of Heaven!"

Lisette laughed. "Take it down a notch. Save it for your next audition."

"Fine! But let's not waste any time."

Together, they spread out the velvet cloth, fully covering the space between the door and the beds. Painted on the fabric was a gold pentagram with various symbols filling in the angles created by the star.

Lisette pulled a table made of dried sticks and leaves out of the closet, placing it in the center. "This is my altar. I made it from the trees out near Mount Ranier."

They all sat in the lotus position within the circle, enough room for all to fit but they still were touching toes. Lisette turned to Aida.

"Black Rose, please take the lead."

"Since this is a full moon, we planned to give praise and sacrifice to the Goddess, one in particular." She pulled out the re-purposed Guadalupe statue and placed it on the altar.

Lisette looked freaked. "Are you two Catholic or something? Because I'm Jewish and—"

"Relax." Aida was surprised at her own calm. "Look at her face. The Goddess was co-opted by the Spanish and their church. We shall ask blessings of her true name, Tonantzin."

Using Mina's smart phone, they faced the statue true south. They each took a glass-enclosed prayer candle and set it before the altar. Lisette passed a plastic lighter until five flames stood before the statue.

Aida told them to link hands and close their eyes. "First, we shall call upon each direction: North, South, East, West. Center ourselves where we are within them. And wherever paths cross, the Goddess will be there."

In her own mind's eye, Aida flashed back to her awakening, the living statue within the garden of roses. Aida spoke directly to her.

"O Mother of Death, Mother of Rebirth, on this night lend us your power. O Protector of Women, shield us against our enemies. O Snake Woman, help us shed our skins and be reborn in your light!"

Tonantzin replied in the heads of all the young women, "The seeker has returned."

"What the—" Gilly's outburst was shushed by Aida.

"Once again, child, you must choose your paths. I shall remain your guiding light."

Within her mind's eye, Aida could see all five of them sitting around the rose garden, surrounding the goddess. Each lit up in different colors. Aida's fiery red was the strongest and Gilly's golden glow the weakest, but each woman had some color radiating around them. Aida took note: Lisette green, Spex blue, and Mina indigo.

"Lead us, mother. Open all paths!"

The rose walls split, showing too many corridors to count. Aida thought it looked like a maze, but she couldn't see any paths crossing. Each choice would influence where she ended up.

"Give thanks to the Directions," Tonantzin bellowed. "Give thanks to the Winds!"

Aida could feel her hair lifted by a strong breeze. She saw her friends' locks were also flowing, except for bald Spex. Still, she smiled in the warm, soothing air.

Aida could see the deer peeking out of one of the rosy paths. She wanted to smile but instead felt annoyance. She shook her head, then the deer scampered off.

"And that is a choice," the Goddess said. A windy tornado swirled around her statue, encompassing everything until the woman opened their eyes and found themselves back in the dorm room.

Gilly rolled out of the power circle first, balling up in the corner. Tears dribbled on her cheeks. "Holy...holy shit. I...I..."

Lisette went and embraced her while Spex snuffed the candles. Aida let out a breath. She felt like she'd been holding it for fifteen minutes or me. "We must give an offering."

Lisette sat Gilly up. "She's right. Pull it together."

"Was there acid in the candles? Did we trip or something?" Gilly verged on panic. Aida crawled over and cupped the blonde woman's head in her hands, staring deep into her eyes.

"Whatever you were before has evolved. You're on the other side now. Don't run from it. Embrace it. Embrace me." She pulled Gilly into her arms, Aida feeling her breath slowing. Finally, Gilly seemed in full control.

"I don't know you. And I confess, you scare me. But that? I wasn't expecting that."

"Were any of us?" Mina laughed. "I thought we'd have a little fun and bond. But I feel reborn! The light of my aura burned away something. I didn't know I was empty until that light filled me."

"The sacrifice!" Spex picked up a sage stick, igniting it with her lighter. The smoke filled the room, calming the whole group.

As they sat together, taking in the aroma, Lisette gripped Aida's hand. "I'm shocked and surprised. I also didn't know what to expect. But if this is a peek at your power, then maybe we'll all benefit." Lisette opened her dorm fridge, pulling out a six pack and a cake pan. "I know we're supposed to do wine and cake, but all I've got is stout and brownies."

As they drank the beer and sliced up the confection, they heard a rattling at the door. As it opened, a woman wearing a sweatshirt and leggings stopped in the transom.

"What are you bitches doing in my room?"

"Witches," Lisette said. "We're witches, Britney. Get that shit right."

Over the next few months, the coven solidified their bond. Although they never had the same vision as the initial ritual, they still prayed and practiced together once a week. After one month of searching, Mina found an apartment. It was cheap, on the other side of the 110 from school where the redevelopment hadn't reached, but that made it easier for Aida and Spex to pay their share. They had to sacrifice some, sharing a bedroom in a two-bed layout, but anything was better than living on the street.

Lisette drove them to Burbank, springing for two single mattresses from Ikea. She said, "You gave me so much confidence after the ritual, I'll do anything to keep the coven together." The apartment building was square and brick with walls even more generic than the dorm room, but after two weeks, Spex and Mina turned it into a witches' roost.

They painted the walls deep purple, foraged cheap furniture and painted it black with white stripes, and bought cheap linen and tie-dyed it, hanging it from the ceiling. Lisette's power circle rug was moved here so the newly-formed coven could call this place their headquarters. Then came the big debate as they sat on the floor of the new place while drinking a bottle of wine.

"We need a name," Gilly said.

"That's silly," Mina said. "The practice is most important."

"Here's my thing," Gilly said. "I walked away from Greek life. That shit was too much with the hazing and rules. But it felt really empowering to say, 'I'm a Kappa Phi.' It sturdied my attitude. If we could have that power! Then we'll feel at our best."

"She's got a point," said Aida. "The vamps have a name: the Muer-tos."

"That's bad-ass," said Spex.

During the months of searching and meeting, Aida had slowly revealed the supernatural realities. Gilly dismissed it all at first, but hearing Aida's stories brought her around. By this time, they had all agreed on Aida's revenge plot, but they didn't agree on how to do it.

"I'm feeling the name thing," said Spex. "It ain't just sororities. Think about the gangs. Crips, Bloods, names have power beyond just the neighborhood."

"Semiotically, it makes sense." They all stared at Lisette. "I'm sorry, but most of us are in college. I can have academic reasons for liking a name." She crossed her arms. "I said exactly the same thing Spex said, just in different terms."

Mina sighed. "Fine. But the name should reflect our philosophy. And we're still arguing about that."

They all naturally turned to Aida. As the most spiritually-attuned of the group, she had assumed de facto leadership. "I know the books talk about left-hand and right-hand paths. But that seems unnecessary."

"May I?" Aida ceded the conversation to Lisette. "That's the definition of a false dichotomy. But..." And she turned to Aida. "In our pursuit of the vampires, we'll need to employ mostly left-hand tactics."

Gilly looked worried. "It's very hard for me to join the dark side. I mean, duh! Star Wars kid! I see where we have to go to achieve this short goal, but what are we sacrificing in our pursuit? Can we all keep our souls intact through this?"

"I understand, Gilly." Aida spoke calmly but felt the rumble within. "But those motherfuckers killed me. I know that part of the reason I'm back is to take care of this scourge. I hope you can follow."

"I... I have nothing that compares." Gilly hung her head. She gulped from her glass. "Power can be fulfilling. But I'm worried it will be temporary. Then where will we be?"

"She's right." Mina looked like she didn't want to agree. "We have to set an endpoint. I've seen so many friends who can't deal with their depression. They think the prescription drugs will help, then the drinking, then the dope. They either end up dead or crazy. I'm doing this so neither will happen to me."

Lisette raised her glass. "When a majority vote for an end, we quit. Agreed?"

They all clinked glasses, their new way of setting rules.

"The Sinestros!" Spex giggled at her proclamation. After getting blank looks, she said, "Our name. We hang left, correct? So, sinister in the Latin..."

"Impressive," said Lisette.

"I may not be in school, but I studied, girl! Plus, Sinestro is the arch-villain in Green Lantern. Fuck a bunch of space cops!"

"Sinestros!" After speaking it in unison, the women clinked glasses. Lisette had chosen to journal all of the group's rituals and rules, vowing to burn it if they ever split. She used the classic black-and-white marbled composition notebook. She grabbed a Sharpie and wrote "Sinestros" in the name blank.

"Okay. What's next?" Spex had taken on the job of keeping things moving.

"Okay, we've all decided Halloween is for poseurs." Lisette read from a to-do list within the journal. "But there was talk of *Dia de los Muertos*. A ritual?"

Aida leaned forward. "While that would be good, why don't we just go party?"

"Now you're talking!" Specs rubbed her palms with anticipation.

Two weeks later, on November 2nd, they spent an hour at the headquarters fixing their make-up. Gilly had the most experience with grease paint, but they were shocked Aida didn't know the patterns. "Mama never let me do this. We did all the usual stuff, but without costuming."

Internet searches gave each of them inspiration, so after the skull paint and colorful dresses, they hopped on the Metro heading into Downtown. They were heading for Grant Park, one of the few green spaces in that zoo of high rises where people could get some relief from stomping on concrete. When they arrived, they saw many people dressed as they were, some better and some worse; two stages, one for mariachi and one for *Norteno* bands; a line of tents for food and goods; and a quiet corner where families set up their altars.

After getting some food—Aida had taquitos while the others snacked on churros—they walked toward the altars. Some were minimal, low benches with pictures of the deceased. Others were in tableau form, telling stories from the last year. President Donald Trump appeared in many places as a devil trying to steal Mexican children. Or the altars were peons to the undocumented. And others were very ornate, piled up like pyramids with the descendants surrounding great-grandfathers and grandmothers.

As they walked through the displays, Aida froze. Off behind one of the gaudier altars was her mother, sitting alone. Next to her was a footstool with Aida's picture on top and a candle featuring Our Lady of Guadalupe burning beneath. She couldn't help but cry, each of the coven embracing her as they realized what they were seeing. Spex pulled away, motioning the group to come with her as she approached Mama. Aida hid but got within earshot.

"Mrs. Menedez?" Spex softened her voice as best she could.

"*Si?*"

"We knew your daughter. From college." She started to falter, but Mina rubbed her shoulder. "I know she misses you very much."

Mama cried, her head drooping into hands. "Thank you." She spoke in halting English. "I talked to her *tia* who can speak with those beyond. I was assured she was happy where she was. But I miss her so much."

As the coven consoled Mama, Aida became overwhelmed. She walked out of earshot, unable to control her emotions. As she staggered away, looking to get a beer or comfort food, anything to stabilize her, she spotted a leather-clad group wearing full face paint. The Muertos with Tamar in the middle, laughing as if nothing was wrong in the world.

Looking around but not able to spot her group, she walked up to

Tamar solo, glaring at her adversary. After a few seconds, Tamar's senses kicked in and she whipped around to face Aida. But she smiled at the younger woman.

"Hey." Tamar nodded and looked put off when Aida wouldn't speak, just staring right at the vampire. "What do you want, kid?"

Aida shook her head because she didn't know what else to do.

But then Tamar smiled. "I know you! You're that little girl from across the street. What's up?"

Tamar reached out to shake Aida's hand. Both turned when they heard a splashing sound to their left. Papi, Tamar's brother, stood there with his mouth agape, two paper cups on the ground spilling out their beer.

"What the fuck?" Papi pointed at Aida, his face pale.

"What's wrong with you, Papi? It's just a kid."

He pulled Tamar close. "That's the kid. From like four months ago."

Now Tamar looked shocked and turned to Aida. "What's going on?"

Aida spoke through clinched teeth. "The Mother Goddess brought me back."

Papi looked genuinely scared. "Tamar! She's a *bruja*."

"A witch? Whatever." Quicker than Aida could react, Tamar was behind her, taloned fingers digging into Aida's throat. "You died once. I'll kill you again and again until it takes." Tamar dropped her voice to a whisper. "I don't want this. I'm different now. We'll both just let this go and we'll all be happy, _si_?"

Tamar didn't wait for Aida to respond. She gathered her crew and pushed Papi away, getting him to walk as fast as he could by her side.

In that moment, when the nails threatened her throat, Aida was scared. All of her power, all of her visions meant nothing when faced with a real enemy. But the fear turned to stone in her belly. She vowed right then and there she would never be scared again.

Aida wandered around until she found her friends. After telling them what happened, her eyes hardened. "But I'll tell you one thing. I don't care what she says. This shit is on."

Chapter Seven

Since the Glamazon Ball dominated the Halloween season (which includes Day of the Dead), Jeremiah and the Vampirates crew decided to make Winter Solstice their big launch. The longest night of the year had always been a big part of the vamp social calendar, so why not debut a major new vamp-only bar then?

Maisie and Horton fretted over the invite list. The three had decided to have a VIP section, but without clear social distinctions like councils and other indicators, making such choices without insulting somebody would be impossible. Jeremiah, of course, had little clue who was who and vowed to work the entire crowd, not just the specials.

"But, y'know, the sheriff has a spot at the adults' table," he told Sophia when explaining what would happen.

"The Solstice parties in New Orleans were so boring. Dragos always gave these long speeches followed by these endless ceremonies. All anyone wanted to do was drink some blood and dance, but no!"

"I'm thinking this one will be fun. We've got a solid DJ—not just darkwave—and a few new bloods for debut."

So the planning process began, with Jeremiah spending more nights a week in Venice because of it. After long deliberations, they set up the full invite list. After the first round of RSVPs, they had a few tables still open. They decided not to book them ahead of time to see who might show up.

In spite of herself, Sophia decided to get dressy for the big night. Even she knew her t-shirt-jeans-boots combo would be dull for such an evening, so she had Sandy bring her to the Glendale Galleria to shop for something nice but not too extravagant.

Sophia had heard these malls, the monuments to unfettered capitalism, were dying as more people used online shopping, but she couldn't find proof here. Even on a Tuesday night, this expansive indoor mall was busy. She saw such a variety of people: Armenians, Asians of all sorts, white, black. She found one of the truths about L.A. to be so obvious here: wherever you go, you're never alone.

Sandy must have seen her expression. "Yeah, babe. This is California living."

"I never went to malls before. Now I know why. If I hadn't've had dinner, my blood lust would be through the roof."

"I know. Just wave after wave. It's good I don't think of them as cattle anymore." Sandy kept walking past the smaller chain boutiques, pointing ahead. "These places are for the kids. You need something higher class."

They ended up at Macy's and soon Sophia had a handful of dresses for the fitting room. Sandy's style was very form fitting, skirts at knee or even mid-thigh, but not splashy or showing too much. Everything she wore could be for a party or for court. But Sophia wanted something more colorful, so she picked a few paisley-patterned dresses in red, blue and green. The blue one, paisley in white and some gold highlights, had a scoop neck and showed some cleavage. It was also the most comfortable, so Sophia stepped out to show Sandy.

"It ain't my style." Sandy shrugged. "I wore enough paisley back in the '60s. But this one on you? Bingo."

Sandy tried on a few things, all within her wheelhouse, then stepped out in a silvery fish-scale patterned dress cut really short. Sophia felt her jaw drop.

"Yes?" Sandy, usually so confident, looked doubtful.

"I mean...wow."

"You're speechless?"

"I guess."

"Then I'm buying." Sandy strutted back to the changing room, her shapely legs on display.

They arrived at the party together, one glammed up in the latest style and the other more conservative but still chic, and all eyes followed them as they made their way to the VIP.

Pamela waited at their table, half-filled champagne flute in front of her. Her style was simple, a red and green dress that felt Christmassy.

"They'll let just anybody in here," Sandy said, laughing at her own joke. "I mean, isn't this vamps only?"

Pamela shook her head. "As if I had any human friends anymore."

Sophia sat and examined the room as Sandy and Pamela chatted about each other's dresses. The dance floor was full, Maisie and Horton dancing close to each other right in the middle. They still wore their comfy sweaters and slacks, unbending to any fashion. A few Glamzons had a table near the DJ, their bondage wear gleaming. Two of them were shirtless, their white skin like light bulbs. But mostly it was a younger crowd, Sophia sensing few with prodigious power. Half an hour later, Tamar and the Muertos made their entrance, she sticking to her tough girl leather jacket and torn jeans. The majority of her cabal went to dance as the music segued to *bachata*, a Latin style of slower dance music. Tamar paused as they left but eventually turned to Sophia.

"You look nice." Tamar nodded at Sophia's look. "I remember that other time you looked nice."

Sandy's head whipped around. "What?"

"Yeah, the Glamazon Ball a few years ago. She looked nice then, too."

Sophia had to laugh. "So what you're saying is I'm a slob."

"No, I..." Tamar paused to re-examine her statement. "Yeah, I guess so. I've got no room to talk."

Sandy stood. "Drinks?"

They two women nodded, so Sandy strode over to the bar. Sophia could see something dark in Tamar's eyes.

"You okay?"

"I don't know. I've been dealing with a lot of shit. Is it okay to talk?"

"Sure." Sophia hadn't had a sit down with her in a while, especially because Tamar didn't attend rehab regularly. Tamar had resisted her ways when Sophia moved to town, but when Sophia was named the sheriff and worked hard to unite the community, Tamar became one of her biggest allies.

Tamar told her about the reading. "I mean, my thing with Alpha was so short, y'know? But he was intense. And he was at my level. When you lead a cabal, you gotta be tough all the time. You can't let nothing get to you. So when we had time together, alone I mean, we could drop all that shit. It's been close to a year now and I don't have nobody. So all this shit is built up."

Sophia looked to see who was listening. Sandy and Pamela were at the far end of the table, looking out at the crowd. With just the two of them paying attention, Sophia leaned in. "I had my one guy for so long. Back in New Orleans? Yeah, it was like that, but I was second in command. The cabal looked up to David, then he would pass off the work. It was much better in terms of dealing with the everyday shit. I don't lean on Jeremiah as much, but he's a good listener. But if he wasn't there, I don't know what I'd do." Sophia smiled. "Did you try that dating app?"

"What? No. That's for losers."

Sandy turned now. "Thanks, babe. No, really."

Sophia shook her head. "Damn vampire hearing."

Tamar looked shocked. "You use it?"

Sandy pulled out her phone. "After a certain nameless vamp bugged the hell out of me, I decided to give it a try. Babe, it's fifty-fifty, but I've gotten a few good rides out of it."

Tamar took the phone and flipped through the pictures. She laughed. "Fuck, some of my guys are in here. They're so full of shit."

Sandy looked at the picture. "Oh yeah. Diego's been wanting a date with me for months."

"He not good enough for you?" Tamar gave Sandy a hard stare but then dropped it with a laugh. "His mama would have a heart attack if he dated a white woman. Especially one from Orange County."

As all three probed the available males, they heard an industrial buzz, followed by the lights going black. As the room crazed with questions, crackling electricity sparked along the floor and ceiling. Sophia could see it was following sockets and power lines until they all converged on the disco ball. The giant globe exploded, sending glass shards everywhere. All the dancers dropped to the ground, covering their heads.

Everyone at Sophia's table had the same idea, ducking under the table.

Sophia looked at Tamar and Sandy, fear in both of their eyes. "What the fuck is going on?"

But she could see neither had an answer.

A few weeks before, while the other three attended their classes, Aida and Spex spread out to find as much info on vamps as they could find. Aida approached many of the downtown homeless kids, especially the Latinx, but she didn't get far. Most thought she was a kook, walking away soon after she asked. She thought she should have gone back to Boyle Heights, but the idea of confronting Tamar face to face by herself scared her. She knew she had powers, but she didn't have the bodily strength the vampire had.

Spex went south. Working South Central and Compton, she hit as many botanicas and herb shops that she could find. The Mexicans didn't want to talk to her, but she found the African woman who sold exotic spices and magic charms along Normandie, in the center of the Nigerian neighborhood in South Central, was more than willing to spill. She gave Spex an earful about demons visiting people when they sleep, how only Jesus could prevent soul rot, and, most importantly, about a cabal of vampires nearby. She gave Spex an address along Vermont Street, so Spex staked the place out one night. She saw four people leave together, all wearing leather but looking out of time. Most of their clothes looked like the '90s, like something out of a Public Enemy or NWA video. After spotting them, she went back to the Nigerian lady the next day to see if she had any lore.

"To the best of my knowing, they celebrate the Solstice. Longest night of the year."

Spex didn't ask how she knew it, but she decided to take that info back to Aida.

She also checked back in with her family. Her mom wasn't thrilled to see her as her heavily Christian lifestyle only allowed for Gospel music and church three times a week. Spex hadn't seen the inside of a chapel since her fifteenth birthday, so they always butted heads. But her mom did have some news for her.

"Your uncle's coming back soon."

"Really?" He had been back and forth between L.A. and New Orleans since he was a kid. According to Spex's mom, he would wear out a welcome then move.

"I'm giving him about a week here. I won't put up with his nonsense too long."

That spurred something in Spex. She remembered the book he'd given her years ago, so she went into her old room to look around. Most of her childhood stuff was gone, the posters and CDs removed because they were "Devil music" in her mom's estimation. But the bed was the same one as her childhood. Reaching between the mattress and the box spring, she found the slim volume there: a Voodoo primer.

Her uncle had been a Black Panther and had dabbled in many Afro-centric movements. He really dug Voodoo but couldn't be too open in this household. Spex slipped the book in her inside jacket pocket, not wanting her mother to see. But she figured if Aida was gonna bring her Mexican stuff into their magic, why couldn't she add some Yoruba?

When she met Aida at the apartment, Spex took the book out. They passed it back and forth, eyes almost breaking at the power of the *loa*, the main gods worshipped in Voodoo. A small section on Divine Horsemen, the ceremonies where the *loa* possess and "ride" their worshipers, had them rolling.

"You have to read more, Spex. They could really help us."

There and then, they planned their Solstice surprise for the vamps.

Aida wondered why Spex's uncle was drawn to Voodoo, and Spex laughed. "Almost all of black people have Louisiana roots. Some come from New Orleans, others from the northern parts, but we all have a bit. It's almost a fetish with some of us, calling ourselves creole or whatnot. It's not untrue, but it's funny. Anyway, anything New Orleans plays big here, so Voodoo ties in too."

Spex worked her way through the book, attracted almost instantly to Shango, who controlled thunder and lightning. She likened him to be Thor but much more powerful.

"He does exactly what we want to do to the vamps: shed light on them. Burn them from existence! Once we unleash the power, he'll take care of the rest."

The coven gathered together everything they deemed necessary: red and white cloth for the cloaks; red and white beads plus some cowrie shells for the necklaces; an ax from the hardware store, Shango's weapon; and the ingredients for a sacred stew: okra, dried shrimp, and coconut oil. The recipe said to use palm oil, but they couldn't find any in the local stores.

Gilly sewed the robes, having made many costumes for her plays. They looked close to altar robes which they all agreed was close enough. Lisette strung the beads together as that was the easiest task. She made sure a cowrie shell hung in the middle so it would be the focal point. Mina and Spex worked on the mask, the most important part of the ceremony. Spex would have to be mounted by the *loa* for their ceremony to work. They searched Google and watched old videos, especially the ones made by Maya Daren back in the '50s which showed the dancers in action. They decided to use the horned style, Mina working on the paper *mache* part.

"This is like back to summer camp," she said.

"I wish," Spex said. "Summer camp for me was television while Moms was at work."

"Yeah, they never let me leave the house," said Aida.

"That's sad," said Lisette. "Maybe that's a project we could do. Summer camp for the poor kids."

"I don't know," said Spex. "We all was pretty wild. You need some real patience."

They tabled the idea, while Aida got cooking. She was the only one who had kitchen experience and knew what to do with the dried shrimp. Okra was new to her, but once she got it stewing in the pot, it looked like *nopales*, the chopped-up cactus bulbs that her mom cooked all the time. After cooking it down for a half-hour, she had the witches taste it. Spex looked most troubled.

"It's okay, but it needs something more. I think Shango would want some more fire." She walked down to the corner store near campus and came back with some Cajun seasoning. After a few shakes, Spex said, "Now we're cooking for black folks." The others agreed the seasoning was worth it.

Finally, the Solstice was upon them. It was also important because it was the last day the Sinestros could meet before the holiday season whisked them all away. They wouldn't all be in the same city until mid-January.

At 11 pm, they dimmed all the electric lights and lit the candles. Spex had collected actual Shango candles from the Nigerian store, so they circled them up and watched the fire glow. Since they couldn't afford drums, Lisette had gone to Spotify and put together a Haitian drum playlist. Placing the altar in the middle of the candle circle, they placed a bowl of stew in the middle.

The plan was twofold: Aida would use divination to see where the vamps were, then Spex would get mounted and attack them remotely. Aida cradled a bowl of water in her lap, calling on Tonantzin to give her sight.

Staring into the bowl, Aida could only see shadows. She chanted prayers to the Mother, then felt her head being thrown back. Later, Mina would talk hushedly how her eyes had rolled into head, hiding her irises. Aida saw was a dark room filled with twisting bodies. She had no idea where it was, but she knew here was their target.

As the other three chanted from phonetically-spelled creole, Spex stood and circled the group, dancing cautiously as to not spill anything, especially the candles. She'd been studying the dance from videos, but she could never be sure how authentic her moves were. Maybe dedication would overcome the lack of talent.

As she shimmied, shook, and shuddered every part of her body, she felt a presence enter the room. The chanting became more intense as Aida started whooping in an incomprehensible language. And then Spex's mind was blank, gone in the moment that Shango entered her body.

The others could see the change. A lambent glow surrounded Spex as she continued to dance. But she would stop and throw her hands out. In her water bowl, Aida matched these lunges with the lightning firing in the club.

First, it blew out the lights. Then the disco ball. Spex could feel Shango peering though her, centering a giant ball of lightning on the roof.

"Yes! Yes! Yes!" Her spirit swelled as the sphere gathered power. "Death to the vampires!"

And she waited for the big release.

Sophia looked at the spot on the ceiling where the disco ball had exploded. All around her the electricity jumped from the wires to bodies, and, worst of all, bodies fell to the floor with their hair singed and no sign of consciousness. Vamps yelled and screamed, pushing around the crowded doorways.

Sandy and Tamar had their hands over their heads even though they were beneath the table with Sophia.

"What the fuck is going on?" Sandy, usually so cool, had completely lost it. She looked ready to stand and bolt. But someone ran by them and an arc of electricity fried them on the spot. Sandy retreated to the wall, eyes wide and mouth screaming.

"You have any idea who's doing this?" Sophia still stared at the ceiling. She could see the electricity swirling and gathering into a ball on the ceiling above the dance floor.

"I... I... Fuck!" Sandy was completely useless.

Sophia finally looked at Tamar, scared and angry at the same time. Tamar curled into herself but banged her fist on the carpet. "Goddammit, goddammit, goddammit!"

"I need you, Tamar! Look at me!" Sophia grabbed her by the shoulders and turned her so they could talk face to face. "What's going on?"

"I think it's a *bruja!*"

A witch? Just like in The Caballero's notes? Sophia's mind started racing through her recent search. If this was magic, it must have a source, usually from beyond the veil. But she needed a safe place to find the source.

Sophia crawled over to Sandy who was still in shock. Jumping up, Sophia sprinted to a table. A champagne flute was still upright, the scarlet dregs of a blood drink still at the bottom. Grabbing it, she slid next to Sandy, grabbed her by the chin to open her mouth, and poured in the ruby liquid. Sandy felt the jumpcharge and locked eyes with Sophia.

"What do you need, babe?"

"Get another table to surround us. I think I can do something, but I need to be protected from those bolts." She turned around. "Tamar, help her!"

Using their vampire speed, they took only 30 seconds to build a makeshift fort from tables and chairs. Sophia took a moment to survey the situation. About twenty bodies were on the floor knocked out, fifteen more looked alive but hiding, and a mob crowded the door not using the best emergency exiting strategies. The ball of lightning on the ceiling continued to grow, now about three feet in diameter.

Sophia put her back to one of the tables. Sandy and Tamar were on their stomachs and looking up at her. Tamar groaned. "This is all my fault."

"How?" Sandy looked ready to tear her apart if it was true.

"Never mind that now!" Sophia forced them to concentrate. "I've got to figure the source. Start naming gods of lightning!"

"Thor! Zeus! The Thunderbird?" Sandy's list didn't seem right.

"Xolotl? He's Aztec." Tamar's choice seemed closer, but Sophia didn't feel that was right.

She closed her eyes and tried to shut out the complete chaos around her. Digging deep into her consciousness, she found a spark which was crying out to her. Somehow she knew it was the last remaining connection she had with Lastie, the Voodoo priest in New Orleans who she'd bitten to gain extra power. And within that spark was the recognition.

"Shango!"

She jumped to her feet and stared into the glowing ball, now seven feet in diameter. She didn't know why, but she could see the red shading within the blue glow and knew the *loa* was feeding this attack. She used her connection to Lastie to unleash his source.

"I call upon you, Papa Legba, master of the crossroads and holder of the keys to the spirit world. Take this opened door and close it. Close the door! Close the door!"

She put all of her remaining energy into that spark until it grew inside her. Soon, she was enveloped by a white light. She pointed her body toward the lightning.

"Please by all I have, Papa Legba, close the door!"

Spex continued to circle the group, dancing in such a way that Aida knew she was possessed. She'd looked up from her scrying, knowing that the electric bolts were causing havoc among the partying vamps. But Spex's ax swinging was scaring the other coven members. While the attacks never came close to contact, they were angled enough for the other three to duck from the swings. Aida, now spiritually back in the room, could see Lisette and Gilly were on the verge of breaking the circle.

"Have faith," Aida shouted. "We must stand strong to achieve our goal!"

Aida looking directly at the two women bolstered their resolve and they re-invested in their chanting. Aida could see Mina relishing the danger, her indigo aura creeping closer to black.

Aida joined the chants. With her added voice, the room crackled with static. She peered into the bowl and could see the ball of lightning grow: two, three, four foot around. She tipped the bowl to see around the room and smiled. All of these monsters were scared, probably for the first time in ages. She looked hard for Tamar, but her nemesis was hidden. Maybe behind those tables and chairs circled for protection? She couldn't tell now that her main connection was severed.

Regardless, the moment was ready and she turned to try and catch Spex/Shango's attention.

"Destroy them!"

But as she yelled her order and peered back in the bowl, she spotted a woman in a paisley dress standing. As this woman extended her arms, she became enveloped in white light with streaks of green flowing within it. This light released from her hands, heading straight to the ball lightning. With a push through the scry, Aida was knocked back, the water spilling over her robes. When she looked back in the bowl, the water was clear. Any remote vision had been disconnected.

Spex fell straight to the ground mid hop. Crashing down with an "oof!", she rolled to her back. The other four immediately surrounded her. Spex pulled back the mask to reveal her bald head glistening with sweat.

"Did we do it?"

Aida's face fell. "I think one of them cut us off from the power."

"Who?"

"Some white woman."

Spex looked mad. "How could she know the spell?"

"We'll have to find out. I guess we can add another enemy to our list."

After Spex washed her face and all the others disassembled the altar, they all sat on the floor eating the okra stew.

"What did it feel like?" Mina said, leaning close to Spex.

"Truth be told, I don't remember a damn thing. I just know my body hurts from all that dancing." She laughed. "That shit was like half an hour in a mosh pit!"

Aida looked at the other three. "What did you guys feel?"

Gilly giggled, but Aida could tell it hid her nervousness. "That was really intense. I mean, when Lisette told me about this, I thought it would be chanting and bonding. But this? Like, whoa!"

"I gotta admit, I've never felt so empowered." Lisette set her bowl down. "But are we doing right? I know those are vampires, but did we see them hurting anyone?"

"They hurt me." Aida felt her insides turn to rock.

"Yeah, but maybe we just take care of, what's her name? Tamar?"

Lisette looked away from Aida. "This is getting very scary."

Aida saw Mina smile, the most genuine look of anyone in the circle. "They are predators. When we were raining Hell on them, it felt right to me. This isn't for weak souls, Lisette. This is a war."

"Mina? Come on. I've preached peace my whole life." Lisette sat up straight. "You're sounding like those militaristic douchebags polluting this country."

Mina softened. "You're right. I've just felt weak my whole life. The power we held in our hands? That was intoxicating."

"Yo, girls! I had a god inside me!" Spex's loud laugh got everyone rolling, but Aida only smiled. Even though this coven had real power, she could see cracks forming. She'd have to make sure everyone was with her plans. If not? Then only those with the will could carry on.

Rosalinda jumped up in her bed. She'd been dreaming about walking in the desert, each of the cacti she saw blooming brightly and smelling of roses. She felt her connection to the Mother increase with each step she took. But the sky darkened quickly to a crepuscular purple with bright flashes of lightning bursting all around her. One bolt hit a seven-foot-tall Joshua tree near her which set it to burning.

As rain stormed down and winds blew in all directions, the fire remained lit. She approached it, brushing back her soaked locks to see within the flames. She had a picture of the Mother, her usual placid face enraged. Someone had called upon her, riling up her vengeance as a protector. But then the flame shot out and she woke.

Something was setting off the spiritual energy in the town, so she took out her cards and pulled three while sitting up in bed.

First was the world, the ball/sphere which makes a great mob. Whoever was acting in the Mother's name was aiming for something big. This project would have effects far from just their little life.

Next came the cello, which isn't a violin. The actor was reaching beyond their grasp. They wanted to be the grand player, but they don't have the power yet to perform what they wanted to do.

The final card was the mermaid, but Rosalinda saw it as the siren. Her call would draw the sailor to the rocks. But her song was so sweet, so powerful. But listening to the siren was always trouble.

She thought about who could be doing such work? Listening to the wrong sources, acting beyond their means?

But then the biggest question of all entered her mind. Was any of this her concern? But the way the Mother had contacted her told her yes.

She could hear her voice now. "You must be my voice in the material plane. Act on my behalf to do right in your world."

She meditated on this for a few moments, then sprang up. Waking this early always drove her to the bathroom.

Part Three: He was a hairy man...

Chapter Eight

The party was over. All the vampires still awake and not knocked out by the energy surges tended to those who had succumbed to the bolts. Jeremiah went to the fuse box and found that the fuses had been blown, but the system hadn't. He replaced all the busted ones and the lights came back on. After such a traumatic event, all that was left was to clean up.

Sophia needed answers and wanted Tamar to supply them. Since Sandy still had a long drive, she excused herself, but Sophia handed the Mexican vamp a broom and gave her instructions: "Talk while you sweep."

Tamar went through the whole thing: the burial, the resurrection, the confrontation at the park. Sophia couldn't believe all that power was concentrated on someone not old enough to drink. But Sophia could see something was nagging Tamar.

"Do you remember the night of the first party? When you came to Boyle Heights?"

"Yeah."

"So the kid was there. Across the street. One of the Bomb Squad tried to attack her but got dusted by the helicopter lights." Tamar looked like she was trying to remember something just beyond her grasp. "It was all over the neighborhood that she went into a coma. Papi still talks to a few of the humans, y'know. Just to keep the heat off the house. But not that family. Anyway, her brother came over and I whipped them 'cause they was macho little shits who needed it. You seeing these connections?"

"Well, something happened to her. Something supernatural."

"I guess I gotta believe that."

Sophia wrinkled her nose. "The vampire has to be convinced that witches exist?"

"Wasn't until I met ya boy that I believed in werewolves. Or possums. Whatever."

"The point is we all tap into this power from beyond. We can call it God or whatever, but we need this power as much as they do. Or other things which we don't believe in." Sophia paused. "Nothing is off the table."

"Not even zombies?" Tamar laughed, knowing Sophia always joked about them.

But Sophia was serious. "Not even zombies."

Jeremiah walked up. "Hey, it's getting early. Come to the bunkhouse."

Maisie, Horton, and Jeremiah put as much trash out as they could—getting all the little shards of the disco ball would take weeks—then showed Tamar and Sophia to the bedroom. Four sets of bunkbeds lined the wall, the room as long as a train car and just as narrow. As the others laid down, Tamar tugged on Sophia's sleeve.

"Can you stay up a little longer?"

Sophia looked at Jeremiah. "The place is great, but we need to get to the bottom of this." He shrugged, so she kissed him softly.

Jeremiah stretched and rolled into a bottom bunk. Tamar and Sophia sat on the one furthest from the drowsy trio of Jeremiah, Horton, and Maisie. They whispered so as not to bother them.

Tamar looked at her feet as she sat on the bed. "So, I went to see this psychic lady."

"Really?"

"Yeah. I thought she'd would do Tarot, but it was *loteria*..." Tamar waved her hand. "Forget it. But what she told me hit home. I really haven't dealt with losing Alpha."

"Fudgie blew the whole grieving process. Not just for you but others, too." The mobster Fudgie Whaloosie had been so unrelenting in his quest to take over L.A. Sophia thought of all the friends they'd lost: Jim—did Pamela have enough time to grieve on that loss?; Alpha, the leader of the all Black Bomb Squad and the only man Tamar had ever loved; the whole Church of Light, the positive vampire sect who thought that one day they could see daylight again. So many undeaths ended because of a singular, destructive will of a vamp who only wanted power. Now that the remaining community was finally catching its breath, Sophia knew they had to reflect on those lost and give more time to processing it.

"How did you deal with losing, what was his name, Chip?"

Sophia thought of her companion, gone two years now. As she thought about him, something clicked within her. "I loved him so much, but really? David was the loss. We never had the physical ties, but he held my heart."

"And then they were both gone?"

"Within weeks. Not just that, but my cabal was destroyed, too. Seventy-five years, then poof." Sophia could feel Tamar leaning into her, so she put her arms up and let Tamar slide in. "See, we have an advantage over the humans. We already know what death feels like. But then we get so much power that we forget how vulnerable we all are."

"That's what I miss about Alpha. We were both leaders, so we had to be tough with the cabal. Kick ass, yell and scream, make them do what we want. Sometimes it's easy and other times...well, you gotta do shit you don't wanna do to get the respect you need. But when we were together? I mean, we got naked and all 'cause, y'know."

Sophia looked across the way at Jeremiah. "I do. I definitely do."

"But we was naked in spirit, too. I'm just now seeing it. We could turn off all the bullshit and be ourselves." Tamar laughed. "Like, Alpha really loved Urkel." Sophia shrugged and Tamar laughed again. "I forgot. You don't know TV. He was this nerdy kid who caused trouble for a family on the show. He said he felt that way sometimes. Alpha made all A's in school."

"He did?"

"Yeah, I was surprised, too, 'cause I didn't. Anyway, he got bullied until he was turned. But he was smart enough to use the power of his mind and his fists to be head of the cabal. So he always joked that Urkel would've been a badass vamp." Tamar put her head on Sophia's shoulder. "I wish I could cry."

"Me, too. Let me tell you one last thing, then we'll call it a night." They both sat crossed legged to face each other. "Remember the night we met? When you ruined my job at the mansion?"

Tamar looked sheepish. "Yeah. You kicked my ass."

"Do you know why?"

Tamar looked confused. "No."

"Because I called you out. Somehow I knew—call it instinct, call it wisdom—that if I directed my challenge to you, I'd get the one on one battle I needed. A lesser leader would have sacrificed a few of her cabal to make sure the new threat would be destroyed. But you knew that stepping up to me would prove something—my guilt, my strength, hell, maybe my worth. You showed your people love without it being mushy."

Tamar nodded. "And they could see it. I got beat, but they still stood behind me."

"Lost the battle but won the war. And it looks like we're gonna have to do it again. And we may lose more friends. But I need the smart leader to help me. You've got the biggest target on your back, but your little enemy also went after all of us. She doesn't know what she did. Because now all of us have something to prove."

Tamar hugged her, then looked in Sophia's eyes. "I think you should meet my psychic."

"Why?"

"'Cause I think she can help us."

Sophia didn't know how, but Tamar's instincts were worth her trust. And with the power this *bruja* threw around tonight, they'd need every ally they could get.

With the place cleaned up and their bellies full, Spex opened a bottle of wine. "Two buck chuck," she exclaimed as she unscrewed the top. Aida found the drink sour, but she knew she wanted something to take the edge off her high. Her heart was still racing and she needed a come down.

She sat on the sofa next to Spex who had her head on the back and her body splayed wide. She looked emptied. "Man, if a fucking god can't take 'em down, what else can we do?"

Mina sat cross-legged in a papasan chair which she'd brought from her parents' house. "We did well. And we did everything correctly. But I think I know the problem." She carefully sipped from her wine glass. "It was indirect. We should have been right there, right where they were."

Gilly laughed. "You think we'd survive that?"

But Lisette, who sat in the webbed camping chair she kept there so she could have a place to sit, reached toward Gilly. "It would be scary, but Mina has a point. Think about electricity and resistance. The longer it has to travel, the weaker it becomes. I'm still convinced some of our magic has at least a basis in real world stuff. So maybe we do have to close the gap."

"Shit, if it was that easy, we could get some dynamite and blow them up." Spex made a rumbling sound with her mouth and threw her hands out in imitation of a blast. "Boom. I know some people who could get that."

Aida shook her head. "While the bold statement would be impressive, we'd have to deal with the cops after that. They can trace that stuff."

Spex nodded. "Yeah. But you know me. I like big."

"One of the problems I'm having is scale." Lisette leaned forward. "Aida, you're obviously tapped deep into the well. Spex, you're growing stronger every day. But I feel the rest of us are getting left behind."

Mina turned to Lisette. "I'm growing. You just haven't seen it."

Lisette opened her palms. "Share! Please. I'd love to see your progress."

Mina stuck to cross-legged position but straightened her back. Looking like a Buddhist in meditation, she chanted and put her hands on her knees. Her fingers extended in heavy metal horns. Her tone crescendoed from mumble to yelling while she circled her hands. The rest of the women could see a ball of energy forming in the middle, the tornado-like movement helping it grow. The soft white light made each face in the room look ghostly as Mina moved the ball from her lap to the center, hovering just over the edge of the coffee table.

Gilly had a huge smile on her face. "Wow! Keep it going."

Aida knew they all needed to help Mina keep it going, so she tucked in her legs, made the same gesture with her hands, and tried to latch onto the ball. Lisette and Gilly also helped, but Spex looked drained, unable to add any more magic to the mix.

Working together, the four inflated the ball to the size of a car tire. Mina called over the droning hum created by the ball. "Can you feel it, Lisette?"

"Yes!" Her curly hair was standing up from the static electricity.

"Lisette, Gilly, take in some of the energy." Aida couldn't see her friends as the light blocked her view, but she knew this would solve part of the problem they were having keeping it under control.

The globe elongated, changing from circular to oblong with pseudopods extending toward the two white women. Mina's eyes began to roll back, so Aida yelled at her.

"Mina, push the energy away. Lisette! Gilly! Pull as hard as you can." Aida didn't want the ball to grow any larger because Mina wouldn't be able to wrangle it.

The ball extended until it was flat on top with two rays feeding into Gilly and Lisette. Mina leaned forward as did Aida. Both extended their hands as if lifting a giant cup. Lisette began to hyperventilate while Gilly gasped with laughter. With one more push, the energy broke and flowed into the two women. Gilly's chest expanded and the white light passed through her. She glowed, her golden aura now like some treasure room in an adventure movie. But Lisette? She let out a whooping scream and collapsed on floor.

Mina was the first to her, rolling out of the papasan and grasping her friend. "Are you okay?"

Lisette breathing slowed over a few moments as it returned to normal. She sat up, looking right in Mina's face. "Well, there's a first time to everything."

Spex sat up, the energy ball giving her new life. "Yeah. Magic can give you life."

"Well, yeah, but Mina knows what I mean." Lisette's mouth looked like a comma.

"NO!"

"Yup."

"What the ..." Spex sat at the edge of the couch.

Mina hugged Lisette around the shoulders. "She came!"

Aida could feel her jaw drop. "You had an orgasm?"

Lisette nodded furiously. "Quite a big one."

Spex slapped Aida's shoulder. "Bitch, we been doing it wrong all this time."

Lisette held up her hands to calm the room. "Mina knows this has been a real struggle of mine. I'm not a virgin, but I haven't had that level of trust necessary to release myself."

Gilly nodded. "I understand. It's hard for me, too."

Spex let out a loud raspberry. "White people! Damn, when you getting some, you got to get yours. That motherfucker ain't going nowhere until I get off."

As they laughed and resumed drinking, Aida thought about what they were saying. She kept her virginity to herself, knowing that her rebirth didn't happen just so she could get a boyfriend. But that same idea brought her back to the vampires. She finished her glass of wine and poured another.

"Spex is right."

"About what?"

"With the vampires. We can't get it for ourselves. They're just too powerful. So we gotta find something who can get them."

"Like a monster?" Spex laughed at the idea, but Aida pointed at her in agreement.

"Yes! If there's vampires in the world, then surely there's other stuff. Like werewolves."

Lisette shrugged. "I guess. We always hear about them being at war."

"In the movies," Mina said. "We don't know what's happening out there."

Gilly put her hand to her chin. "And we just wasted the full moon. What else? Elves and dwarves?"

"I don't know if *Lord of the Rings* was very accurate," Lisette said. "But we know about the veil. Maybe the fey can help us."

Mina shuddered. "If the myths are true about them, we'll probably all disappear. No, we need something scary. A real monster. Like a *rokuroburi* or something."

Aida said, "What's that?"

"It's a monster that's a flying head and entrails. It eats the heads of its victims and assumes their bodies." Mina smiled at her scary thoughts.

"Not sure where we'd find one," Lisette said. "But maybe there's a Mexican thingy. If the myth comes close to matching the reality, then something could be true."

"The big one my mom warned me about was *la llorona*, the weeping woman." They all looked interested, so Aida told the tale. "She was a young woman who fell for a soldier and let him make love to her on the night before he left. When he returned, she had a baby waiting for him, but he said the baby wasn't his. So, to be with the soldier, she took her baby to the river and drowned it. She told him what she'd done, but it only repulsed him more. He went away, saying he never wanted to see her again. So she returned to the river and threw herself in, dying while missing both her love and her baby. She's supposed to haunt riversides, looking for her child. And if she sees you, the child by the river, she'll kidnap you and take you away forever."

"Wow," Mina said.

Gilly laughed. "Obviously, Mexican mothers didn't want their children near rivers at night."

Lisette wrote in her notebook. "There is so much feminism to unpack there. I think I just found my senior thesis." But then she looked up. "Would she help us?"

"I doubt it," Spex said. "That ghost is probably crazy. What we need is a goblin or a boogeyman of some sort."

"Boogeyman!" Aida snapped her fingers. "*El cucuy!*" The rest of the woman stared at Aida. "It's like a hairy man with red eyes who snatches children."

"Again with the children snatching," Gilly said. "Are all lessons in Mexican households 'never leave the house'?"

"You have no idea," Aida said. "But maybe one of those could at least take out the Boyle Heights vamps. It would be a good start."

"Where would we find one?" Spex looked to each of them until ending at Aida.

"I'm not sure," Aida said. "But it's probably somewhere dangerous."

Tamar gave Sophia the address for the card reader and she noticed it was very close, just over the river, so she had Jeremiah drop her off. He was headed toward Long Beach anyway and this stop wouldn't be too far off the track. The squat building looked a little low rent, but Sophia knew telling fortunes wasn't about making big money.

Sophia pulled open the door, setting off a collection of bells tied to the inner doorknob. Entering the reception room, she heard, "Just a minute" from the back room.

The woman who entered was very elegant if a bit out of date. Her flowing gown reminded Sophia of the '60s, even though she still wore jeans and boots back then. Her face was made up with strong mascara, but she had seen the look on Tamar also. Sophia guessed it was cultural. But as the woman gazed at Sophia, she bent into a deep bow.

"*Bon soir, madame.*"

"I'm not married." Sophia hated the *madame/mademoiselle* separation as it made a woman's life seem like nothing without a man.

"Please excuse me, but my mother did teach me to respect my elders."

Okay, she's good, thought Sophia, knowing that she still looked mid-30s. She had been turned in her 20s, but the hard Storyville life had packed on some extra years. Still, Sophia returned the bow. "I was sent here by one of my companions. You helped her a great deal, apparently."

"The young one? The weight of her pain was obvious. But you?" Rosalinda laughed. "Let's just say the river is deep." She turned and held open the curtain separating the two rooms. "Come, let's sit."

Sophia looked at the walls as she moved into the room. Original art and psychedelic posters hung here. The art featured a lot of roses. One caught her eye in particular, a framed copy of the Grateful Dead's album *American Beauty*. As Sophia lingered, Rosalinda walked up behind her.

"Are you a fan?"

"Me? Not really. But one of my ca... best friends was."

Rosalinda looked far away as Sophia turned. "Mr. Garcia was a friend. I met him when I was young and we had...an intense experience." She sighed. "I think this album cover is a reference to it, but we had lost contact by then."

"Fritz would've talked your ear off about him."

"Your friend has passed?"

"Yes." Sophia could feel Rosalinda's eyes boring into her.

"Along with a few others, I see." Rosalinda pointed to the reading table. "I don't have anything to offer you, but would you mind if I had tea?"

"No. Go ahead."

As she poured water into the kettle, Rosalinda said, "If your kind are going to keep coming, I guess I'll have to keep some...beverages around."

"It goes bad too quickly, so don't worry."

"Good to know." She returned to the table having poured water into a teapot, the string and card of the bag hanging over the rim. "Now, why are we here tonight ...?"

"Sophia."

"Sophia. I'm Rosalinda. Do you want your fortune told?"

"Yes, but we need to talk about something else first."

"As you wish."

Sophia told her about the attack in Long Beach. She left out how she used her connection to Legbah to shut down the magic but shared the rest. "Tamar is convinced a *bruja*—her words—was behind it."

Sophia watched Rosalinda withdraw, going into a trance for a few seconds. Rosalinda said, "I felt this exact event coming through the veil. It was very powerful." Then she paused. "I'm at a crossroads with this..." When Sophia flinched at the words, Rosalinda said, "Did I say something wrong?"

"No. You're very much on point."

"Anyway, I think it's my niece who's behind this." As Sophia leaned in to speak, Rosalinda held up her hand. "I don't know where she is. She came here a few months ago with the story of how one of your kind killed her, but the power of the Mother Goddess brought her back. The same Mother who's represented in all this art."

Sophia saw the Guadalupe virgin in a few of the paintings. "Aren't those Catholic?"

"Yes and no. Yes and no." Rosalinda's words faded. "It's not important. What is important is you've revealed to me how strong she's become. When I saw her, her power was too raw. She must have concentrated her studies."

"Let me tell you this. I have a very strict agenda. I'm working to save the souls of the vamps. Me and mine are not hunting humans anymore. We're finding alternatives to our predatory instincts. So when I hear her story, my first thought is to negotiate."

"Even with an eighteen-year-old girl?"

"Especially with them. The young see things in black and white. They want big, dramatic changes with sweeping acts. You and I both know some ideas need to move slowly."

"Agreed. But you will see the fire is deep within her. I can try to set something up, but I can't guarantee any movement on the issue."

"I'll talk with Tamar. This is her mess more than mine, but I hold a position of...power within the group."

"Why do you hesitate?" Rosalinda leaned forward.

"Because it still grates on my personality. But somehow..."

"You're the boss?" Rosalinda smiled. She looked like she knew how pointed that word was with Sophia. But how could she?

"Yeah. I'm the boss." As Rosalinda drank some tea, Sophia looked into her lap. "I'm in charge, so I will lead any negotiations."

"If you don't want the burden, don't take it." Rosalinda put her mug back on the table. Then she smiled. "I've just said something very silly, haven't I?"

They both laughed. Sophia gulped some air. "Yup."

"You must know that I won't allow my niece to be taken or… worse."

Sophia nodded. "Yes, she did a vary bad thing, but I only want to talk. For now. If she reacts differently…"

"I understand," Rosalinda said. "We should see what the cards say."

Rosalinda laid out three cards after Sophia cut the deck. The first one showed a tree.

"*El arbol.* He who nears a good tree is blanketed by good shade." Rosalinda peered up at Sophia.

Sophia was unsure, but said, "I mean, maybe that's me? I'm certainly the one who protects everybody."

"You have the roots in a rootless culture, yes? You've been here for a very long time. It shows in your patience and your ability to see many sides. Trees are also gathering places, so they attract crowds even if the tree doesn't want them. You will need to stay firm as the chaos swirls around you."

Sophia watched as the next card turned: a picture of a bird. Maybe a parrot?

Rosalinda said, "You have me hopping here and there, like a bird on a branch." She tapped the card. "This one is obvious. The bird will come to a branch on the tree. It will cause some chaos because it can't sit still. But it's a bird, so it can't bring the whole tree down. Remember that when you first encounter the bird."

Finally, the third card came up: a hat?

Rosalinda looked a bit confused. "The bonnet. *El gorrito.* Put the bonnet on the baby lest he catch cold." Her face didn't look like she solved this riddle, but then something clicked and she snapped her fingers. "Your friend. She's something of a baby vampire, yes?"

"More so than me, for sure."

"You must protect her. She's the one who will continue to instigate, especially when you don't want it. You must keep her safe so that she won't get a cold. And what is more cold than a permanent death?"

Sophia nodded. She paused for a moment, then stood. "I want to meet with your niece. If we can cut this thing off at the bud, then maybe we can avoid trouble."

"You really think she wants to avoid trouble?"

"No, but I do. And you do. And we're the adults around here." Sophia left her number and hoped she would hear from Rosalinda soon. The card reader said she didn't know how to get in touch with her niece, but she would make it happen. Sophia hoped it would happen soon before things got so out of hand that she couldn't stop the war from coming.

Chapter Nine

Before they looked for the monster, Aida wanted to expand their magical connection. The power that Mina had tapped into the other night showed her that they all needed more spells as a backup if pure muscle didn't work. They were witches after all.

While sometimes it was hard to remember her time with Tonantzin, she knew the magic they could access was in the four elements—earth, air, fire, water. So they took a weekend retreat, as they called it, to fine tune their senses. Through the Internet, a few library books, and one self-published grimoire found in a downtown bookstore, they each pushed themselves to connect to the elements.

Spex had already touched the divine, so her fire magic was strong. After seeing that, each one could see specialization came about naturally. Attunement to more than one element was nearly impossible.

Aida was surprised to find her specialty was air. She thought her connection to the volcano would give her fire, but fire cannot exist without a source. She found she could extinguish candles, blow objects off tables, and, most surprisingly, float above the ground. The "flying" as she called it lasted only seconds, but the thrill was visceral.

"Maybe this was the witches and the brooms thing," she said. "Combining wood with air. They must have been really advanced."

"Or the more natural world allowed for a closer connection to magic." Lisette looked pleased with her connection and Aida could see no dispute with her findings.

By the end of Sunday, each of them had accessed the energy. Mina formed fiery shapes but couldn't get them to hold. Lisette could manipulate dirt and rocks with her powers, making patterns in a mini Zen garden. Gilly had some ability to push water around, but it was still weak. With all four elements within their grasp, even if they didn't have mastery, now was the time to seek the creature.

They combed through the library and looked online again, but information about *el cucuy* was scarce and contradictory. The only thing any scholar could agree on was its love of high perches, like rooftops or spires, but not necessarily in crowded areas where it might be spotted in its child snatching. So they debated a bit until Spex made a possible connection.

"Bridges. They're high here and they can hide a monster." The group agreed she could be right, but they wondered where to search.

Aida thought about all the old stories. "There's always a river in these tragedies. And what's more isolated than the L.A. River?"

They looked on Google to see a variety of bridges: the Cesar Chavez overpass which connected Downtown to Boyle Heights; Colorado Street coming into Pasadena with its multiple suicide attempts; and the Hyperion/Glendale connector between Silver Lake and Atwater Village. The first was over a train track, so they discounted that. And since the last one went right over the river, they thought to go there first.

Climbing into Mina's car, they tried to figure out the best way to access the bridge. The maps showed two places: a staircase leading up to Hyperion and a short foot bridge over the 5 freeway which led directly to the river. Each was accessed at Riverside Boulevard in Los Feliz right near the Mulholland Fountain. They decided to go to the river first, thinking the higher street might have too much traffic.

Parking near where Riverside intersected with Los Feliz Boulevard, they spotted a recessed field, about seven feet down, with a children's playground near the street and a series of tennis courts straight back.

Gilly shivered in the cooling night as they passed the slides. "The idea that a monster may be watching the kids playing? Fucking creepy."

"Everything in that light is creepy," said Lisette.

They kept walking back, past all the courts to a trail that led alongside a soccer pitch, empty at this late hour. Finally, they saw twisting stairs surrounded by fencing which they climbed. This stretched over the freeway where cars still streamed like an endless school of fish. They all paused at the center while Gilly took a few pictures, including a selfie with the traffic behind her.

"So L.A.," she said. "I'll get a ton of likes for that one."

Finally, the path opened onto the river. Though immortalized in many films and television shows, especially *Grease*, in the 21st century the concrete paths keeping the trickle of water flowing had been left to grow wild. They approached a fence run through with three parallel wires to see a few things: another thin bridge leading into the heart of the Atwater neighborhood, giant bushes and reedy plants blooming from the river trench which was about fifteen feet across, and the Hyperion bridge which was about ten feet above their heads here with the path leading up to its walkway. They climbed through the fence and walked down the 30 degree concrete incline to where the river ran.

The first thing Aida noticed was they weren't alone. At forty-foot intervals, tent clusters sat on the incline, homeless people tucked in for the night. She knew they wouldn't camp by the river because any small rainstorm might mean a heavy flood as this canal drained everything from the Valley to Long Beach. But it was clear the campers definitely avoided under the bridge.

"Think that's a sign?" Spex was joking, but Aida agreed there must be danger under there.

They walked two by three, Aida and Spex in the lead with the others close by their backs. Even Aida felt creeped out here, all of the power surges she'd felt lately disappearing in the face of a true monster. But she stiffened. She'd looked a vampire in the eye. *El cucuy* shouldn't be any worse.

In the shadow of the bridge, each of them examined the nooks and crannies, or at least as much as they could being that the trestle was twenty feet above their heads. Spex clapped, leading to a small echo. Aida stepped forward.

"Anybody up there? We want to talk to you."

She heard an echoing groan, probably from within a drainage pipe about ten feet up the incline and right in the middle of the two sides of the bridge. Aida's boots clung well as she climbed as did Spex's. The black woman snapped open a six-inch knife.

"Are you crazy?" Lisette swiveled her head. "That might be illegal."

"So's stealing kids. I ain't going up here unarmed."

Spex caught up to Aida and they surrounded the pipe which was about six feet around.

Aida leaned forward. "Who's there?"

The groan gained power, followed by a rustling within the pipe. Aida and Spex crept closer, each uneasy at actually entering the hole. The groan became a congested roar. As they looked at the trembling leaves, they leaned in even closer until a head popped out. Aida stumbled back, losing her footing. She rolled to the bottom and the other three helped her quickly.

Spex was still there, looking into the grizzled face of a man, smiling at his jape, gap-toothed grin and wheezy laughter vibrating his whole body. He dug a backpack out of the detritus, scampered down the incline, and bowed to the group who helped Aida stand back up.

"That's whatcha get for disturbing a man's sleep. Evening, ladies."

Spex slowly walked down, joining her friends. "Asshole. You okay, Aida?"

She had dressed in long sleeves and denim for tonight's adventure, so the only scratches were on her face and surface level. As she dusted off her pants, she said, "That was a bust." But then their heads all went skyward as another sound echoed near them, a metallic bonk of someone grabbing a girder.

"You've ruined his hidey hole, girls. But I'm guessing that wasn't your intent." The voice was scratchy but high registered. Aida felt her arm flesh goose up at the sound of it, like nails on a chalkboard but amplified with the bridge cover.

"We're here to see *el cucuy,*" Aida said. "Are you him?"

"I've gone by many names. That's certainly one of them."

Spex, knife held against her forearm for a quick in-fighting strike to hide the blade, stepped forward. "Show yourself. I don't like talking to shadows."

He swung from the bottom of the bridge, out of the shadows and into the dim light. Small, maybe four foot five, but completely covered in hair, the creature had elongated hands and feet so he could easily cling to the girders. He hung upside down and had swiveled his head so he could look at them directly. His eyes glowed red in the darkness and one ear was quadruple the size of the other and pointed like a bat's.

Aida felt her mouth dry as she looked at the abomination. But she swallowed what little spit she could muster. "We've come to make a deal with you."

"Why should I deal when I see my meals for the next month right in front of me?" The gibbering laughter sent a wave of fear through the group and they tightened their formation.

"Simple." Aida choked on the word, but she soldiered on. "We have magic in our circle. Enough to keep you from harming us."

"I don't believe you." He dropped from the overpass and into the shadows. They could hear his feet scraping the concrete. Aida pulled her friend into a circle with her in the middle, chanting as quickly as she could, "*Fiat lux! Fiat lux! Fiat lux!*" They all joined in, gathering their voices together. The ball of light formed within the circle, rotating it towards the incline. They caught the creature in their bright spotlight only five feet from their pack. He put up both hands to block the bright blaze, screaming as the illumination surrounded him. The ends of his hair started smoking. "Stop! Stop! Your magic is strong."

They cut the light and he scrambled back up to where the bridge made the incline. The gasoline smell of burning hair persisted. He started to move away from the bridge, but Aida yelled at him to stop.

"What do you witches want?" He sounded semi-afraid and semi in pain.

"We want your strength." Aida could feel her confidence surging.

"To do what?"

"To kill vampires."

The *cucuy* laughed. "I have no argument with them."

"But we do. And we need muscle to enhance our magic."

"Then it will cost you." He stroked his chin with his webbed hand. "A sacrifice, at the very least."

"One of us?" Gilly sounded frantic despite their close circle.

"While I'm sure you taste fine, you're tough old chickens. I'd require something more young and tender." His slurping sounded vile.

Lisette leaned in to whisper. "He can't be fucking serious. We're not giving him a kid."

Gilly's head whipped around. "That's monstrous."

Aida turned to face them, but she kept her voice way down. "And he's a monster. Don't worry, I'll find a way out of it." She turned and raised her voice to the creature. "Fine. But only after you help us."

"Then return here tomorrow with your detailed instructions. But don't you dare double-cross me!" He popped up, his gnarled face within the circle. They all screamed and jumped. "If you do, you all shall die!"

As the circle spread out, he ran away, a shambling, hunchbacked gait carrying him toward downtown.

The women each looked around and regained their composure. They walked back to the car, Lisette fuming.

"Dammit, there's empowerment and then there's murder! I agree the vampires should pay for what they did to you, but you're promising that thing too much."

"Grow up, Lisette." Mina's face had darkened considerably. "We're at war and war requires sacrifices."

Gilly moved closer to Lisette. "War? I wanted to get closer to the earth, feel the energy run through me. I didn't sign up for war."

The two white women stood by each other, facing down the other three. Spex spoke up. "I didn't know y'all a few months ago, but this chick pulled my ass up. I'm sticking with her."

Mina nodded, her arms crossed and her right foot planted in front of her body. "Definitely."

"Slow down." Aida separated herself. "I'm not killing any kids. I have the grudge here. Anything I do or sacrifice will not harm another. That's the code. We do what we can to rid this world of monsters. We'll make both of these predators pay for feeding on the good people of the world. Agreed?"

Lisette and Gilly looked skeptical, but they nodded agreement. They all joined hands.

"The Mother will see us through," Aida said. "She will guide us to a place of strength and beauty."

Aida broke the circle and they didn't speak more than a few words as they returned to the apartment.

After their trepidatious start, the relationship between Tamar and Rosalinda grew. After their first meeting, Tamar went twice more before finally settling on a monthly schedule. They had scheduled their meet in the week between Christmas and New Years, but Tamar was still troubled by the Solstice attack.

Rosalinda decided Tamar needed to know the truth. "I think I know who did this."

"So do I. It's that little neighbor of mine."

"Wait. You live by the Menendez family?"

"Yeah. When the girl went into a coma, one of the boys blamed me. He came over and I beat the shit out of him. And now she blames me for every evil in the world."

"Well, there's something else." Rosalinda blew out her breath to relax herself. "She's my grandniece."

Tamar's face looked like all of the muscles were contracting at once. Her fists flexed and she looked on the verge of breaking everything in the shop. But then she shook her head a few times and waved her arms in a dismissing motion. "You didn't know she was gonna attack, right?"

"I definitely would have told you. I don't like violence in any form."

Tamar nodded. Rosalinda was unsure if she was forgiven, but she saw Tamar had settled into a slow simmer.

The vampire said, "You may not like violence, but I ain't sure we can avoid it."

"Let's cross that bridge later." Rosalinda stood. "I'm going to have tea. You may indulge in your refreshment."

They'd set some guidelines. Rosalinda knew Tamar was drinking blood, but they agreed that only animal blood would be okay. Rosalinda couldn't control the vampire, but Tamar had hinted she was in some sort of rehab program where these vamps were weaning themselves off their predatory nature. Sophia had told her the outline, but Rosalinda didn't know the full story yet.

Tamar said, "Before we have the reading, I gotta question."

Rosalinda's ear pricked up. Tamar had used the readings mostly for counseling, digging into the loss of a mate and helping her to process her feelings. But as well as that work had gone, Tamar had many other questions. This sounded like one of those times. Rosalinda sat at the table, specifically keeping her gaze on the vampire instead of the cards. She opened her palms and Tamar began.

"Y'know, there's no handbook for being a vampire. They don't have...what's that thing on the first day of school?"

"Orientation?"

"Yeah. We don't get any of that. So I'm asking you. Where does all this magic come from?"

"That, my young friend, is a good question with a very long

answer. But I'll give you the short version." Rosalinda went and grabbed her drawing pad and a pencil and brought it back to the table. "In its most simple form, magic comes from the beyond. Here's the best I can come up with."

Rosalinda drew a rough picture of the planet, then drew three squiggly lines next to it.

"Imagine if the night sky was a curtain. We here in L.A. see only a few stars and a few of those are the planets. That's about as much magic that flows from beyond and into our sphere. Most of it is sourced from the divine."

"You mean God is real?"

"The Christian God? Sure. Because of this." She drew a series of parallel lines as if the Earth radiated light. "All of that energy put into prayers and sacrifices feeds Jehovah's being. But it's easier for the divine to receive the energy than to reflect it back on the living. And from our studies—I mean those of us who can pierce the veil directly—that entity has no interest in funneling it back except as general goodwill. Ironically, it's because the smaller deities have fewer followers that they work harder to empower humans. That's why this knowledge is so hidden."

"So..." Tamar paused, processing a thought. "There were more miracles in the Bible because Jehovah was smaller and working just with the Jews."

"*Loteria!*" Rosalinda liked using that phrase instead of "bingo" to make her clients laugh. It worked on Tamar. "Now, there's too many demands, so focusing that much energy—and believe me, it's a lot—just doesn't happen. So when I invoke the Mother or any of the others, she can give me the power in small bursts."

"But what about me? And the other vamps?"

"You may not like what you hear, but I'll give it to you straight. The beyond has many avenues, both in and out. My power, as with many practitioners, is from the divine. Yours, my dear, is infernal."

"The Devil?"

"I don't like that name, so let's refine it. Think of the atom. It has a positive charge and a negative one. The divine works through positivity, meaning this energy exchange is creative. The infernal's power comes from destruction. Like your soul..."

"Wait. I still have a soul?" Tamar looked hopeful for a second, but Rosalinda needed her to know the truth.

"No. Your eternal life is fueled by the soul's destruction. All creatures of the night, your supernatural brethren, have made this sacrifice. Do you remember yourself before getting turned?"

"Of course."

"What were you like?"

"I don't know. Normal, I guess. What's any teenager like?"

"But then something happened. How does young Tamar differ?"

Rosalinda could see she was giving it some real thought.

"It's hunger. It's why I always feel...what's the word? Predatory? Every time I see a human—even you, I'm sorry to say—my stomach bubbles. I can't fill it, so I hunt. All the time. Mostly with my eyes now, but that feeling never goes away."

"You are feeding the void. Your spirit needs food just like the body, but it's a different form of sustenance. Unfortunately, your kind is incapable of filling up."

Tamar smirked. "You know, Sophia's got this convergence thing. We all hum together and the sound grows and grows. It actually does fill me up. For a bit, anyway."

Rosalinda was shocked. A vampire had found a way to access the divine? This Sophia was special. She'd need to find out more.

But Tamar had more questions. "When you say children of the night ...?"

"Lycanthropes, ghosts, those things. There's also a few beasties I wouldn't want to meet up with."

"Zombies?"

"I've never seen one. But I'm not closing myself off to any ideas."

Tamar looked like a high school student in math class trying to make sense of all the ideas. "Okay, you have divine and infernal. Sounds like another binary. But you said..."

"I'm glad you're listening. There's still many things I don't know, sources of beyond energy I can't understand. The only other one I can confirm are the eternals."

"Who's that?"

"They populate the veil, living in the in-between. They aren't sources of power but can access it for humanity. Sometimes there's a price, but others do it for goodwill. The English called them the Fae. Icelanders talk of elves. The *loa* in Voodoun or Santeria or Candomble, depending on your preference. And, of course, the Catholic saints. I mean, don't we call on our ancestors on *Dia de la*

Muertos?"

"Never thought of it that way."

"Humans don't live long enough to fully comprehend the levels of the beyond. Maybe you might get many insights I'll never find."

As Rosalinda reached out for the deck to give Tamar her reading, they both heard a banging on the door.

"Get your ass out here, vampire!"

The voice was young, but it wasn't Aida. Maybe it was that black girl Rosalinda had met before? They both stood and went out, Rosalinda feeling the air turn colder as Tamar let her predator rise to the top.

The five young women stood on the street, just beyond the curb. The two blonde ones looked nervous, but Aida's sneer dominated her face. In the months since she'd seen her last, Rosalinda could see the transformation. Yes, her power source was divine, but something cast a sharp, deep shadow over her soul. Aida's aura crackled with this energy.

"*Hola, tia.* Why you hanging out with this trash?"

"Those who come to me for help get my help. You don't get to judge until you know them as well as I do."

"I see one thing—another victim." The Asian and black girl laughed, their auras getting drawn into Aida's darkness.

"It's not too late, Aida. The left-hand path pulls you away from the Mother, not toward her. You can still find her light." Rosalinda could hear Tamar growling, her fangs and teeth grinding.

"Yeah but look at this fucking animal! Mad dogs get put down." Aida's friends snickered with the insult.

Rosalinda put her hand on Tamar's shoulder. "Easy," she said to the vampire. "These kids are playing a game."

But another scent hit the soft wind. Rosalinda looked at Tamar who could smell it too. The foul stench—rot, garbage, unwashed animal—swirled around them. Rosalinda's breath caught.

"What did you do, you stupid girl! What did you do?"

Chapter Ten

Aida thought the look on her great aunt's face was hilarious. While *Tia* Rosalinda wasn't one of those women who tried to keep her down, her words betrayed exactly what Aida knew: everyone underestimated her. The only ones who had believed in her were the Mother and Tonantzin, so she strove to be as fierce as those gods.

Her aunt's street was wide and open but not busy because of the time. Aida had been training her body to keep late hours because she had to know her enemy. Without so much sun, her skin had paled, her hair as dark as midnight in comparison. She wasn't sure if the *cucuy* had an advantage or not, but the surprised look on the vampire's face showed a level of concern that Aida knew was a positive for the battle. And just like that, the creature sprung from Rosalinda's roof onto Tamar's back.

Right before the tendril-like claws could grasp her, Tamar ducked, grabbed the *cucuy*'s right wrist, and slammed it to the ground. But the little monster looked rubber as it bounced off the sidewalk, rolled away, and jumped back to its feet. His laughter curdled Aida's blood.

Tamar looked focused even if she couldn't keep the anger out of her face. Hiding her fangs for now, she crouched into a fighter's stance.

The rest of the coven squirmed to get out of the way, crowding around Rosalinda's door. Her aunt did the same but looked defiant, standing tall in front of the beast.

The hairy creature looked at Rosalinda for a quick second. "The *bruja* comes by it naturally, I see." He let loose that weaponized laugh once more, Rosalinda covering her ears and crouching down in its wake.

But the monster knew it couldn't keep its eyes off Tamar for too long. The vampire closed their gap in a flash, slashing at the *cucuy*'s throat with her claws. He ducked and kicked. His oversized foot caught Tamar in the stomach, throwing her back 20 feet. Sitting in the middle of Eagle Rock Boulevard, Tamar looked to see if any traffic was around. Headlights glowed about a half mile down the road.

She looked down her nose at the goblin-like thing. "Let's take this somewhere private. Follow me if you dare."

Tamar turned misty in front of everybody. Her cloud lifted into the air and drifted north. The *cucuy* went down on its hands and knees, looking like the biggest, meanest dog in the junk yard. He sniffed a few times, pointed its gargantuan ear in Tamar's direction, then leaped to the roofs, disappearing into the night.

"What's that way?" Aida spoke to her aunt.

Rosalinda looked so pissed off that she might not answer, but through tight lips she said, "The cemetery. At least no one else will be harmed."

"Let's go!" Aida turned so the coven could return to Mina's car, but Rosalinda's grip on her shoulders felt like hawk claws.

Swinging her niece around, Rosalinda shouted, "You careless, stupid, callous little..."

"Say it, *tia*! I'm a bitch. I'm a bitch and I love it."

"You don't know what mess you could cause. Those things are paid in blood."

"Give me some credit. I've planned the whole thing out."

"You can't control a *cucuy* anymore than you can ride a tornado. Mark my words, something will go wrong and you'll have to pay for it."

"Fuck you, lady!" Spex now stood right by Aida. "My girl's got power."

"She's a toddler holding a firehose. The damage you can do is immense." Rosalinda opened her door. "Come back to me when you're ready to mature. This path isn't just dangerous, it's self-destructive." She looked at the other three. "I hope you aren't as blind as Ms. Spex here. Get out now while you can." Rosalinda closed the door and locked it with a snap.

"That old rag don't know you." Spex said, pointing at her door. "She doesn't know what it takes to change the world."

"No, she doesn't." Aida looked serious now. "Let's go find those two. We need to make sure our charge finishes the job."

#

Tamar landed in an open field. To either side of her, gravestones filled symmetrical lines, little lanes for the mourners to walk up and find their passed loved one. But this empty area gave Tamar advantage by keeping the monster out of the shadows. She smelled him before she saw him; for the first time, she wished her sense of smell was more in line with her pre-vamp days. The caustic fog wrapped up every sense above her neck.

"Do you feel more at home here among your dead brethren?" The taunt came from a line of trees about 25 yards from where she stood, but she used her super hearing to pinpoint his location. In an instant, she stood beneath him.

He clung to the trunk as easily as a monkey on a pole. His smile, or at least his exposed teeth, was sinister.

"Go back to wherever you came from. We don't need to fight." Tamar wanted to rip this thing's arms off, but she tried to conjure her inner Sophia. That one would negotiate.

"But then I get no reward. Those skinny popsicles promised me flesh and I'll have it."

"You trust those bitches?"

"That would be preposterous. But I'll extract payment. Of that, I'm sure." The *cucuy* dropped to the ground, its short legs bouncing like springs. "Besides, I've always wanted to see if you vaunted vampires were as strong as advertised."

Tamar saw just how quickly this squirt could move. Not as fast as her but still, it closed the gap between them before she could set. Two open-clawed swings came from the right and left and all Tamar could do was retreat. Ceding ground went against her nature, but she also wanted to stay in one piece.

When the next right-handed swing came from below, she planted her foot in his open palm. She sprang over her opponent, delivering a mule kick to the back of its head. She knew it was a glancing blow because the *cucuy* rolled forward and away from her. At least she knew she hit it. He stood and faced her, right hand forward and left hand massaging the back of its head.

"Hmmmmm." The monster looked like he hadn't been hurt in a while.

Now more wary, the *cucuy* realigned itself with both hands forward but with a more stable stance: right foot forward and left foot back and facing the side for better balance. Tamar was unsure if the fighting was training or instinct, but she didn't take her eyes off it. Still, he leaped with no telegraphing.

She felt the two mitts clapping together, trying to box her ears, but blocked the strike with her forearms. The creature's left hand gripped her wrist. She could feel herself lifted and flipped, her back crashing to the ground, one of her ribs cracking. She knew she was lucky she didn't need air because she'd be gasping now.

The pain was bad, but she knew she had to fight through it. Kipping up in one motion, she felt the thing trying to hold her from the back. Pivoting around and going to one knee, she struck his midsection, connecting solidly with flesh. The *cucuy* was thrown back fifteen feet onto its back. She charged in, trying to keep it on the ground, but those damn feet came up and flipped her away. She used some of her power to pull her knees in and land on her feet.

But he had also regained his balance and was in her face when she landed. Grabbing her from behind, he somehow managed to lift her into the air. His grip, tight as a pliers, popped one more rib sending more waves of pain through Tamar. For the first time, she thought she might have been too cocky to stand and fight alone.

The only limbs free were her legs. Her boots flailed and she connected with a knee cap. The *cucuy* didn't lose its grip, but now Tamar could feel the ground. She pushed backwards with both legs and fell with her whole-body weight on top of the *cucuy*. She heard his breath whoosh out and felt his grip loosen. She wriggled her arms free and threw both elbows back, trying hard to strike the side of his head. She finally smacked his throat. She broke the grip and rolled away.

She heard the *cucuy* huffing, but her own pain made it difficult to stand. She could feel her ribs stitching back together, but it would take a few more minutes for them to heal. The goblin jumped on her back before she could get off her knees, riding her like she was a horse. He circled his right arm around her throat.

Throwing elbows only made her fall prone. He tightened his grip. The choking maneuver didn't hurt her, but she felt trapped beneath him.

Tamar used the *cucuy's* compact torso against it. She brought her knees under her waist and lifted. She ran forward and shook everything she could: arms, neck, head. But the damn thing's grip was too much and he was heavier than she thought he should be. She tried to get to the road, to maybe use the asphalt as a weapon, but she stumbled when she got 20 feet away. She crawled closer, but the *cucuy* planted his feet and drew back her head.

With her neck pulled back and her eyes upward, Tamar could see the jagged claw above her, ready to decapitate her. She had seconds to live and squirmed with all her might, but the monster's coiled body held her in place. But just as he moved to drop its cutting blow, a car's headlights flooded over them. The creature screamed and loosened his grip. She used her last strength to scoot onto her back. She took the last of her conscious thought, focusing on shrinking and soon found herself airborne, bat wings flapping a hasty escape.

She would live to fight again. And next time she'd bring a shitload of help.

Mina's car swung around a bend in the road and Aida could see the two beings struggling in the night.

"Over there," she called out. For some reason, the two looked like they were coming to meet up with them, but then she saw the vampire fall.

This was it. Aida knew her goal had finally been achieved. She let out a little "yes!" as she saw the *cucuy* ready to strike the vampire down. But Mina pulled the car over and the headlights shined right at the battle.

Aida could see the *cucuy*'s eyes close and his head pivot away from the illumination. It was too damn bright for the night creature.

"Dammit!" Aida jumped out of the car, closing fast with the fight, but she felt something around her head and dropped to her knees. She looked up to see a bat flying away, into the dark sky and out of sight.

"You idiots!" The *cucuy*'s angry voice was much less intimidating than his normal tone, but the thing was right in Aida's grill. "I had her! She was dead and I'd be a legend. But you ruined it!" He reached out to slash Aida, but she conjured a puff of air that blew both of them back five feet. She hoped it would calm him at the very least.

And it did. The weirdly ironic look returned to its face. "No matter. I have done damage to her and will soon complete the mission.

I assume you have my payment ready."

"The payment was for death."

"She is dead." The monster's smirk was loathsome in Aida's eyes.

"Permanent death."

"Oh, that." The two front claws of its right hand danced along his chin. "Let me remember. No, I said help. And I have fulfilled that bargain."

"Really?"

"Yes, I have helped. But I'm feeling gracious. After that little scuffle, I know I can take her. You'll get the finishing for free." He pressed his claws together, forming a pyramid with its hands. "But I will get my payment."

"We'll need ..." Aida couldn't finish her sentence. The *cucuy* had wrapped its claws around Gilly's neck, lifting her off the ground. Aida saw her friend gagging and turning purple.

"I figured as much. She won't be as sweet a meal as what I was promised, but, well, we all must make due." He looked at Aida. She saw his face resembled the Grinch from the Christmas cartoon. "But I'm fair. You have a day. Then she dies."

With power they couldn't comprehend, he pulled Gilly over his shoulder and lumbered off at great speed, an ugly but swift retreat. As Aida turned back to the group to strategize, she felt an open hand strike her cheek. Lisette looked ready to kill her.

"You knew this would happen, but you had to go too far. Didn't you?"

Lisette pulled back to hit her again, so Aida took the air from her lungs with a quick twist of her wrist. Lisette fell to her knees.

"I have complete control here. Maybe I took too much for granted, but that thing won't beat me. We'll make a plan and get her back."

Lisette, still gasping, rubbed her throat. "A plan? That's how we messed up in the first place." She looked at Mina and Spex. "Come on! We're fucking kids! We're in over our heads."

"You are." Spex's face looked angry. "I'm with her. Mina, too."

Lisette stood. "I want to help Gilly. What do we have to do?"

"We need a spell," Aida said. "And after that, we'll need someone who we can actually trust."

Silver Lake was just over the river and freeway from the cemetery, so Tamar headed to the ZLVG Center straight away. She wasn't concerned with getting back to fight the *cucuy*, more she needed a strong hand to make sure she was alright. Revenge would have to take a breath.

As she transformed from bat to human on the front sidewalk, her feet failed her. She collapsed, able only to get her hands up to protect her face. Shimmying up to her knees, she managed only to knock on the door while sitting on the sidewalk. Her healing powers worked while she waited for Sophia.

It took only a few moments for Sophia to open the door and help Tamar into the front office.

Sophia looked extremely frazzled. "I've got a meeting going on, but I'll ..."

"Don't." Tamar set herself in the padded chair in the newly designed room. "I'll be fine. They need you just as much as I do."

Sophia looked like she wanted to do more, but she acquiesced, letting Tamar recover at her own rate. However, once Sophia disappeared behind the meeting room door, Jeremiah slipped out and lay across the love seat.

"Damn. You look about spent," he said.

Tamar looked at him. He'd changed since his turning, looking slicker and gaining an edge that made him much scarier, but that farm boy voice still stuck in his throat.

"You know about *el cucuy*?"

"Uh-uh. Is that a lycanthrope?"

"Nah. It's a straight up monster. He's a ... what do white people call it? A boogeyman."

"Something from up under the bed?" Jeremiah sniffed a laugh.

"Yeah, if your bed was on top a hell hole." Tamar tried to giggle, but her ribs weren't yet whole. The stitch sharpened her groan. "I've never seen one before, but the legends have been around for centuries. You got that thing, *la Llorona*, *el chupacabra*, all this crazy shit. They ain't got monsters where you're from?"

"Sure, but Bigfoot ain't never beat up one of my friends." Jeremiah leaned in. "The fuck is all this? You become a monster hunter now?"

"It's a long story."

"Got time." Jeremiah leaned back, crossing his legs and looking like an analyst waiting for the juicy problems.

So she told him as much of the story as she could remember, including the club catastrophe which made him look angrier instead of helpful. Then finally, he said, "This little girl going that far out of her way to piss you off? Hell, sounds like she needs a good spanking. I'm ready to go at it when you need me."

"You sure Sophia ain't gonna, like, try to negotiate with the damn thing?"

"Not everything is up to her. Besides, it'd probably make the world a better place if we cleaned out this bugger."

"You ain't wrong."

As they talked about where she met the monster and how to kill it, Sophia's meeting ended. As the recovering vamps filed out, Sophia joined the conversation.

"Are you sure we can't talk to it?" Sophia didn't understand why the two laughed and Tamar handed Jeremiah a dollar.

"Look, boo, this thing is downright evil. Tamar tells me they like to eat babies. You want to have coffee with that thing?"

"Fine." Sophia looked like she wanted to drag this out, but Tamar was glad to have Jeremiah on her side. "Did you talk to Rosalinda?"

Tamar snapped her fingers. The old lady might be seriously worried.

After calling her and checking in, Tamar heard Rosalinda sounding relieved.

"That girl, my niece? I gotta warn you, she looks like she wants to take this to the end."

Tamar didn't want to hurt Rosalinda, but she knew the psychic understood what was going on. "That girl is gonna have to pay for this, but we'd rather take out the *cucuy* first."

"Nothing wrong with that. But that means Aida will have to go to a higher level in your fight."

Tamar said, "I'm putting my people together. When you're already dead, fighting ain't no big thing."

Rosalinda hung up and Tamar faced Sophia. "Seriously, you with me?"

"Yes. But I am worried about fighting magic. I don't have much experience with that."

Tamar folded her arms. "I only know one way. Fight to kill. She started this fight. I aim to end it."

Chapter Eleven

At the ZLVG Center, they plotted their next move. Since they had little idea how to find this creature, Tamar went through the folklore. Like most Mexican baddies, *el cucuy* was associated with rivers.

"Makes sense," Sophia said. "All of our monsters were in the middle of the swamp. Don't want your kids wandering off, so a few ghost stories set them in line."

And even though Jeremiah scoffed at calling the L.A. River a river, they decided to head down there. It was only a few blocks away, but they had little time before sunrise, so they set to the air, flying there in bat form.

In the short flight, Sophia pondered their actions. What Tamar described was a monster, but did that mean it was all bad? Sophia had been tasked by Carmen to take care of all supernatural beings. She thought back to those old stories her father would tell. The *rougerou* was nothing but a werewolf and until recently her boyfriend had been just that. Weird things like the Grunch or the Lutins were also probably monsters. But would she attack them? The only thing she knew she would fight would be the *feu follet*, the little fairies posing as swamp light that take your soul. Nothing good comes from dealing with the fey.

They landed right under the Hyperion bridge, less than half a mile from the Center. They all started sniffing, but the funky green smell of the water overpowered everything.

"Dang, I wish I still had my possum nose." Jeremiah got down on all fours. "This vampire smelling just ain't as powerful."

"Still better than humans." Tamar went under the bridge, quickly crawling up the incline. She saw signs of some sort of nest, but it looked abandoned. She smelled around there. The *cucuy*'s musky smell was all over this. She dropped back down to her friends. "He was here, but he's gone. I bet he moved so the girls couldn't find him again."

"Well, shit. The river goes all the way down to Long Beach."

Sophia looked around, trying to picture the neighborhood. "Okay, toward the valley, the river actually is fairly deep. So I'm thinking we head south a bit."

They walked the bike path above the river. The bridge at Glendale Blvd was also empty, but they kept on. Tamar said, "He was strong, but he couldn't fly. I don't think he's too far away." Her hunch was rewarded when they all heard a young woman screaming.

Just off the bike path were small sitting areas surrounded by desert flowers and cacti, an attempt to bring the local flora back to the street. Benches also sat within these mini-gardens and that's where the *cucuy* struggled to wrap Gilly with vines and cast-off ropes. The young woman kicked again, her booted foot crashing into the monster's jaw. It wheeled back with its claw to put a stop to the screaming, but Tamar grabbed its neck and pulled it away. But his greasy hair was hard to hold and the monster wiggled free from her grasp.

As it stood, his rictus grin returned. "Back for more?"

"Yeah. But I brought help this time." Tamar looked beyond the *cucuy*, hoping Sophia and Jeremiah were closing in, but she only saw the grinning goblin. She glanced up to see Sophia trying to untie the girl. "Jesus, Sophia, can you help me out just once?"

"She's a child."

"She's one of the witches!"

Sophia found it hard to believe that this little moppet was an evil witch. Even if she was, she still shouldn't be in danger. Sophia pulled out her claws to cut the ropes.

But the *cucuy* hissed when it saw this. "The girl is mine! I earned her for my dinner." With a bounding leap, the fuzzball cleared the bushes in his way and landed next to Sophia. With the back of his frog-like hand, he smashed Sophia across the nose, sending her through the bushes to roll right to Jeremiah's feet.

Sophia felt her nose: broken and bleeding. As she looked up, she saw Jeremiah's usually goofy grin had become evil. "You ready to fight now?"

"Yes." Sophia rolled on her back and sprang to her feet. Tamar was already on the path to confront the little being, he crouching as low as he could to make her attacks that much harder.

He sprang, legs like tightened coils. Tamar had to bend over backwards to avoid getting clocked in the chin. He bounced around like a beachball and flailed his limbs. None of the three vampires could get close enough to strike.

"Never wished I had a gun so bad," Jeremiah said. "Although I have no idea if that would work."

"Let's get the girl and get outta here." Sophia was dizzy from the monster's bounding but saw Tamar's face.

Her look said it, but still Tamar spoke. "No way! I'm getting payback."

Sophia had heard her grumbling earlier. Tamar wanted action and, at this point, anything less would be surrender. Sophia needed to put this to an end quickly. She transformed into mist, settling her cloud around the bat-like face of her opponent. He started choking. Sophia knew she couldn't hold this form without putting her own life in danger, so as soon as it started coughing, she pulled back and reformed herself. Tamar didn't wait.

The Muertos leader pinned the creature to the ground, left hand on its throat and right hand free to beat it senseless. After three successive blows and blood pouring from his turned-up nose, the *cucuy* looked about ready to pass out. Sophia moved to pull Tamar off, but Jeremiah held her back.

"This is her fight," he said.

"It's going to die."

"No it won't. She just wants to make sure it don't fuck with us no more."

As the fifth and sixth punches landed, the creature's breath became ragged.

"This isn't punishment anymore. This is revenge." Sophia looked exasperated.

Jeremiah looked disappointed, but he knew Sophia was right. "Okay, let's stop her."

As they moved to pull Tamar off the *cucuy*, they saw Tamar freeze at an odd angle. She was fighting the paralysis, but it wasn't doing any good. Sophia looked down to the riverbed to see the three other witches. The young Asian woman, face set fiercely, using her magic to hold Tamar. The black girl then swung her arms forward, creating a big gust of wind to blow Tamar off the beast. Finally, the young Latina raised her arms, levitating the *cucuy*.

With a crumbling voice, he yelled, "You broke the deal. Not me!"

The young Mexican smiled as she moved it from the path to the river. "You stole my friend. And I'll make you pay."

With a quick flourish, she whipped her hands toward the water and the *cucuy* dropped face first into the stream. He struggled and flapped but couldn't get free. In a few moments, he slumped, drowned in the river and defeated by the spell.

Sophia saw Tamar was still paralyzed, but Jeremiah was ready to attack the witches. He zipped down the path, only to hit an invisible shield. Sophia now saw the young white girl magicking a protective barrier the vamps couldn't cross. Sophia knew it was time to negotiate. She grabbed the tied-up girl and dug her vampire claws into her neck. "Truce, kids. Truce."

The Mexican girl checked on the *cucuy*. Sophia could see the creature was dead and the girl was ready to talk.

Aida stepped forward. "What needs to happen here?"

Sophia hoped she could take charge but had yet to deal with these girls. "We'll stand down once you drop your spells."

"And Gilly?" She nodded to the girl in Sophia's arms.

"When we're all safe, she'll be released."

"Dammit, don't surrender!" Jeremiah was as angry as Sophia had ever seen him. His change to vampire was complete, all of the old him erased.

"It's not a surrender! We're gonna have peace." Sophia was surprised to hear herself shouting, but Jeremiah was going too far.

"Fuck that!" Jeremiah beat against the invisible shield and three of the girls flinched. The Mexican one didn't even stop smiling.

"See that? That's why we're gonna kill all of you."

"Jeremiah, get up here. Now!" She saw he didn't want to do it, but she was in charge. She knew she'd whup his ass if he didn't stand down, but did he? The answer seemed to be yes as he walked up the incline. But he did it at human speed, not vampire.

Sophia cocked her head to the side. "Drop the spell on Tamar."

The Mexican girl nodded and the Asian girl pulled her hands in. Tamar fell to the ground. Sophia looked at her: Tamar was pissed, but she wasn't girding for further battle.

"Good. I'm going to put your friend down and then we're going to fly out of here. Okay?"

"Fine." But her smile turned extra sarcastic. "But you've been added to the list, you old hag!"

Sophia was as surprised as anyone when she said, "How old do you think I am."

"Like, real old. Thirty-five or forty."

Jeremiah's goofy guffaw erupted between them. He was almost doubled over with laughter. He pointed at Sophia who could feel some weird anger bubbling within her. "You may be an old lady, but you're my old lady."

"Shut up."

Sophia put Gilly back on the bench without untying her. She figured they'd rush up to help without using more combat magic. And she was right. As soon as she put them down, the three vampires all changed to bat form and headed away from this battle. But Sophia knew she was going to hear it from the two of them once they were safe.

As Mina and Spex untied Gilly, Aida looked around. "I think they're gone."

Lisette had wandered closer to the river. The *cucuy's* remains were falling apart, becoming muddy silt on a slow voyage to the Pacific Ocean. Aida approached Lisette with caution. She still needed Lisette's help and thought maybe some kid gloves were needed here.

"Okay, that didn't go as planned."

"Ya think?" Lisette still didn't face Aida. It wasn't clear if her eyes were open, but her head was hanging very low.

"Maybe I acted too rashly. But you have to understand-"

Now Lisette whirled around. "I understand fine." Her eyes were rimmed red, but the rest of her face was set with fury. "You don't care about the coven. You don't care about each of us. You have a one-track mind and if one of us dies in the process, well that's just how war goes."

"I care about you." Aida wasn't sure if she was telling the truth or just trying to convince herself it was true.

"I wanted to find meaning in my life."

"I have meaning: kill those damn vampires."

"You've sacrificed your sanity for revenge. I'm done. You may have access to real magic, but it's not worth it." Lisette ran her hands through her hair. "None of this is worth it."

The other three approached carefully, but lines were being drawn. Mina and Spex lined up behind Aida while Gilly stood next to Lisette.

Gilly rubbed her hands, red marks from the ropes still tattooing her wrists. "I won't be your martyr anymore, Aida. Your fight is not worth my life."

Mina scoffed. "Sure. Your beautiful white life is way too important."

Gilly screamed wordlessly, then calmed herself. "All of our lives are important."

Spex laughed. "You're right. All lives matter."

Lisette said, "Don't put words in our mouths. But you've got one thing right: I have too much to live for. I'm out."

Lisette and Gilly turned to leave. Mina yelled out, "I drove! How the hell are you getting home?"

Gilly held up her phone. "21st Century style. Uber."

Before they walked more than five feet, Aida thrust out both of her arms, twisting the air out of Lisette's and Gilly's lungs. She walked in front of them as they gasped. "Tell me why I shouldn't kill you now."

"Why?" Lisette's voice was a gurgle.

"Your privilege lets you walk away from this. Go back to your rich kid school and your rich kid friends and leave us to fight for our lives. Maybe you should see how we all live, right down here in these streets."

Aida saw Mina nodding, her point hitting home.

But Spex was waving her off. "Stop it! If you kill them, you're just as bad as the vamps."

Aida was hurt by the words, but mostly because they were true. She dropped the spell and the two women huffed as air returned to their lungs. Aida crouched to look the two right in the eyes as they stood on all fours.

"Know this. You have never met us. Never even heard of us. When you walk away, this whole time together disappears. Because if you think of getting in my way, even just a little bit, I won't hesitate. You'll be dead." Aida stood tall. "Now get the fuck outta here."

Gilly and Lisette ran as fast as their legs could move. Soon they were over the bank and out of sight.

Aida stood in front of the other two. She focused her gaze on Spex. "Don't you dare question me again."

"Bullshit." Spex stared right back at her. "This ain't no damn dictatorship. I see wrong, I speak up." She turned to Mina. "Am I right?"

Mina hesitated. Aida could see two ideas fighting in her mind.

She blew out a strong breath. "You're the leader, Aida, but Spex is right. We have to do this the right way."

Aida wanted to set them both aflame. She knew just the spell to do it. But she tamped down that anger and let a calming spirit run through her. "The Mother and Tonantzin live inside me. But they react differently. I need to use the volcano's power while keeping the Mother's attitude." She nodded. "Thank you for keeping me in line."

"Yeah, but those bitches had to learn." Spex pointed toward the road. "They don't know what we know. Like you said, they got their world waiting for them. We just got us."

"Word." Mina's face was set in agreement.

"We need a new plan. Something to really disrupt their world." Aida's gaze drifted into the sky. "Something we know we can survive but would knock them right out."

Spex kicked the ground. "I didn't want to say it 'cause he's crazy, but we might might need to see my great uncle."

The three vampires didn't even make it into the door of the ZLVG center. They collapsed just outside the door in the cool evening breeze. Jeremiah was the first to stand.

"I'm gonna get us all a drink. We need it."

As he went inside to get some pre-bottled blood, Tamar crouched forward.

"Sophia, I love you, but you're gonna get us all killed."

"Serious question—have you ever dealt with magic before?"

"No, but—"

"I've stared a god in the face—channeled through a human, of course, but still. So I've seen a few things. But this? I got nothing."

Jeremiah came out with the bottles and they all took big slugs. Renewed by the life-giving liquid, they went inside and sat in the conference room. Sophia rolled out the white board to get some ideas flowing, but Tamar grimaced.

"Ugh, I didn't pay that much attention in school twenty years ago. I don't want to relive that."

Sophia pulled out a few markers. "I also want Sandy on this." She dialed the table-top phone and put Sandy on speaker.

"Are you kidding me with this?" Sandy sounded as mad as Tamar. "Babe, they're tearing us a new one. Monsters? Spells? We got to start giving it back to them."

"I know none of you want to hear this, but they're kids."

"Look, I was turned when I was sixteen, okay?" Tamar took another pull from the bottle.

"You don't look a day older than that," Jeremiah said and laughed. Sophia felt a little twinge—was he flirting?

"Whatever, dude. I still have to dye my hair. Anyway, I know what it's like to have that much power and that many, whatcha call 'em? Hormones?"

Sandy's short cough of a laugh echoed through the speakers. "Shit, if I were human, I'd be begging for some of them now."

"That's my point, right? Sophia, your age is your strength, but you can't remember what it's was like to be that young. I kinda do. Even when I was little, the first thing we all did was fight. Over nothing, man. Some boy look at you the wrong way? Gotta throw. Every little drama was huge. I know these girls are a little older, but my neighbor girl? She grew up in all that. And she ain't gonna stop 'til one of us dies."

"It'll be her, anyway." Jeremiah's statement got a nod from Tamar, but Sandy piped in.

"We can't know that. Sounds like she can tap into some volcano or something. We lost a bunch of us just fighting each other. Who are we going to lose when we go up against witches?" Sandy paused, choking a bit on the words. Sophia had never heard her so emotional. "Sophia? You, Tamar? Jeremiah? Who else needs to die in this fight? And can you live with yourself if you sacrifice someone over a grudge?"

Tamar paused at this. "I miss Alpha every day. Seriously, any little thing would set me off. But he died fighting. Not cowering in a corner, too scared to act. He was claws out, teeth popped, and in it."

"That may be." Sophia sat now, no brainstorming getting done tonight. "But I'm going back to the charter on this one. We've stopped killing humans. We can find a way to short-circuit her plans and still save her life. Because she's sick! I see it and you do, too."

"Sick dogs get put down." Jeremiah looked so serious that it scared Sophia. "And sick dogs attack people. You ain't seeing the big picture."

"But she's not a dog! She's human." Sophia had no intention of backing down.

"But I ain't. Not anymore." Apparently, neither did Jeremiah.

"What comes after? Do we go back to hunting humans for food?" Sandy's tinny voice quieted the table.

Tamar laughed. "I wouldn't ever do that." She stood. "Don't you trust us, Sandy? Sophia, don't you see that when our lives are threatened, we need to fight back? Or are you the ones who's scared? That you can't control yourselves?"

Sophia paused. Who was this all about? The kid? Tamar? Hell, did seeing Lastie turn into Legba that time have her cowed? "I don't know, Tamar. I only know I'm not ready to kill someone I don't understand."

"I am. The rest is your problem." Tamar walked out of the room and out of the center.

Jeremiah stood.

"Are you going with her?"

"I think I am." He straightened his coat. "I think you're wrong this time."

Sophia needed more time. Desperately. But even more, she needed him like he used to be, the one who would listen and comment while she worked out a plan. But she could see that Jeremiah was gone as he walked out the door.

"Babe? You still there?"

"Yeah, Sandy."

"I can't see his face, but I think you're losing him."

"I know. He doesn't like to talk like he used to. But I'll go through the scenarios and he'll see what he needs to do about the witch."

"No, babe. Listen. I think you're losing him to her. Tamar."

Sophia had known what Sandy meant, but she wasn't ready to say her friend was right.

Part Four: Beyond the Grave

Chapter Twelve

"I don't know where my niece is." Rosalinda had been expecting one of the vampires to return to her shop. Or was at least hopeful. *El cucuy* was no small matter when it came to fighting. But she was expecting Tamar, not Sophia.

"No, don't worry. We're all safe."

"Sarcasm from the elders. I guess it's something we all have to get used to."

Sophia walked into the shop and went to sit at the reading table, but Rosalinda stopped her.

"Let's go in the back room. More comfortable."

As they pushed through the tie-dyed curtain, Sophia did see a much more relaxing place. The walls were midnight blue with frescoes of the desert at night, lots and lots of Joshua trees, filling the empty spaces. Two overstuffed armchairs were centered in the room. As Sophia sat, Rosalinda went to her vinyl record player and set a disc spinning. Soon, Carlos Santana's guitar tones filled the background.

"I'm not gonna lie. I think this room is better than my apartment." Rosalinda, as usual, started her water boiler. Tea would be forthcoming.

"Same here. I don't know if you've seen my place, but it's in Silver Lake. I live right above an office building."

"The benefits of not needing a kitchen."

"That and I own it."

"Then regardless of comfort level, you're very lucky."

As Rosalinda settled into her chair with a steaming mug of chamomile, she felt the weight of the situation descend upon her. "We're in for some very bad times, aren't we?"

"'Fraid so."

"Tell me your end and I'll try to figure out mine."

"Tamar is pissed. As you know, she's been working on her issues, but she doesn't like backing down from a fight." Sophia looked at the ceiling. "And when I say backing down, I mean anything short full victory."

"Which usually means death."

"I came here to stop that. And she's been listening to me. But this niece of yours pushes all her wrong buttons."

Rosalinda swished the liquid around, forgetting there were no leaves in the bottom because she's used bags. "The Volcano speaks to both of them, but with different voices."

Sophia chuckled. "Okay, talk to me like I have no idea about this stuff."

"It seems when my niece was transitioning to her power, she had a vision of her two birth signs, the deer and the volcano. You can tell which one she's favoring." Rosalinda sipped to give Sophia a chance to laugh. "Anyway, this is a powerful being in the Aztec pantheon. And while we Mexicans are nominally Catholic, some of us like to keep these older traditions alive."

"This is like Voodoo, where the *loa* became saints."

"*Loteria!* I can feel the volcanic energy in Tamar even if she knows little about it. So, yes, she will not take kindly to someone trying to kill her and may want to do a preemptive strike."

"That's exactly what she wants to do. And she has most of the others on her side." Sophia sat forward, not content with the relaxing vibe of her chair. "I have real reservations about killing someone so young because she's talented way beyond her years. But she's also claiming that all vampires need to die."

"If you are representing a new way forward for your kind, then I don't want to see all this death either. But I'm not sure I see any way to stop it."

"That's my problem, too. Tamar and Jeremiah said you put down a bad dog—"

"Aida said the same thing."

"Then we're having a further problem. If they don't see each other as people but only as monsters, then their actions are much easier." Sophia plopped back in the chair. "But we're never gonna get them to talk it out."

"Old people talk. Young people act. It's the way it's always been."

"Wait, she had those others with her," Sophia said. "The one who was captured? They didn't look happy with your niece."

"They said something about USC. It's a big campus, but you have better senses than most."

"Still, they'll be powerless to stop Aida. So we need to find a way to disrupt her powers before things get beyond our control." Sophia felt an idea scratching at the back of her head.

"Oh, we're in control, are we?" Now, it was Rosalinda's turn to be sarcastic.

"In a very broad sense of speaking, yes."

"I actually believe you, Sophia. But you may be overestimating my powers. Aida's far beyond me. Even now. I can do a few things, but seeing the future isn't the same as pulling the life force from another being." Rosalinda thought for a second. "That being said, cutting off her access to the divine might be something I can do. For a short time. In a limited capacity."

"Don't oversell it."

"I'm being realistic. What can you do?"

"I wish I knew." Sophia stood. "With any luck, we might be able to short-circuit this thing."

"Luck is what drives the cards. Truth is what's behind the process." Rosalinda finished her tea. Sophia disappeared wordlessly into the night, the worry clinging to her like plastic wrap. Rosalinda liked this one, but for the first time in a long time, she had no vision of the future. And all the calming tea in the world wasn't gonna help with that amount of worry.

Even though she was pissed off at Sophia, Tamar was exhausted from the fight with that hairy monster. Jeremiah offered to drive her home, saying he didn't want to be alone with Sophia. Not right now at least.

"I don't know how I'd feel if I was still a possum guy, but as a vampire, I'm pretty sore at her."

Tamar agreed but kept her mouth shut. She liked Jeremiah but felt anything out of her mouth would soon make it to Sophia's ears. She couldn't trust him just yet to be completely on her side. Although she definitely felt he was more on her side than Sophia's right now. Still, the most she wanted to do was collapse into her coffin.

As she directed Jeremiah to her house, she started to nod out. Dawn was imminent, but she realized he needed to be inside, too.

"You need to crash here?"

"Naw. I can make it to Long Beach within the hour. I think you should come to the club tomorrow night. I'll get all the VampAmp people together. They need to know what's going on."

Tamar nodded but was doubtful. Again, cool vamps to hang with, but they weren't the strongest in a fight. Her gang would back her up and she trusted them, but these ones, the white and middle-class ones, might not get what's happening here. Still, she could use the help. This girl was something more than a nuisance. She was a threat.

As she woke the next night, Tamar felt a lot better. Before she was turned, a night of fighting—and there were more than she liked to admit—would mean two or three days of recovery. She needed to ice down the bruises, stretch her hurt muscles, and just sit still to let time do its work. But the vampire's body had an accelerated clock and on this night she felt fully refreshed. She texted Jeremiah that she was up and made an appointment to meet at the club at midnight. It would let the workers get some stuff done but still give enough time for debate. Not that she wanted to argue, but she figured some healthy back and forth might focus her own ideas.

She got Papi to drive her down, mostly so she could talk things over with him. His still being human always helped her with perspective.

"You regret what you did to that girl?" Tamar tried to be gentle even if it didn't come naturally.

Papi shook his head. "Next time, I make sure she's completely dead. Head off, body scattered."

"Damn. That's cold even for me."

"I know. But that's why we're in this mess. I let myself be soft. Someone comes for your family, soft is a vice. Soft is for people with privilege." Papi's eyes didn't waver from the road.

"Sophia is getting soft. At least I think."

"See, I get that from her. She don't have a family. She has to stand outside everything and run this joint. That ain't a job for a hard ass like you. She needs to be a diplomat. You, sis, are the fighter. 'Cause that girl ain't gunning for Sophia, now is she?"

"I think she is. She wants to kill all vampires." Tamar was sure of that at least.

"But she's starting with you, *mija*. She might run out of enthusiasm after you're gone." He paused for a second. "Which you won't be. Not on my watch."

"*Gracias.*"

Papi dropped Tamar off in front of the club and went to find a parking spot, an increasingly rare commodity in this beach town. The downtown area south of the Pacific Coast Highway was tightening up as more people wanted cheaper rents and an accommodating lifestyle. As a result, an already-packed area was getting overstuffed and more cars than parking spots filled the streets.

Tamar entered to see the upstairs moderately filled, maybe twenty vamps at the bar and in the booths. Jeremiah was serving and he poured her a pint glass from a tap.

"It's the latest from the farm up north. Wild deer blood mixed with some organic pig. Got a nice little acorn finish to it."

This whole scene was weird to Tamar. Ever since Sophia got her off human blood—although, the occasional thrall ponied up when times were tight—she'd been getting chicken and cow blood from a local *carniceria* who Papi paid under the table. But the stuff in this glass was like drinking Coca-Cola when her diet tasted like tap water.

"How much does all this cost?" Even though she ran a cabal, Tamar wasn't rich. All their money was in the house.

"It's a bit premium, but why go cheap?"

This seemed quite similar to a lot of the world. She knew Papi drank whatever beer was the cheapest. To him, even a Modelo was premium. But this was a snobby microbrew version. But when she drank it? Yeah, it was good. But she didn't want this every day.

She took the pint to the table where Maisie and Horton sat. There were a couple of the other VampAmp programmers there, but she didn't know them by name. But the young couple she did know had shown some mettle when fighting against Fudgie Whaloosie's gang, so maybe these hipster types could be good allies. As she sat, they turned the conversation to Aida and her coven.

Maisie leaned forward. "I went through a witchy period in high school—Jesus, was that ten years ago? Anyway, died my hair black, learned a few spells and such. But... nothing. I came to believe magic wasn't real."

Horton nodded. "Obviously, getting turned showed me the supernatural was real. I never was a believer in anything. But still, it's like an onion, where you keep peeling back the layers and all these new things are real—ghosts, magic, zombies..."

"We still don't think zombies are real." Tamar said, certain Sophia's words were on her tongue..

Horton said, "Something happened in New Orleans about a year ago. The normies don't know, but the vamps were all chatting about it."

"Isn't that where Sophia's from?"

"Yeah." Maisie had her phone out, confirming the story. "Vamps in New Orleans have to watch themselves because they have a council, but a few post anonymously to our boards. Anyway, it's linked to that Voodoo priest she knows."

"Fuck, man. Zombies." Tamar took a big pull from her glass. "Ain't that some shit."

"What's next, right?" Horton laughed as he spoke. "Is the Boogeyman gonna come get us?"

"Uuuhhhhhh..." Tamar took another sip to keep quiet.

Horton slapped the table. "Is that what you and Jeremiah fought? A real-life boogeyman?"

"The Mexican version, yes."

"Oh, damn!" Maisie was smiling, but more out of wonder than happiness. "This shit's getting real, yo."

"And on that note..." Jeremiah had walked over from the bar. He picked up a knife and tapped on a glass until he had the whole room's attention. "Hey, y'all. I'm glad you could come. This isn't a regular meeting, but we have something serious to discuss.

"Last night, Tamar, Sophia and I got into a scuffle with a bad little mother called the *cucuy*. And get this! We didn't take it down. These little girls—okay, they're like college age or whatever—they used magic to finish him off. But they sent him after us to begin with."

Jeremiah motioned for Tamar to stand.

"Y'all know Tamar and the Muertos ain't nothing to fuck with. But this magic thing's over all of our heads. Hell, even Sophia don't know what's going on." That brought audible gasps from the crowd. "So we gotta band together and help our friend 'cause this don't just end with her. This witch is coming for all of us and we need to unite and take her down."

Jeremiah ceded the floor to Tamar. As she moved to the center of attention, Papi walked in. He stayed in the back of the room while she spoke.

"You guys know I'm Mexican. Pretty fucking obvious, right?" This got a smattering of laughs. "What you may not know—aside from the tacos you used to eat were white bread garbage—is that everything we do is *por familia*. Family comes first.

"But I'm starting to learn something from all of you. Family don't mean just blood. In my culture, it does, but we may have some learning to do. I can see that family extends to those who you put your trust in. I trust Sophia. Sometimes it's hard for me not to call her *tia*, but I'm sure she'd hate that. But Sophia isn't thinking about family." She saw Papi nod as his words came out of Tamar's mouth.

"She's gotta think about all the families, not just ours. But this little *bruja* came into my house and threatened me and mine directly. I offered her peace and she chose war. So I'm asking you and Jeremiah is asking you—" He gave a little wave to confirm her assertion. "We are both asking you to fight. 'Cause families fight together.

"Imagine what you would do if some witch attacked the person next you. What would you do? Don't answer 'cause I know. Fangs out, bitch dead. I know it. You know it.

"When all this is over, we'll let Sophia talk it out with the authorities or whatever. That's what she does and that's why we love her. But we're taking the fight to the street and I need to know that my family, *mi familia*, has my back. What do you say?"

The small crowd whooped and hollered. Horton stood. "Yeah. Let's kick some witch ass!"

Tamar nodded as the energy grew within the bar. She took a page from Sophia's book to make sure the feeling would remain.

"Let's converge! Show me we're all in this together!"

Hands joined throughout the room while Tamar began the moaning drone. Soon, the harmonics built and the chandeliers began swaying. At the final crescendo, everyone threw their hands in the air. Tamar felt like a pact had been made.

As she sat, Papi sat beside her. He smiled. "I know you got them. And you've got our gang. You need anyone else?"

Tamar nodded. "We need at least one more cabal in on this. I need to go see the Bomb Squad."

#

As Mina drove to down the 110 Freeway toward Compton, Spex told them what to expect.

"Like everything, it's starting to change. Used to be mostly black people, but Mexicans are here, too. Thing is, people only hear about gangs, but there's lots of houses. Don't mean it ain't dangerous, but you can go block to block and see completely different shit."

This storied neighborhood, so big in the American consciousness because of N.W.A. and other gangsta rappers, is actually quite small. Bounded in the rhombus between four freeways—110 on the east, 710 to the west, 105 north, and 91 south—it sits between two very different cities: Gardena, a lower- and middle-class Asian neighborhood mostly populated by Koreans, and Long Beach, the rapidly changing but working-class enclave.

Aida could see this neighborhood was distinct from Boyle Heights. Many smaller houses and big-block apartment buildings were scattered through the streets, but just about every block was anchored to a tall Victorian with their steepled structures and side turrets, much like the vampires' place next door. But as they drove down Long Beach Blvd, the streets now numbering in the hundreds—Aida remembering they lived near 29th Street—she could see the leftovers of previous times. The blocks were filled with Craftsman houses: one story high, angled roofs covering the whole footprint, small front porches, and metal gates. These were left over from when this was a new suburb for white working-class people to live their American dream of owning a house. Time and migration patterns had clouded that dream, but still, the people here could have something of their own even if the overall neighborhood was dilapidated.

Spex's mom had such a place. She lived near City Hall, with its collection of columns decorating the front of the building. As they pulled up, Aida saw her on the porch, looking near 40 although Aida couldn't fully tell her age. She was definitely younger than her mother and looked as tough as her daughter in an overlarge black t-shirt, gym shorts hanging past her knees, and slides. But she had a huge wooden cross hanging around her neck and Aida could see the t-shirt said "Jesus" in very large letters. Maybe she always looked tough, but the real possibility was she didn't want to see her daughter and her weirdo friends.

Mina and Aida stayed in the car while Spex got out. She left the driver's back door open so her friends could hear the conversation.

"What you doing here?" Yes, Mom's tone was unfriendly.

"We're here to see Uncle Ibrahim."

"His name is Moses."

"Mom..."

"A-ight, if you need to call him by a heathen name, go right ahead. Y'all be cooking in Hell together, I suppose."

Mina whispered to Aida, "Is this not going well?"

"I think this may be normal. We'll see."

Spex still hadn't entered the front gate. "Can we see him?"

"Did he invite you? Because this is still my house and I get to choose who comes in."

Spex shook her head. "No. But we all want to talk to him."

"Brought the whole fucking United Nations, I see." Mom pointed at the car but afterwards looked over her shoulder. "What you want with that sinner?"

"I just want to talk to him about something. You need to know?"

"Probably best if I don't." Mom yawned. "He ain't here. There's one of them community gardens up the road. He spends most of his time there with some chickens they got going."

"Okay. Thanks."

As Spex got into the car, Mom said, "Come back when you ready for some Jesus in your life."

"If she only knew," Aida said as Spex closed the door.

"Yeah and she ain't gonna."

Spex knew the place her mom described, just about five minutes away. The garden was on a corner lot in the middle of a neighborhood, the remains of a concrete foundation stretching along the western edge. The place was enclosed by a metal fence and a sign hung over it: Sankofa Gardens with a stylized bird reaching its beak back. Spex pointed at the sign.

"I think it's from Ghana. There's lots of that Afrocentric stuff from the '60s still around here in the names of non-profits. In fact, that's what Uncle Ibrahim is: a throwback."

They didn't see anyone in the rows of tall plants from the outside, but Aida saw lots of vegetables amid the rows and raised beds, including corn, onions, tomatoes, okra, and all sorts of herbs. The gate wasn't locked, so they walked in.

Aida could hear the clucking of chickens toward the rear of the garden. The back of a building, stacked concrete blocks, was the end of the garden, although someone had put fencing up against it. A wider open area with a smaller wooden fence enclosed the chicken run and coop. Five birds picked at the dirt as an older black man fed them by hand. He leaned on a raw wooden cane which held baubles and strings tied from the top.

He was bald underneath a round *kente* cloth hat that matched his dashiki colored with geometric lines of red, yellow, black and green.. He wore jean shorts and leather sandals, but the most impressive thing about him was his long gray beard, one big bush from his chin to his sternum. He looked up and smiled when he saw Spex.

"Tamala? Is that you?"

She opened the gate and gave him a hug. Joy filled his face, but Aida could see behind that. He had deep lines hidden by the beard, not from age but from a rough life. Power radiated from these facial runs, showing that he had learned many things, but the price was high. She knew instantly that he would help them.

Spex introduced everyone. While they talked, he continued spreading feed for the birds. Aida could tell he was avoiding her gaze.

"What makes you want to come see an old man like me?" His voice was gravelly.

Spex took lead. "We're having some problems and I thought you might be the one to help us."

"I ain't getting involved with gangs or anything like that. I'm happy to be above that and work the Earth for a natural bounty."

"We ain't like that, Uncle Ib. It's something else. Something... magical."

"Why would you think someone in your family would have a hand in magic? Isn't Jesus the way for true spiritual enlightenment?" His face was stoney now. Aida could tell he knew what was being asked, but he had no interest in addressing the question.

"I thought you was Muslim." Spex looked confused. Maybe she had thought this would be straightforward, but Aida could sense his reluctance. What was holding him back?

"Many books lead us to the same conclusion. We are meant for higher purposes. Access to the divine comes through hard work and self-reflection. It isn't a favor."

Aida stepped up to the fence. "We all have accessed the divine. That's not what we're asking for."

Now Ibrahim looked at Aida. The facade was still rock solid, but she could see behind that face to the true question.

"No, that's obvious." Ibrahim removed the feed bag and placed it in a locker. He perched himself on a wooden bar stool. "I can't quite tell your sources, but I see the end result. My niece here has called upon Shango. That I can tell. But you..." He paused to look at Aida, cocking his head. "You are connected to this hemisphere. The older ones who waited when the white men came. Who exactly is unclear, but that's how it should be."

He then turned to Mina. "You are the least refined one. But I see the potential. I can help you the most."

Mina smiled. This had been an ongoing discussion—how could she progress? Aida didn't know and they'd lost any hope of Rosalinda helping. If this man could bring her in line with the others, they would be so powerful.

But Ibrahim now was ready to ask the questions. "Who is after you?"

Spex looked all around to make sure nobody was listening. "Vampires."

His face squinched, not pained but intrigued. "I haven't met any children of the night. Why do they hunt you?"

Aida smiled now. "The predators will be my prey."

"Hmmm, this sounds like a story I need to know." He stood. "I'll help you. I've lived long enough to know what some consider right means doing harm. I can help. But there will be a price."

Aida looked deflated. "Money is something I can't magick."

"Money has never been my priority, girl. We'll do the deed first. Price will come later. Now, for y'all, what do you require?"

Aida said, "Some sort of aid in the fight. There are plenty of them. We are just us."

"How many are they?"

Spex shrugged. "Dozens at least. Maybe 50?"

"So you need a small army."

Spex leaned in and whispered. "I'd heard something about New Orleans..."

"I will tell that tale soon. That was a failed experiment. To truly battle the undead, you need to fight the enemy on its own turf."

Aida asked, "What does that mean?"

"Very simple, my dear. The right tool for the job is necromancy."

Chapter Thirteen

With Tamar and Jeremiah gone, Sophia canceled her meetings. She needed to track down these two girls and see if she could get any info to bring down their coven.

She started at the river. Fresh out of bed and full of morning blood, she walked over there as soon as she woke up. She went directly to the old nest and put her nose to work.

Boy, was the *cucuy* rank. The odors, very animalistic, were hard to pierce, but she could perceive an underlying scent: patchouli. These Wiccans were never far from hippies, were they?

But that wouldn't be enough. Not on a college campus, at least. There were other markers, more personal notes of sweat. Surely the heat and the fear generated both. Combined with the oil, she was pretty certain she could track one of them. Now to get to campus.

When she got in the Uber, the driver pinched her nose. Maybe fumbling around in a sewer grate added some extra funk to her style.

"Take me home, real quick. I'll clean up before we go to USC."

"Please?"

After the change and a silent drive down south, Sophia was deposited by the front gate. It was only 8pm, so the campus still had people walking about. This place was huge. She might have to do this a few nights in a row or maybe find a human to track her down during the day. But she was here, so she started.

She went to the large dorm first, the one which looked closer to a skyscraper. As she walked near the front door, her nose tweaked. Had she gotten this lucky? Outside near the fountain, she saw a young blonde woman looking at her phone and talking excitedly. She swished her arms back and forth as she spoke to the electronic device.

Sophia slid as close to her as she could. With her hearing, she could tell this woman wasn't talking to someone. She was reading lines from a play or something, paused after every line. This was definitely the one who was captured.

Sophia got very close, then spoke. "Getting right back to normal, kid?"

Gilly jumped, then turned around. She went into a fighting stance. "I don't have the power the others have, but I will fight you."

"Do you recognize me?" Gilly nodded. "Then you know I helped rescue you."

"You were the one who tried to talk everybody down," Gilly said. "The older one."

"Yes, the old one." Sophia tried not to groan. "And that's why I'm here. I'm trying to prevent a fight, not start one."

Gilly stood straight. "That's okay. The two of us aren't with them anymore."

"Which two?"

"Me and Lisette."

"Is she around?"

"She should be upstairs."

"Then let's talk."

"Okay. But down here. Out in the open. I still don't trust anybody."

"That's your right."

After ten minutes, Gilly returned with Lisette who wore a hoodie up like she wanted to hide her face.

Sophia was confused. "What's all this?"

"Too many eyes around this place. I don't know who's where anymore."

"I just have a few questions. Like why you recruited the *cucuy* to begin with."

Lisette looked at Gilly, then turned back to Sophia. "That was Aida's idea."

"We'd never heard of the damn thing." Gilly embraced herself, looking as scared now as if she'd been tied up. "Is was something that could fight like... you guys. Vampires." She whispered the last word.

"It was tough. No doubt." Sophia shuddered inwardly at the thought of trying to fight that thing again. "I think one of us could have been seriously hurt if Aida hadn't killed it."

Lisette's face was very sour. "Killing, killing, killing. That's all she wants to talk about. Look, I understand the beef she has with the

Mexican one..."

"So do I." Sophia was trying to be understanding.

"I just wanted to tap into something beyond me. Something divine."

Gilly nodded. "We wanted to bring light to our world. But Aida and Spex... and Mina, too. They just want darkness."

"I'm just as scared of Mina as I am of Aida. She has so much anger that if she gets half as powerful, things will get ugly." Lisette laid back on the concrete step. "Aida and that vampire just need to fight this out and be done with it."

"Do you two know what they're gonna do?"

Gilly shook her head. "We both decided to get out. Cut off all ties. I'm not built for something that dangerous."

"Yeah, we have lives outside of magic. I don't know if those three do." Lisette sat back up. "I can hear Aida's voice in my head, giving me shit for having privilege. And it's true. But being privileged and being blind are two different things. Aida's blind from fury. And if my privilege can keep me safe, well it damn sure will this time."

Sophia was convinced these two weren't a threat anymore. But the remaining three seemed capable of anything. Sophia had one last question. "Where do they live?" She wasn't after a fight, but she knew she needed to keep an eye on them before the real fight started.

Instead of going back to Spex's mom's house where Uncle Ibrahim was staying, they all agreed they needed privacy. The three decided to bring him back to the apartment where they could really hash out the next step's details. As they drove up Exposition Blvd, Ibrahim fell into a fit of nostalgia.

"I been gone so long that nothing feels right here." Ibrahim laughed. "Of course, I loved being in New Orleans. I wasn't born there, but the roots go deep. Spex'll tell y'all, just about everybody here in South Central and Compton has some sort of family from Louisiana or Texas. But the New Orleans people feel it the strongest."

He laughed and pointed at a sign that advertised Louisiana fried chicken.

"First thing people told me when I saw that was, 'They Chinese, y'know.' But they still go there. Just to get that taste." He looked at

Mina while she kept her eyes forward. "No offense now."

"That's okay. I'm Japanese."

"Sorry, sorry. It's funny, though. We see those Koreans in the corner stores and the Chinese in the restaurants and we see invaders. Like we own this shit. But they just like us. Pushed out of the city. Gotta work and scrape to survive. We all got pitted against each other in some sort of war and the only winners is them rich motherfuckers."

Aida turned around to face Ibrahim. "It's happening in Boyle Heights, too."

"I heard all about that. Truth is that money always wins. One day, all of this city may be white people ringed by communities of black and brown. But it isn't about race—some of it is, but not all. It's like ole Woody Guthrie said. Gotta have the dough-ray-me."

They parked in their space and headed up to the apartment. Spex filled a bowl with tortilla chips with small cups of salsa and Aida pulled a pitcher of iced tea from the fridge. The women squatted on the floor while Ibrahim sat on a chair. He leaned forward on his cane.

"My friend Israel was the one who put this idea in my head. When I went to New Orleans back in the late '60s, I was part of the Black Panther Party. They didn't want us down there and they went to war. You can guess who won.

"Now, Izzy was part of the Party, or so I thought. Turned out he was a cop the whole time. Now I got off light—couple years in the stir. Not like one of us who got framed for murder. But when I got out, I had vengeance on my mind. Izzy was gonna pay for all the bad stuff he did.

"I got back to find a broken man. Haunted. The ghosts of four little girls who were blown up in a church visited him every night, asking him questions. I must say, it broke my heart. He needed help and I was the only one willing to do it."

"Wait, ghosts are real, too?" Spex looked surprised. "Damn. This world is full of stuff we never see."

"The more you do magic, the more you find. So now we're getting to the mid-'70s. Izzy needs something to help him. So he goes to a local Voudon. She says he needs to get right with his roots. Take up the practice. He asks me to join him.

"As you know, I'd already been a Panther and had joined the Black

Muslims in jail. But none of that felt right. This did. The two of us dived in, trained and studied, learned how to draw the *veve*, and practiced every week. We even went down to Haiti to be initiated. It worked on me. I was never happier. Izzy? He still had troubles.

"Come way forward to the late '90s. Izzy's mind has started to deteriorate. He gets it in his head that being a practitioner wasn't enough. We had to become *bokor*, magicians. Light or dark makes no difference. Magic was the end goal, an access to the divine. To that end, he knew—just knew—we had to make zombie powder. He saw a war coming where black people would have to fight against The Man and we needed that tool for our side.

"It took us *years*. Almost a decade. But we finally found something that would work. But while I was working the assembly, Izzy was falling deeper into the dark side.

"I had some idea how we would use the stuff. We'd find a few people, drug them up, and take from them. It wasn't a noble plan, but it would get us some money to keep the revolution going. Then Hurricane Katrina hit.

"Izzy talked all sorts of crap for years, that he summoned the hurricane to cleanse the soul of the city. I indulged him in this because he was my friend and we'd been tight for so long. Then we finally found the right time for our revolution. We teamed up with some young guns and took our shot.

"But the problem with the powder is you need live people to work on. And Izzy and the kids didn't care nothing for the people in the neighborhood. We was hurting other black folk. I hit the road before it all got too out of hand. I heard Izzy died. But I don't want to do that. It's too risky.

"We need to connect to the gods. Let the bodies of those passed to do the work. That way we don't hurt the community. We only hurt those who hurt you."

Ibrahim sat back while Aida pondered what he said.

"They feed on us," she said. "They feed on life. I like this plan. Use death against them. What do we have to do?"

Ibrahim closed his eyes. "It won't be easy. This is the darkest magic there is. We'll need to call upon some spirits who will demand a lot from us." He rubbed his face. "The energy I've used in my magic has run me down. This might just rob you of youth. But if you are ready to make the next step on your journey, nothing but power awaits."

"How do we do it?" Mina looked really charged by this challenge.

"We need to do a little study. But we also need to find a grave-yard."

The apartment was near USC so Sophia decided to walk over there. She checked her phone and saw the easiest route may be over a bridge on Adams Street. She hadn't spent much time down in this neighborhood, so she thought this would be a good time to see how the students lived.

She went up Hoover, a street which extended almost to Silver Lake. She saw a brand new mall, apparently built by the university, just across the street. It had the same style as the school's build-ings—red brick and wide walkways. It seemed designed for stu-dents even though it technically wasn't on campus. She saw groups of kids around tables, relaxing and eating. Not a whole lot of study-ing, but this wasn't a library,

As she continued past a soccer field, empty at this time of night, she came to a street where a few houses had Greek letters. She knew it must be the frat row. She seen something similar back home, with most of Tulane's Greek houses on Broadway Avenue just across the street from campus. But this was something different.

These houses were on the same level as the mansions on St. Charles Ave, those antebellum monsters with their columns and wide porches. Huge places filled with kids who didn't have to worry about where their next meal was coming from. Most of the hous-es weren't of Southern design, but they had the stately elegance of something older, something traditional, something unreachable.

She paused in front of one which could be from back home. Eight gabled windows lined the roof, perfect for looking out on the street for a midnight suitor or something romantic like that. Four square columns, two on each side of the front door, stretched to the sec-ond story, framing a small Juliet balcony over the entrance. And if that wasn't enough, a magnolia tree stood in the center of a brilliant green lawn—something the southern California climate would nev-er allow without big bucks to maintain it—with a small stone bench under it. The whole place felt like a fairy tale sold to the young women who saw themselves as trophies.

But as she got further down the row, she saw not all of the houses mirrored that mansion. Some were downright junky, no doubt where the boys lived. Also, a lingering smell filled her senses, something awfully familiar which she couldn't quite identify. Finally, it hit her—Bourbon Street, that ungodly combination of stale beer and bodily fluids. The facade may be old world and romantic, but the true nature of this life revealed itself quickly.

She left behind the row for Exposition Blvd which looked like any business stretch: fast food, bars, strip malls. She went up the few blocks to Adams where a huge Catholic church was on the corner. This looked art deco, maybe from the '20s or '30s. Its spire was huge, nearly four stories tall, with two belfries on top of each other with a dome above that. Doric columns surrounded the area for the bells as well as the front of the church which was carved with statues and other filigrees. Someone had spent a lot of cash on this back in the day.

Leaving the church behind, she crossed over the 110 Freeway to the neighborhood where Aida and her friends lived.

And how quick the transition was. Like the wrong side of the tracks of her time, this side of the freeway was a completely different world. One of the first places she passed was labeled "Department of Public Services," looking to be the place where welfare recipients and other poor people went for help. Exposition Blvd may have been a bit grungy because of the traffic, but over here on Grand it was grimy. This whole block looked like it needed a power wash and she still wasn't sure if that would erase the problem.

As she walked towards Downtown, the signs turned to Spanish, although she certainly recognized corner liquor stores and mechanic shops as part of the cheaper lifestyle. Some of the buildings looked abandoned which wasn't anything like packed-to-the-gills Silver Lake.

She wasn't surprised to see monied enclaves sitting near poor sections. New Orleans was like this. But the difference in wealth was so much more. Certainly, USC was sitting on close to a billion in assets, but only a few blocks away, people were starving.

Yet how long would it take for the needs of the rich to stretch across the freeway? Los Angles proper was losing most of its poorer sections. Soon, this patchwork of cities would coalesce into a full city of privilege and push the poor as far away as possible.

Sophia chose not to dwell on it. It would only depress her. Like her time in San Francisco, she wanted to take these blocks and save every last one, living or dead. But she had to concentrate on three young women who wanted her destroyed.

As for the future, she could certainly live long enough to see it happen. But those were for times when her life wasn't threatened. As she finally found the ugly brick apartment building, she took to the air, turning to bat form and landing on the roof opposite. She needed to know their plans and hopefully a little spying would reveal just what they were thinking.

Chapter Fourteen

Aida looked excited when Ibrahim ended his story. "I think I know where to find the power. We should call upon Quetzalcoatl."

Ibrahim smiled at the idea. "The feathered serpent? Tell me more."

"He created humankind by stealing the bones of the dead and soaking them in his blood. Sounds like a way to raise corpses."

Spex looked like she'd swallowed chicken bone. "Are we sure about this? I'm like all for using our own power to fight the vampires, but this sounds like we're messing with something we shouldn't be touching."

"The untouchable is where I live." Ibrahim wasn't smiling anymore. "Any time someone tells me I shouldn't do it, that draws me in further." He turned to Aida. "What would such a ceremony entail?"

"Let me find it." She'd been researching Aztec gods to see where else she could focus her power. The volcano was a never-ending source, but the other gods could expand her skill set. She opened the bookmarks she'd set on Mina's computer. "I know this may sound strange, but I found this Masonic rite..."

Mina laughed. "The Masons? Are they a bunch of white dudes looking for an excuse to get drunk?"

"Don't discount their wisdom. After all, they hold the secret to Jesus' family." Ibrahim cleared his throat. "Besides, the brothers have been infiltrating their organization for a couple of decades. Soon, we'll have all their wisdom to use against them."

Aida was confused by all Ibrahim had to say, but she soldiered on. "There's a whole lot going on here, but we'll need some corn and *pulque*. Fuck, where can we find that?"

"You showing your age, girl. I just need to pop down the liquor store and grab some tequila. We need anything else?"

"No, we have all the other stuff we need."

"Alright, then." He stood and looked at Spex. "Wanna take a

walk?"

"Sure." She stood and they left the place for Aida and Mina to get together the rest of the ingredients.

As they got to street level, Ibrahim fell in step with Spex. He seemed much more serious out here than he did in the apartment. Maybe because he was trying to charm the other two and didn't have to do that with Spex. But she felt something was up right now. The shoe finally dropped.

"You trust these two?" He was looking forward, keeping his eyes to the street probably because this neighborhood wasn't his own.

"I've seen things this past few months that blew my mind. They might not be family to you, but I'm in a whole new world here."

"That's not what I asked. I asked if you trust them."

Spex had to think on this. Mina hadn't shared as much as Aida. She was dark when they started, into all that Goth music. But the witchcraft had reformed her into something else. The rage dam she'd built through high school had sprung a leak and now she was soaking in it. But it was unfocused, chaotic. If that dam crumbled in addition to her power growing, she might destroy something Spex considered valuable. She had to share that much with Ibrahim.

"Mina's cool, but I don't know if I trust her. She was something fragile that could break and now she's trying to break herself."

"I can see that. Her aura is so dark." He rubbed his chin. "Take this as a lesson. Rage is tool, a means. It can't be the reason to be. But at least she's not as powerful as Aida. Not yet, at least."

"Mina probably needs some help. It's beyond me, that's for sure."

"That's a colonial mindset. She needs training. That's something where we can really help her." He let out a sigh. "I've known too many who succumbed to rage. My New Orleans friend was one of them. He wouldn't let me help him. In the end, it all swallowed him."

"You sound like you're happy he died."

"His passing was a boon. His suffering is over. Mine is still going." He looked at Spex now. "Okay, beyond her power, what about Aida?"

This was something that had been gnawing at Spex. Where Mina had no outlet for her rage, Aida was obsessed with the vampires to the point of ignoring anything else. After hearing the story, Spex believed Aida's revenge was justified. After all, they were monsters. But they could have been studying the magic more, not just as a tool but for greater empowerment. Maybe even to help other people, like Aida's aunt does. And now that the fight had gone from her neighbor vampire to the whole damn race, Spex thought Aida was losing her grip.

Maybe the white girls were dilettantes. Maybe they didn't have what it takes to be real with magic. But they certainly didn't need to be taken hostage by another monster. And Aida seemed real quick to sell them out for her goals. She felt very close to Aida, her first real friend since she took to the streets. But she could see the tree roots turning into branches and she wasn't sure which way she was growing.

"I know her heart. I can vouch for that. But, yeah. Maybe once we kill that Mexican vampire, she'll calm down and we can go back to studying and practicing."

"Do you really believe that?"

"I can have hope."

"I think you're misplacing it. She won't stop. I know she was good for you, brought you further into your practice. But we have to see these powerful souls for what they are: users. She'll change the goals over and over because it's the power move. Israel did as such with me. I followed for way too long." He paused and stopped. The store was in sight, about half a block away. "Let's follow this path. I feel destroying this monster will close some doors for Aida. We'll give her the chance to stop. But we must be ready when she disappoints us."

Spex thought he would keep walking, but he now turned to her.

"The big question comes next. Do you trust me?"

"Moms says I shouldn't."

"She puts her trust in her faith. Like Aida is blinded by the vampire, my wonderful sister is blinded by Jesus, the way and the light. For her, it's all encompassing, but for me it is a torch down a dark path I can't follow."

"You were gone for so long. I thought you were one kind of person and now I'm seeing a different one."

"I'm definitely not the person I was back then. Remember the proverb: you never see the same river twice. I've learned a few things and I've gained some new knowledge. But my dark path has fewer lights. You may not want to follow."

"I'm at least ready to see where it goes."

"Okay. But don't say I didn't warn you. Let's grab the booze."

They went inside. The bottles were lined up behind Plexiglas as a smaller Arabic man looked at them suspiciously. Ibrahim knew what he was looking for.

"There." He pointed to a tequila that was cheap but still one hundred percent agave. "Hopefully, that will be enough for our prayers."

As the counter man pulled down the bottle, Ibrahim stepped to the front shelves, disappearing for a second. He returned with a clear bottle containing bright green liquid.

"What's that?"

The old man smiled. "Margarita mix. Hell, after the ceremony, we should have a few cocktails."

Sophia perked up when she saw Aida's black friend and the older man leave the apartment. She debated flying over to the window to peek in on the remaining two, but all the windows were covered and set into the wall with no ledges. She didn't feel like hovering around, so she decided to flutter down to street level and follow the walkers.

At about twenty feet above their heads, she could only pick out fragments of what they were saying. But two words focused her: New Orleans. Was this guy from back home? Did he know Lastie? She laughed at herself, muttering, "Yeah, all black people know each other. Jesus, could I be more cliche?"

She paused as they went into a corner liquor store. No way she was heading in there, so she retreated to the apartment building. Maybe this was a party? They were kids after all.

No, she knew something big was brewing, but she'd have to be patient. The hour was still early, but she would have to be concerned about where she would crash if they went somewhere else. Living the night life wasn't all glamor, now was it?

She saw them coming back, so she went around the corner, transforming to her human form at street level. If they were going to act, it would be in the next few hours. She just needed to stay calm and let them do their thing.

She saw a bar about a block up with windows to the street, the cover she would need. As she entered, *ranchero* music blared, filling every nook with its accordion flow, and a line of older Mexican men occupying the bar. She thought about Montana as she closed the door. Hopefully, her song was keeping San Francisco in just the right amount of drama. She ordered a beer and sat at the perfect window seat, hoping that she could be alone until those kids left their place.

As Spex and Ibrahim went to the store, Aida and Mina started setting up. Mina went to her computer while Aida got the main components together: a bowl full of masa—the finely ground corn meal used for tortillas and tamales; cups for the liquor; and a circle made of dirt from their house plants. She laughed as she completed the final task.

"Spex will be pissed if I killed her cactus. But we need the dirt and there's none outside."

Mina called Aida over. "Look. This is a later picture of Quetzal-coatl."

Aida had always pictured the winged serpent from the myths, but here was a human with a feathered coat, a duck-billed mask, and, most important to Mina, a conical hat. "That looks important. Check your rites to see if that's something we need."

Sure enough, the Masons who led this right had such hats, specifically ones with a five-pointed silver star up front.

"Do you think it's necessary?"

Mina looked at the picture. "I have no idea, but it's better to cover as many bases as we can."

Aida texted Spex who still hadn't returned, telling her to stop at the drug store to see if they had any birthday party hats.

"Really?" was the reply.

"Yeah. The cone kind."

"Okay."

Mina went to her bedroom and pulled a few sticks of nag champa incense. "We need this, right?"

"Always."

They sat within the circle as they waited for the other two to return. Mina was usually reserved and remained that way tonight, so Aida knew she needed to see how she was feeling.

"Are you worried about this at all?"

"No." Mina looked quite certain. "I know it's cliche for the Goth girl to be all into death and stuff, but ever since we started fighting the vampires, I've never felt so right."

Aida paused and stayed silent, not wanting to stop her friend now that she was finally opening up.

"I don't have any particular thing I'm mad at. It's just something inside of me that sees the negative in everything. The way my mom wants me to be passive. The way the world sees Japanese girls as an erotic fixation. But most of all why I could never be happy."

"That's intense. I felt some of that, too. But I didn't see the alternatives."

"Aida, you were sheltered. So was I. I mean, we don't get to think like that. That there's anything wrong or, even worse, that there's something wrong with us. The Orange County high school crowd was so vapid. So when I found the subcultures and the music and the... the... energy. Man., I felt free. Not happy, but free. So when you say let's go to the dark side, I've been doing that for years. You're just catching up to me."

Aida held out her arms. "May I?"

Mina held her so tightly. Aida had never had such emotional friendships before. Or at least ones this deep.

"I don't know what happened to me." Aida blew out a big breath. "There's no one I can talk to about this transformation. But it can't be me alone. One person is not a circle. I need you all. Can you see that."

Mina nodded, verging on tears. "When we kill the vampire, we need to go away. Remember the Tarot. The three of us have to be The Hermit and really focus our energies."

"What about school?"

"I'm thinking it isn't a priority."

"Will your dad stop paying for the apartment?"

"We'll figure that out later, okay?"

Aida was cool with that. The task in front of them was the first of many mountains. Each would be a difficult climb, so why fear the one in the future? She needed to concentrate on the now.

Spex and Ibrahim returned from the store, with Spex still weirded out by the party hat request. Even though Mina showed her the picture, she was still skeptical, all the way up to the point where they sat within the circle wearing the newly-decorated hats. Mina had added silver stars to a dark coat of watercolor.

Spex frowned. "C'mon, guys. We look like dorks."

"It's all right there in the picture." Mina sounded mad. Aida couldn't tell if it was because she made the hats or by Spex's resistance to the ceremony. "I know I did these quickly, but it was the best I could do."

"Young lady, it's best to concentrate on what's inside your heart than on your outside." Ibrahim was probably one of the few who could get away with calling Spex "young lady" and not get a fist to the nose. Aida could definitely tell how much she respected her uncle.

"I'd be happier if the hats didn't make me crave cake and ice cream." Spex laughed to break the tension then picked up the incense. "Regardless, I'll light the candles."

As the scented smoke filled the room, they all quieted. Aida looked to Ibrahim. "Do you want to lead this?"

"These are your gods. I defer. I'm here only as a guide."

Aida took the moment to soak up the ever-rare compliment from an older person, but then she was ready to dive into the summoning.

After a bit of chanting, formless sounds meant to bring the group together, Aida spoke, "I call upon Quetzalcoatl, grounded in earth as the snake but part of the air as the bird. Oh, winged serpent, open your spirit to our prayers. Feed upon the maize which you showed humans how to harvest."

Hearing her part, Spex took a pinch of masa and sprinkled it over the burning incense. A popcorn scent added to the incense's perfume.

Aida continued, "Now we shall take part in the Drink of Equal Parts. We offer a liquor made of all the elements—fire, water, earth, and wood. This sacred drink represents your conjoining of earth and sky. We shall all take drinks of equal portions *pulque*."

They each leaned forward and took up the shot glasses, drinking down the tequila within. Aida heard Ibrahim let out an involuntary "aaaahhhh," but she let it go. The alcohol numbed her tongue a bit. Tequila and beer were the drinks of choice in her family, but this liquor smelled and tasted better than the cheap rotgut her brothers kept around. While not making her drunk, it certainly gave her a small swirl.

They all returned their glasses to the reserved space in front of them and Aida started again. "We greet you from the four compass points." She and Mina had made sure that each spot lined up exactly with the primary directions. "Come to us, oh god of wind and rain, of art and learning and present to us the knowledge that we seek."

They all chanted again, something Mina had found in what was assumed would be the Aztec language. Their voices became one and, after a few minutes of synchronizing, a wind circled through the room. Since the a/c was off, Aida knew they had been successful in their ritual. She opened her eyes.

The smoke emanating from the incense spread from the tight pattern off the sticks and fluctuated within the circle. Aida could see it twisting and forming. As they continued their chant, the smoke coalesced into a floating snake form with the fabled wings spread from what looked like the back. In the hissing voice of a cartoon serpent, the cloud spoke. "You have summoned me from a long rest. Who gives you the authority to call upon me?"

Aida looked into its cloudy eyes. "The Mother. Tonantzin."

Quetzalcoatl nodded. "Yes. I see her spirit within you. And a few others, too."

"You honor me and you honor us with your presence."

"I accept your offerings and I will listen to your supplications."

"Mighty Quetzalcoatl, we seek knowledge. We seek to learn how you raised dead bones to become human."

"Have the tales of my accomplishments been so lost so you don't know them?"

"We have heard the actions but not the specifics. We seek such power."

"I shall tell you all the story. What you learn from it may not be what you wanted, but I shall recount my trip to the underworld."

Chapter Fifteen

Listen to me, children, as I tell you of how the gods created humans so very long ago.

My brother Tezcatlipoca had a need. He came to me with his great plan to create a new race, the humans, who would live to serve and worship us. After creating the earth and sky from shedding our skins, it was up to us to populate it. My brother didn't know what to use to create such a people, but I had my own idea.

I knew the bones of the Great Old Ones had long been buried. Certainly, using these to construct our new creation would not only pay homage to the elders but would also infuse humans with some of their power. But these bones were not out in the open where any could find them.

They had been buried long ago in Mictlan, the underworld, where the Lord and Lady kept them. Some said they were for safe keeping while others said the rulers considered these remains a great treasure that should not be shared. I took my leave of my brother and traveled below, keeping my reasons secret for the present.

Both Lord Mictlanteuctli and Lady Mictlancihuatl, their bony faces so unreadable and therefore hard to fool, wondered why I had come all that way. I told them I wanted to visit the Old Ones' burial site and perhaps use a few spare bones to help contact them. They said that even visiting the site required a trial. The Lord pulled from his pocket a conch shell and, lipless though he was, blew a resounding note. He said I needed to do the same before I could visit. He held out the shell and I took it.

And now I knew he had tried to trick me. The ends of the conch had no hole to blow upon and the spiral was tight so that no air could be released. Only the Lord and Lady's magic could make a sound from such an instrument.

I took the shell away from their empty, uncaring stares. I sat in a corner, trying to figure a way to create any sound. I scratched the ground and, as this was the land of the dead, I found the dirt teeming with worms of all kinds. With some deeper digging, I acquired a handful of maggots and placed them onto the shell's end. In a few minutes, they had penetrated the outer carapace and had hollowed out a portion of the shell. Still, no noise could be made because no outlet for the air existed.

I searched Mictlan further. Soon, I came upon a tree whose branches were dead but whose trunk seemed alive. As I got closer, I saw the life was a giant beehive, swarming with workers among the empty trunk. As I got closer, their buzzing lifted, so loud that normal talking would be drowned out. Any attempt to get close was met with a swarming attack. While I knew they wouldn't kill me, I still didn't want the stinging pain.

Using the dead branches on the ground, I quickly built a fire. The smoke lifted to the hive and the bees calmed. In that quiet time, I approached the hive. With care, I took some of the bees and pushed them into the shell until the small chamber was full. I hurried back to court.

"My lord, I will accomplish your task." I blew into the chamber of shell and the bees awoke. Packed in tight and away from their queen, they droned so loudly that it filled the chamber. Mictlanteuctli, betraying no emotion, pointed me toward the cemetery. I left the conch at his feet and went down the tunnel.

The burial site was a giant mound, but it was easy to see the bones within the dirt as there were as many of them as ground cover. I picked through them, taking care to separate the male and female parts, and put them in my bag. When the bag was mostly full, I returned to the court.

The Lord and Lady waited for me. She said, "Quetzalcoatl, those bones are sacred and they belong in Mictlan. I hope you didn't try to take any."

"Of course not, my lady. I am always respectful."

I heard what sounded like a contemptuous laugh and Lord Mictlanteuctli disappeared. He had transported himself to the burial site and cried out, "Stop him! He has what is ours!"

I flew off at the alarm, passing through many tunnels on my way to Earth. Up ahead, I saw the ground crumble into a pit meant to trap me, but I laughed. I would fly right over that. But as I was hovering over the pit, the cave's roof collapsed and held me. I managed to stick my head out and, before the Lord or Lady got there, a new goddess arrived, Chihuacoatl who ruled over the snakes.

"Brother," she said, "What has happened?"

I pulled free the bag of bones and spilled them in front of her, the male and female mixing together.

"Gather some maize, great goddess." She found some quickly as it grew everywhere. As the falling rocks had injured me, I spat blood upon those bones and told her to mix them together. As she combined the raw materials, I worked my way out of the pit. Using my arts, I formed the bones and corn meal into humans, injecting them with life from the power of my blood.

When the Lord and Lady arrived, they saw no bones but instead found these newly formed creatures.

"We owe you an apology, Quetzalcoatl. You did not have our bones. But where did you find these?"

"Lost among the underworld, good lady. They need to live on the Earth."

And with that, I led them to the world above to grow and multiply.

Aida listened closely to the god. As he finished his tale, she said, "And that is all? Blood and corn?"

"And the gift of my power."

"Can you grant me that gift?"

"Humans already exist. Anything you make would be...something different."

"I ask again, great god, grant me your power."

The smoky figure paused. "No, you must use your own. But I suggest you don't." As the smoke turned to wisps, they heard, "You may call on me again, but only if you use your powers wisely."

The smoke returned to its vertical power and the rustling air stilled. Quetzalcoatl was gone.

Aida felt devastated. The Mother had never denied her. The Volcano had only served her. Why was she now shunned by this god? But then she thought about the second part of what he had said. "I have the power."

Spex looked at her. "Yeah, but so what? He ain't giving you his."

"No, he said I have it. Right now.

Mina nodded. "He did say that."

Aida leaped to her feet, the idea striking like lightning. "We should go. Right now. I see how to do it."

Mina and Ibrahim shared her enthusiasm, but Spex was slow to get up.

"You heard him, right? He said don't do it."

"He suggested we don't do it."

"But that was a god. Saying no. Can't you see that?" Spex held her arms out as if saying *what don't y'all understand about no?*

Ibrahim stepped forward. "If he didn't want us to have it, he wouldn't have given us the tool. We must try and see if it works."

Spex nodded, still unsure but willing to see where this went. "Where are we going?"

They all thought about it, but Mina came up with the solution. "Cherry Hill in Long Beach. I go there all the time. It's old and it's barely used. Nobody will mess with us."

With a destination in mind, they went to the car to complete their new task.

Sophia was glad the beer came in a tall can because the bartender couldn't see how little she drank. None, in fact, even though she pretended to take pulls from it.

The smell of the brew brought her back. The musky aroma filled the street of the modern French Quarter, not unlike what she'd just experienced on frat row, but Storyville floated into her mind now. Even when she was so young, 16 years old, the beer was the easiest and cheapest way to leave reality behind. Whiskey and absinthe also flowed, but they got her so drunk. Just a lightweight country girl who never even had a sip of the stuff growing up, the easy fizz of beer sat better with her than those sticky liquors.

She and some of the other Josie Arlington girls would step out at three in the afternoon, right before the male population began to get horny. Back then, they didn't have bottles but served out pails which you had to bring back. Two pails could cover five of them and they'd drink and make fun of the men who haunted their transoms until the early dawn.

She was never upset she'd left that behind as it was more grief than gain, but those memories were the good ones. She was glad to think back to them. Not innocent, but certainly not cynical. And even as exploited labor, still she had been somewhat taken care of.

She felt a tap on her shoulder. An older man in a pink *guayabera* extended his hand. "Dance, *mi amor*?"

He had a pudgy build and thick, black-framed glasses. Probably 80, he didn't have the usual lusty look of those who usually approached her. She glanced over her shoulder to see a few younger men, mostly in their 40s and 50s, watched, laughing at their elder. Sophia wasn't sure what to do.

"I'm on the lookout. I need to keep my eye on the street."

The old man turned around. "Miguel, keep lookout." His accent was thick but easily understandable. "Who are you waiting for?"

She described the four and one of the guys took her place at her table.

"You owe me a *cerveza*, Gonzalo," the younger one said.

"No problem, no problem. Just let me dance first."

The bartender changed the music from the up-tempo oom-pah music to a slow, horn-filled ballad. Sophia recognized it as a mambo.

"This your music?"

"*Si, si*. He keeps it on the jukebox for me."

"Are you Cuban?"

Gonzalo looked shocked. "I am. How did you know?"

"I know this music. I'm from New Orleans." She always wanted to say "sort of" after saying the city because she wasn't born there, but that was just a quirk of that city and state.

"Alright, then let's go then."

He wasn't spry, his legs stiff from passed years, but he knew where his feet should land. Sophia looked at his footwork and was surprised to see spectator shoes, the black and white leather kind Chip used to wear. She fell right in with him, twirling when he pulled her and shuffling when he let her out.

The smile on his face was infectious and Sophia felt the joy. All of those problems next door could wait for a second.

"Why me, Gonzalo?"

"You want the truth?"

"Always."

"These youngsters needed a little lesson. I make fun of them, saying the Mexicans are like mules. Work, work, work. They need to be more *Cubano*, learn to love life. Learn to love women. They said I couldn't get you to dance but look! It's not so hard if you have the right attitude."

"This might not have worked with someone else. I'm different."

"You don't look so different. Just a young woman out for a drink."

"I'm older than I look, Gonzalo."

"Bah! I'm an old man. I'll be 78 this year." He tilted his head to the men at the bar. "They were all born in America, so they have some of the American to them. But I saw hard times back in Santiago. I know I'm lucky to be here. They think they deserve it."

"I remember the war."

"Castro? He can go to hell as far as I'm concerned."

"No, the one where Spain got kicked out."

"Oh, come on. That was before World War I."

"Look into my eyes, *mon ami*." She turned on that mesmerizing gaze and let him sink into her. She had to use her supernatural strength to keep him aloft during this slow dance. "I said I was older than I look."

She released him from her control. He looked scared.

"Don't worry," she said. "I'm like you. I know a dance is just a dance."

"Hey, lady?" Miguel was calling from the window. "I think those people you're watching are leaving."

She ran to the window and saw them getting into a car.

"Shit." She paused before running out. Gonzalo smiled at her.

"I'll never forget you, that's for sure," he said. He held up her hand and kissed its back. "*Fria*?"

He finally felt how cold her hand was. "*Si*. You know what that means?"

"*Si.*"

"Then *vaya con dios*, Gonzalo." She turned to the men at the bar. "Y'all could learn something from him."

She dashed outside to see the car pulling off. Wanting to conserve her strength, she transformed into a bat, but she flew to the back window and held on with her tiny claws. Hopefully, the people inside wouldn't see her as she hitched a ride.

The cemetery wasn't far away from Compton. Following the main road Willow, it was past the 710 freeway and set into a hill at the corner of Orange Ave. The incline wasn't huge as they turned onto that street but looking down into the park from the visitor's lot, a small asphalt one cut into the road, Aida saw plenty of places to do their work without being caught.

They followed the stairs down, concrete steps flanked by a thin metal rail. To the north at the end of the park, Aida could see oil pumps working, bobbing like those toy birds dipping into a glass of water. They'd been such a big part of developing Los Angeles, but now they were just background noise and local flair in the bustling city. Somebody made a little something from the produced oil, but nobody was getting rich anymore.

Nobody had laid a path between the tombstones, so the markers were set into a grassy field. As they wandered, trying to decide which grave to use, Spex said, "I'm glad I remembered the shovel."

Aida agreed. "This could get real messy if we don't find a relatively fresh grave."

Spex laughed. "Totally normal conversation, yo."

Mina spotted a fresh patch of dirt far enough away from the two main roads. With no lighting within the graveyard, Aida hoped they wouldn't be spotted.

The three women took turns shoveling. Ibrahim said he'd wrenched his back in the garden and couldn't help. Aida wasn't sure if this was an excuse, but she let it go. From the Quetzalcoatl spell formulated in her mind, they didn't need to dig the whole thing up, just create a pathway for the components. They dug a round hole about a foot in diameter and soon struck wood. Here Ibrahim offered his strength.

He spiked down three times, the third one producing a satisfying crack. He'd breached the coffin, so Aida and the other two began setting up the spell.

They used the same components as the summoning: incense, masa, and tequila.

"Hate to waste good booze," Ibrahim said. "But that's what the spell takes."

They used the masa to ring the gravesite, creating a power circle. Once the circle was formed, Mina lit the incense and dropped one of the sticks into the hole. She set four others on the primary directions within the circle. Spex took the bowl with the remaining masa and poured the tequila into it, then stirred to create a paste. She turned to Aida. "Now comes the hard part."

"I know." Aida knew she had the god's spirit within her temporarily, so she would have to be the one to sacrifice. Pulling out her ceremonial knife, she placed it in her palm and squeezed the blade.

"How much blood do you need?" Mina was enthralled by the process.

"Not too much, I don't think." With a quick motion, she pulled the blade from her grip. She let out a scream as she sliced open her palm. They all looked around, but it drew no attention.

The blood flowed quickly into the bowl. Aida thought she might have cut too deep. The wound weeped bright red as she looked into her hand. Ibrahim splashed it with the tequila and she groaned loudly again.

"Gotta clean it," he said. He then wrapped it up with the gauze they'd brought.

Aida looked at Spex. "Pour it in the hole quickly. We don't want to break the spell."

Spex did as she was told. She got as much of the bloody paste out of the bowl as she could although some residue remained. Aida dropped to the ground, feeling stunned by the pain. The other three waited for something to happen.

After ten minutes, Aida saw the disappointment on their faces. Nothing came from the grave, no noise and no zombie. She didn't understand why they'd failed, but it was plain they had.

Ibrahim helped Aida to her feet. "We need to get you home. You don't look good."

Mina looked the angriest. "Now what are we gonna do? Just turn over and let the vamps be?"

Aida saw that Spex almost looked relieved. "I think we go back to the study," Spex said. "Let's look at other empowerment magic. Then maybe we can use that to get our revenge."

But Ibrahim remained adamant. "You'll need something stronger than that. You need the dark path to fight the undead. I can't believe this didn't work."

Just as they got a few yards from the grave, Aida stopped. She felt something stir, energy coalescing that hadn't been there before. She hurried back to the hole. "I think it worked."

She kneeled down and heard a noise. Groaning and scratching came from below the ground. Their hole began to crumble as the earth moved around it. Aida had to scoot forward or risk falling in. As she set herself, a cadaverous hand burst through the dirt right by her face. She screamed from surprise and got to her feet.

Slowly, the creature exhumed itself.

Chapter Sixteen

Sophia had no idea where they were, but she guessed Long Beach. Maybe she had become an Angelino after all because she identified the 710 as they went under it.

It took a bit of strength to hold on during the drive, so when they finally parked the car, she dropped out of sight and rested while they determined where they were going. When she finally saw where they were, she shuddered. What could they possibly do in a graveyard? Did they have the kind of magic to raise the dead? She really hoped not.

She stayed in bat form and flew into the trees around the graveyard. When they settled on a freshly dug site, she guessed that they were trying some form of death magic. She remembered the legends of zombie powder, how the old Voudons had held control over their subjects, but she'd seen nothing like that. *Still*, she thought, *if they are pitting the dead against us undead, we're in for a helluva fight.*

Sophia stayed still as the women and man went through a ceremony. When the one she knew to be Aida sliced open her hand, her protector instincts kicked in. She wanted to run forward and make sure she was alright. And then for a split second, her predator rose to the top. The ride had weakened her. A little taste of witch blood would fix her right up.

But she shook it off. Spending as little time as she could with humans had made her forget the blood lust. *Like any addict*, she thought, *I could fall right off the wagon.* But she steadied herself and went back to her spying.

She felt relieved. Whatever they had tried didn't work. They looked to be collecting themselves and walking off. She would return to their apartment later after spending a good night resting. Sophia's mission, at least for tonight, was done.

But then Aida turned back to the grave. She tripped and fell and jumped back. Sophia could see what had scared her—a bony arm had shot up through the dirt.

The remains which pushed itself out of the grave still retained some humanity. It had been a woman, African American from her facial construction, but her skin had paled to a sickly greenish brown. Long, curly hair still clung to her scalp and her nails had grown into a claw-like sharpness, now smudged and filthy from scratching her way out of the ground. But as she made her way top-side, the real sickening details emerged.

Ragged clothing hung from the skeleton, but the body had re-duced greatly from the burial, her former dress now looking muu-muu sized. All that was left of this former person was skin and bones, the rest already gone or possibly removed in the embalming process. Her lips had receded, bucking out her teeth. But scariest of all, her eyeballs were gone and she stared at her saviors with empty sockets.

Sophia felt her body lock up, paralyzed by the sight of monstrosi-ty. The creature's hideous shamble, moving forward and side to side at the same time like a puppet with a broken string, was slow. Even this far away, she could feel the hunger consuming the creature.

Trying to get her senses back, she looked at the four of them and how they were dealing. The black woman seemed the most freaked out and skittered away from the other three who were reaching out to it. Sophia saw something that made her very frightened—the black woman had scraped her shoes through the circle. Whatever controlling power they might have held over the zombie was now broken.

Fear bolted through Sophia like lightning. They were playing with forces they didn't understand and may die because of it. She couldn't watch what happened next. She took to the air, flying to-ward downtown Long Beach.

As the zombie rose from the grave, Aida felt scared for the first time in a long time. Whatever this was was truly horrific. She looked to her companions. Spex and Mina looked frightened also, but Ibrahim? He looked ecstatic.

"Yes!" He looked like his football team had just scored a touch-down. "Arise and fight for us!"

But the creature didn't look controlled. The opposite, in fact. It leaned toward Ibrahim with arms outstretched, looking like it wanted to rend his limbs. Aida used her insight to look into its aura and was immediately repulsed. This being, whatever it was, had only hunger and nothing else. The spell had given it its pseudo-life, but it sure as hell didn't tell Aida how to wrangle it.

"Ibrahim, look out!" Aida saw that he had turned his back to the zombie, wanting Spex to come closer even though she was frightened out of her mind. He whipped around and narrowly avoided a swiping claw. Now he was as scared as the women.

"Control it," he shouted to Aida.

"I can't!"

"Use the god's power." He turned to Mina and Spex. "Get outside the circle. That will at least contain it."

The three of them scooted away from the zombie. Aida also jumped outside the circle then retreated within herself to find the god's spark to control such a creature. In her meditation, she found the glowing green magic within her soul, the surrounding rainbow aura looking like the serpent's wings.

"I have created life. How do I control it?"

The serpent's voice laughed. "You haven't created life. You've created a mockery. Do you think I'd give you that kind of power?"

"But how do I make it do as I command?"

"You don't." The glow began to shrink. "I created the humans. I didn't control them. You've misused my power. Take this as a lesson if you survive."

And with that, the glow snuffed out and Aida returned to the waking world.

She could tell one thing—the zombie was slow. Its bones didn't connect correctly, so it shambled toward the three of them who waited just outside the circle.

"What do we do?" Spex leaned forward to look closer at the monster. But Aida saw in their hurry to get out of the circle that it had been broken. Spex stood above the space not knowing she was in real trouble.

Aida screamed but it was too late. The zombie swiped across Spex's left cheek, leaving two deep slashes in her face.

Spex fell back screaming and grasping at her face. Those wounds were deep.

Mina acted quickly, grabbing the shovel and swinging at the body. The zombie did its best to avoid the swings. Still, Mina connected with the rib cage, cracking a few exposed bones.

Ibrahim took his cane and swung it like a baseball bat. He smashed at the right shoulder bones but couldn't get it to break. The zombie backhanded the cane, sending it flying from Ibrahim's grip.

Ibrahim went to recover the cane and Mina kept smashing at its body, but the zombie had drawn blood from Spex. It closed on her as she curled on the ground crying in pain. Spex didn't even know it was coming until it was only a few feet away. Spex kicked out, connecting with the left knee and hyperextending it. The monster now leaned forward, its teeth nearing Spex's face.

Aida was frozen. She'd used the bulk of her power in the resurrection and even then, what could wind do against it? It had no breath.

She called out to Mina. "Use the fire! Use it now!"

"But I can't." Mina had been working hard on accessing the magic within flames, but something had been holding her back. Even her spiritual journey, under the supervision of Aida, hadn't torn down the wall.

"If there's ever a time to break through, Mina, that time is now."

"Help me!"

She ran over to Mina and took one of her hands. They both closed their eyes as Aida entered Mina's soul, Mina now glowing in real life as Aida's body crumpled to the ground. Mina held fast to Aida's hand so she wouldn't break the connection.

Mina's aura dominated Aida's vision, the vague indigo edges leading to inky blackness. Aida now knew why Mina did little meditation as it was very easy to get lost in this darkness. She opened her mind to communicate with her friend.

"Think, Mina. Where did you see the fire?"

"I... I can't remember."

Aida saw some flickers, little pops of light like lightening bugs on a summer's night.

"Push! I'm starting to see it."

"It was on top of a mountain..."

As Mina recalled her spiritual quest, the spots of glowing orange grew from tiny specks to candle-like flames.

"Push, Mina! It's almost there."

"Yes! I remember!"

Now the various flickers coalesced into one big ball. Aida entered it and used what power she had left to expand it to fill the soul space.

They both popped their eyes open. Mina looked different now. No fear, no confusion populated her. She was clear and ready. Aida, back in her body, stood up.

Grabbing the shovel by the spade, she ran her hand along the wooden handle, leaving gouts of flame where she rubbed. Soon, the whole thing glowed, a torch in the night.

As the zombie leaned over Spex, going in for the kill, Mina shoved the burning handle through the rib cage then thrust the creature away from Spex.

The zombie tripped over its feet but then stood to face down its opponents. The fire caught the clothing then ignited the flesh.

Aida looked at Mina. She waved her hands, conducting the fire to do its job. With a final flourish, Mina turned the fire into a ball that engulfed the monster. The fire took a minute to burn itself out, leaving only a pile of ash where there had been bone.

Aida saw Mina looked proud in that moment. But then they heard Spex's cries and immediately ran to their friend.

"Get me to a fucking hospital! Now!"

Sophia didn't know why she didn't help them, but the horror of watching that thing rise from the grave and go on the attack had panicked her. Fight or flight had kicked in and her lizard brain chose the latter.

She remembered saying way back about never having seen a zombie. The real thing was far more frightening. And that dead creature she saw certainly couldn't be helped by attending a few of her meetings.

If she had been hesitant before, her fears had been removed and replaced by the shambling mess she'd just seen. If they had survived, which she thought they might somehow, they were way more powerful than she suspected. She would now do anything she could to stop these people from releasing those monsters. She could feel sunrise was coming soon, so she had to get inside.

As she landed in downtown Long Beach, she laughed at herself. She couldn't remember where the hell the bar was. And for that matter, she also couldn't remember the name of the human bar below. She quickly took to Google with "pirate bar Long Beach" and found she was only six blocks off. She walked quickly, not daring to use her vampire powers right now even though the streets were empty. Soon, she was pulling open the doors to the Deadman's Chest.

Maisie and Horton were in the lower bar in one of the leather booths. Maisie was sitting on Horton's lap, leaning in and kissing him deeply. Sophia could smell the blood lust coming off them, but she was glad they were channeling that into sex and not killing.

When the front door closed behind her, both of the young vamps heads swiveled toward her. Sophia laughed at how guilty they looked as if she had any say over how they spent their time.

"Sophia!" Maisie's voice wasn't a question. "What are you doing here?"

"I've been following those witches. We're gonna have to send out a general alarm. But I was too far to get back to Silver Lake. I knew Jeremiah was here and y'all had built emergency cubbies. May get a little snug tonight, but it's not like we're sleeping."

As she went to go upstairs, Maisie was scrambling off Horton's lap. "Sophia, wait."

"It's getting late and..." As soon as she opened the door, Sophia saw why Maisie had been so nervous. She found Jeremiah and Tamar locked in a loving embrace, each of them stripped down to their underwear as they stood over an open casket. Her jaw dropped. Her spirit was cracking within her, so she retreated to an old friend: sarcasm.

Sophia said, "I know my timing is bad, but I'm glad I didn't get here five minutes later."

The two broke their embrace, separating and standing at attention like teenagers caught by parents. Sophia's mind was swirling so much, she didn't feel sadness or betrayal. She stuffed down those two emotions as Maisie and Horton joined the impromptu party upstairs.

Jeremiah took a step forward. "Sophia..."

"Don't. Not now." She held out her hand, not wanting to be touched by him at all.

Maisie put a hand on her shoulder. "Are you okay?"

"Of course not." She looked Maisie in the eye. "But what's going on here will be a problem for the future. We have a problem for right fucking now."

"Is it those witches?" Tamar crossed her arms over her bra, trying to provide herself with some cover.

"They've chosen a very dark path. They found someone who practices necromancy."

Horton looked like he'd swallowed his tongue. "You mean like zombies and shit?"

"Yeah. I saw them doing it at some graveyard up the hill. Thing was, they couldn't control it. Not yet. So that means we have a few weeks. But when they do figure out the magic..."

"It could be the dadblamed apocalypse." Jeremiah put his hand to his face. "*Dawn of the Dead* shit."

Sophia sat in a chair. "Hopefully, it won't get that big. But they would have the resources to raise an army at will many times over."

"Fuck. This is all my fault." Tamar had always been tough around Sophia, rarely letting the cracks show. But this was all too much. Even at her age—somewhere around 50—she still had a lot of little girl in her. Sophia watched as Tamar climbed into the casket and curled up. Jeremiah took a quick step toward Tamar, but Sophia waved him off.

"Let me." Sophia pulled the chair over and rubbed Tamar's back. "You made some mistakes, boo. But no one could have predicted this. This girl is a thousand-year storm wrapped in a tiny little body. Best we can do is ride it out."

Tamar rolled over and looked straight into Sophia's eyes. "Why don't you want to kill me?"

"Over that asshole?" Sophia cocked her face back at Jeremiah.

"Hey!"

"Quiet, boy. I'm talking right now." Sophia said it all through a smile even though the hurt was settling in. She looked Tamar in the face. "I kicked your ass once. I could do it again."

"Like to see you try." Tamar laughed through a tearless crying face.

"If we don't die in the next few months, we'll hash this out. Now go to sleep." She stood and started to close the cover.

"Wait, Jeremiah goes in here, too."

"He'll be here. I need about five minutes with homeboy. Okay?"

"Yeah. Just don't rip his dick off."

"No promises." Sophia closed the casket. Maisie and Horton took their cue and entered their own private space. Jeremiah had slipped his pants on but stood there shirtless in the dim lights. Sophia stood.

"When were you gonna tell me?"

"This just started. But we been dancing around it the last two nights. Since the *cucuy* thing. We were both pissed and that turned into something else."

"I been seeing this coming. Or at least I was warned it was coming." Sophia couldn't look him in the eye. "Was this ever a good idea?"

"You saved my life. That was a good idea. But you did it the only way you knew how. Turning me created a problem we couldn't solve." He reached out and gently took her chin. She allowed it despite wanting to break his hand off at the wrist. "I wasn't saved. I was resurrected. Into a new life with a new way of thinking. I get cloudy when I think back to those years of shape changing and whatnot. But all my memories of you are clear."

"First time I saw you, I said no. Then I said yes. Now you're saying no." Sophia threw up her hands. "Being with someone for 80 years makes this drama seem very weird. I let myself love you. Not like Chip. Not like David. But it was real."

"I know I'm fucking this up. You and me was the best ever. Vampires are forever, but I'm not sure love is. Can it be?" Jeremiah was searching, but she wasn't letting him off the hook just yet.

"Yes, it can be. It could have been decades of what we had." His head hung and now it was her turn to lift a chin. "But I'll let you go peacefully."

"You will?"

"What did you think I was gonna do?"

"Go full Cajun or something. Like when you get really mad."

She smiled and dropped her voice into her old accent. "I ain't not never gonna forget this, no." Then she returned to her flat, accentless tone. "But I think I might be able to forgive. With time."

"Okay." He looked relieved.

"We're gonna do this clean, now. You are officially kicked out of the center."

"For good? What about the meetings?"

"No, dickhead. You can come to meetings." She paused. "After two months, okay?"

"Okay. I'll get my clothes and stuff out tomorrow. I'm gonna move in here if you need to talk to me."

"I will. We got one helluva fight coming, you and me." She pushed him gently. "Now get outta my face, boy."

As Jeremiah climbed into his shared coffin, Sophia knocked on Maisie and Horton's.

"Yeah, Sophia?"

"Maisie, you're gonna have to show me how to use that dating app. 'Cause if he's getting laid, I'm sure as shit getting some, too."

Chapter Seventeen

Ibrahim, in his undershirt, sat in the front seat of Mina's car. He had taken his dashiki shirt and gave that to Spex to hold to her face. The shirt got soaked quickly and drops fell into the feet well in the backseat.

They didn't know of any hospital in Long Beach, so they sped to County USC. Aida thought it was a good idea because it was also a charity hospital where anyone could get help.

Since the time was nearing 5am, they could move quickly along the 710 with the hospital near where the 10 and 710 came together. Spex still groaned at the pain, but she had started to dull to it. That might mean she was heading into shock, so Aida tried to keep talking in order to stay alert.

"What happened with the circle?" Spex slurred her words.

"Somebody dragged their foot when stepping out of it." Aida looked at Spex. "Any of us could have done it, but damn, there was a zombie after you."

Spex looked at Mina. "And what happened there at the end? The fire?"

Mina had a wicked smile. "I know this experiment was a failure, but I finally leveled up with the magic. Aida unlocked what was holding me back."

Ibrahim nodded. "We had a misstep. But now everyone in this car has seen their powers increase. We know what it feels like and how to refocus ourselves so we can make the necromancy work. With a bit more study and maybe some new sources, we can control those things and put them to our use."

While everyone else was nodding, Spex had to keep herself from screaming. "Are you fucking kidding me? I just had my face ripped off by that thing."

Aida did look somewhat repentant although Spex could still see her obsession floating on top. "Yes, we made a huge mistake. But it isn't the one you're thinking. We moved too fast."

Mina pointed at Aida. "She's right. We all want this thing now. But we need to slow down and..."

"Maybe we need to walk away." Mina and Aida gasped at Spex's declaration. "Maybe we need to rethink this whole damn thing." She leaned toward Aida. "How much pain is this vendetta going to cause? I've always said that Mexican vampire should pay for what she and her brother did. But we are way out of our league. Does one of us have to die for this? Huh?"

Aida became very calm. "I've already died. And I wouldn't ask it of you if I didn't think the cause was right."

"So you're saying I could die?"

"Yes. So could I. So could any of us." Spex wouldn't describe Aida's face as cold, more like she had detached from her humanity. She saw the same look in Mina.

"Look at what I've already sacrificed. These will scar up and I'll wear them for life."

"All of our scars are part of our story." Ibrahim commanded her attention. "I have many from my fights through the years. Aida will have one on her palm after tonight. Mina bears her own internal wounds.

"Regardless," he said, "we have set ourselves along a path, a very noble one. We start with the evil in front of us and then move on to the other scourges of life. Those who would take our homes. Those who would hinder our lives. Those who put themselves above others. Once we gain momentum through our magic, all this will be in our hands."

And Spex finally saw it, what her mother had been saying all these years. Ibrahim hid it well, but beneath his hippie-hotep veneer was a mad soul. It hadn't just been Israel's influence. Ibrahim had ridden side by side up Crazy Mountain. She knew she needed the hospital, but she also needed help. She needed to get away from this trio for a little bit and see if this was the way she thought. Because if she meditated on it and found herself agreeing with this plan, she also thought she might have to check herself into a loony bin.

As they reached the hospital and drove into the emergency room's horseshoe-shaped drive, Spex sat up.

"Listen. I don't want any of y'all to get into trouble or have to give your name or anything. I'll just say some crackhead did this to me."

Aida looked like she wanted to protest, but Ibrahim butted in. "She's right. Just call us when you're healed up."

"It's okay. I'll catch a ride share or something."

Aida said, "Still, call when you get out. So I know you're all right."

"You got it, *chica*."

The nurses took her pretty quickly as the wound was deep. They took her into the emergency room and sewed up her face while she went under sedation. When she woke up, the nurse brought the doctor in.

The doctor, a young Indian man with thick glasses, looked very concerned. "You said somebody cut you with a knife?"

"Yeah. Some crackhead downtown."

"There was some bacteria in there. Very dangerous. If you had waited two, three more hours, I'm not sure we could have saved your jaw."

"You serious?"

"Very much so. I want you to stay—"

"Sorry, doc. I'm outta here."

"No, we need to—"

"You don't need nothing. I have to see someone right away."

The doctor tried to talk her down as she got dressed, but Spex didn't want to talk to him lest the truth find its way into her mouth. He finally relented and she walked into the morning sunshine. As she got into the back of the Uber she ordered, she texted Aida who wanted to know if she was coming straight home.

"I'm starving," Spex wrote. "There's a place over here I've heard has good tacos."

But the car wasn't taking her to any food joint. She pointed him to Eagle Rock because she had to talk to Aunt Rosalinda pronto.

Aida's aunt wasn't in her shop when Spex arrived, so she drifted up the road where she found a coffee shop which served breakfast. She could feel all eyes following her, but she understood. The bandages on her face were wrapped and tightened so that she looked like a half-mummy. She was just glad the stitches weren't visible because they might not have served her.

Deciding that chewing would be bad for her, she ordered a green smoothie and slurped it through a straw to minimize any jaw work. The painkillers were wearing off and she wasn't sure she could afford to fill her prescription. They gave her five pills at the hospital, but she was sure they wouldn't last past the pain. This would take weeks if not months to heal.

She thought about the zombie last night, especially how eager Ibrahim had been to continue working on necromancy. She just wasn't sure if this coven was her gig anymore, but she'd gone so far with it. She needed time away because she knew she'd be right back in the thick of it once she got back to the apartment.

She hung out until 10am, new stares coming from every customer who walked in. Finally, she went back to Rosalinda's and found the open sign hanging on the front door.

"Oh, my dear, what happened to you?" Rosalinda swarmed Spex as she entered. The old woman put her hand to the tip of Spex's chin, turning her until Spex felt sharp stabs. "Sorry, but this is bad. I guess you won't want any tea."

"Not today, thanks."

"I assume your injury is why you're here, so... go on."

They sat at the reading table and Spex recounted the full story, including bringing in Ibrahim. When she stopped, Rosalinda looked shocked. But she took a second to compose herself before speaking to Spex.

"Your uncle calls himself a what?"

"A *bokor*. It's tied to voodoo."

"Not my specialty. I've had some friends into *Candomble* and other island religions, but never full-on Voudon. Maybe Sophia—"

"You mean the vampire?"

"Yes. She's from New Orleans."

"That's where Ibrahim was."

"Well, I have some research to do, that's for sure. As for you..." She took out her cards and shuffled. "We need you to focus. On Aida, on the whole situation. Because I think you are in way over your head regardless how powerful your coven has become."

"I'm starting to doubt things, too."

"Pick your cards."

Spex drew out three and laid them out. Rosalinda turned over the first one: *el corazón.* The heart.

"This one's obvious," Spex said.

"I agree. But what do you see?"

"This is me and my love for Aida."

"Exactly. But every love requires a choice. To love or not. Who to love. How much love you can give. So think of this card as you and the decisions you must make soon."

Spex stopped her. "Don't these cards have little sayings?"

"Yeah. This one is 'do not miss me, sweetheart, I'll be back by bus.'"

"What does that mean?"

Rosalinda shrugged. "It's not science. Your guess is as good as mine."

Spex didn't feel like guessing, so she turned the next card.

"The bell. 'You with the bell and I with your sister.' Another obscure one, I'm afraid."

"I don't know. Ibrahim has moved into the group pretty quickly. He's on the verge of taking my place."

"Yes, yes. Because you are sounding the alarm. Have you spoken of your feelings with Aida?"

"I yelled at them. Aida doesn't like being challenged."

"She's changed so much. As a little girl, she was so respectful." Then Rosalinda laughed. "But so was I and that got me nowhere."

"If I keep challenging her, she's gonna kick me out. Or I might make the choice to leave."

"Again, your heart is telling you to make your choice. It won't be easy."

"If I keep getting beat up, that may make the choice hella easy."

Spex could see Rosalinda wanted to care for her, to tell her what to do and when. But the way she worked was indirect and interpretive. She needed to lay out the facts and let the customer decide. Spex knew it would be her own choice, but this wasn't providing the clarity she desired. Maybe the last card would be more definitive.

Rosalinda turned the last card: *la calavera*. The skull. Rosalinda said the words slowly, like she didn't want to put them into the air. "As I passed by the cemetery, I found myself a skull."

Spex closed her dropped jaw and retreated to her sarcasm. "A little on the nose, huh, universe?"

"I know you need to laugh this off, but here's the serious part. Every choice you make will lead to death. Your own. Aida's. The coven. All those vampires—"

"Who are dead already."

"Yes, but they still walk among us. You know as well as I do that my niece is fomenting war. This has been coming since you first met her. No action you take will prevent it, but you can do one thing. Keep yourself out of it."

Spex looked at the card, a skull and crossbones like the pirate flag. "I think I could've figured all this out on my own, but this seals it. I have a lot of choices to make and it won't be easy." She stood to go but lingered in the doorway. "Can you get in touch with that Sophia if I need her?"

Rosalinda nodded. "I'll be waiting for your call."

Spex left the shop and walked toward the train station. She'd head back downtown, back to the apartment. She hoped along the walk that clarity would come, but she had too many doubts. Something would give and she hoped it wouldn't be her head separating from her neck.

After Spex left, Rosalinda decided to retreat to her study. She turned the sign from open to closed, checked the book to see how much time she had before next appointment—two hours—and then, as always, put the kettle on. But instead of filing through the pre-filled bags, she pulled out a tea ball and went to her special stash of *calea zachatechi*, better known as the dream herb.

While she wasn't tired—she's only been up for a few hours—the herb would help her do what she hadn't done in almost decade: commune with The Mother.

She pondered this move as the kettle began its boil. She had no particular reason for stopping her walks in the lands beyond human existence. She prayed to The Mother every night, still using the necklace her *abuela* gave her when she left Los Angeles for San Francisco. And when she was practicing heavily in the Bay Area, she would dreamwalk with others in their search for enlightenment. Maybe it was age and her current contentment. Maybe it was too difficult because her times out of body often left her in great pain. Or maybe she just knew The Mother gave her favor through the cards and, after a dedicated life, that was enough.

But she also knew she had to return and speak directly with her honored goddess. Her niece had been dabbling in the darkest of magic, putting her soul in dire situations, and The Mother could give Rosalinda direction in how to handle her untamed beast child.

The brew was so bitter—it had been so long that Rosalinda had forgotten how unpalatable the herb was—so she gave it a long squeeze from the honey bear and another of Meyer lemon she'd just gotten from the store. It was still lip smacking, right up there with gentian root, but she drank it down. Pulling a few leaves from her peppermint plant, which when dreaming was known to add a prophetic effect, she chewed, cleansing her palate, and settled into her leather chair.

Without knowing how, she woke up to find herself in front of Tonantzin's pyramid. Without hesitation, she walked inside to where the statue stood, its multiple millennia watch still unending. Rosalinda bowed before her.

"Much time has passed, daughter."

"Mother, I speak to you every day, but you don't reply."

"And so it goes. You are one of the shiniest stars whose love keeps me alive. I only wish humans could be stronger for these short trips to see me."

"Mother, I come seeking guidance about one of your other followers."

The statue stayed still, but Rosalinda could feel the spirit before her nodding. "I knew she was close to you when she first appeared. But she had to choose her own path. And, as of this moment, she is not choosing wisely."

"She is under the influence of another magician. Not mine."

"Not just this human who would destroy all before him. She has forsaken my magic for that of Quetzalcoatl."

Spex had shared that with Rosalinda, but she had understood it more as an evocation, a short term fix. But here was The Mother feeling rebuked. This was not good.

"The god of wind and rain like his tricks, Mother. It seems when granting Aida some of his power, he did not grant her control."

"I could sense that. Besides, the young fool wasn't using the magic for its intended purposes. She wants death as a force for destruction. But Santa Muerte is part of our natural cycle. She doesn't like this abominable magic either."

"What of the deathless ones which she wishes to destroy?"

"They are abominations also. Fiends with infernal power. But they should be fought using light and truth. Aida is wandering off the path she took when we first met."

This was what Rosalinda feared most, but she knew she had to hear it from The Mother in her voice. Rosalinda had to hear the unvarnished truth.

"Mother, will you punish the child?"

"If she leaves the path, she is not my follower anymore. All that has been granted will be taken away."

"What can I do?"

"Lead her back to me. This is not irreversible, but consequence follows action like morning coming through night. It's a lesson not easily learned, but one that must be."

Thanking Tonantzin, Rosalinda stood and walked out of the pyramid. As she stepped into the white-glowing door, she awoke in her chair. She felt sore, her consciousness feeling like an ill-fitting bra. But she had to process this vision.

Aida would lose her power if she continued with the necromancy. But that would drive her further toward the *bokor*, especially if he could fill that void with his own magic. In order to save Aida's soul, Rosalinda must intervene. But when? And how? Would her niece even listen to her advice? Since Rosalinda also advised the vampires, probably not.

But she had to act. She had to be there at the correct time to steer Aida away from destruction. She would need to speak to Sophia, to know what the vampires were thinking. She needed to be agile at a time when her brain and body were slow but precise. For the first time in her life, she wasn't sure she could pull off the necessary magic and nothing scared her more than that.

Chapter Eighteen

During the day, vampires were dead, so they always looked forward to the night when they could feel that spark of life energy. But this was the one time when a vampire might have wanted to stay dead. At least for a little longer. Tamar's eyes opened and she felt the embrace of Jeremiah. This felt safe and comfortable while all the ugliness of the previous night awaited her outside the coffin. Nevertheless, she had to face the woman she loved but had betrayed.

"Jeremiah?"

"Yeah?"

"I need to talk to her alone. You have to go away for a little bit."

"I get it. Best I kept my mouth shut anyways."

As they emerged from the coffins, the small group was quiet. Maisie and Horton were dressing for work, to be out of there and on their way to Venice Beach. They said little, ignoring everyone and everything in their haste to get out of the way. After Jeremiah got dressed, he slipped on his leather jacket. Sophia pushed open the coffin set aside for visitors and rolled out.

"Gotta meet up with the butcher."

Jeremiah walked out on the heels of the young couple. Tamar and Sophia stared at each other for a few seconds. Sophia cracked first.

"I'm too old for this shit." She went to the bar, pulling out a bottle of blood and sitting at a stool. "You really coulda picked a better time for this. Especially since you're in the middle of a death feud."

Tamar felt the rage rise in her. "My heart doesn't go by your schedule."

"That's how you're playing this? Anger? Resentment? Who's the wronged fucking party here, kid?"

Tamar felt her canines pop, finding herself crouching and ready to fight. Sophia just laughed at her.

"Put that shit away before you get hurt."

When the rage subsided, all that was left was void. She crumpled to the ground, overcome by all the feeling swirling inside.

"There was no intention. No malice. I just acted."

"Like I said last night, I saw this coming. I just thought the break-up would be on my terms. I'm just learning being in control doesn't mean you have control." Sophia laughed. "I didn't ask for any of this, but I still feel the need to take charge. So I blame me. And you. And him. All of us get some. But blame is useless. It doesn't make anybody happy. Blame is the bitter aftertaste of the chocolate instead of remembering the sweet." She chugged the bottle to the bottom. "Right about now is when I start missing whiskey."

Tamar agreed. Tequila and beer wouldn't solve this problem but would at least numb the pain. She got her own bottle of blood and sat on the other side of the bar, intentionally giving Sophia some distance. "What do we do about the *bruja*?"

"What we've done before. Take the fight to her."

"A challenge?"

"Yeah. It'll be ugly. And we may lose a few friends. But she's not gonna stop until she gets her war, so let's stop avoiding it." Sophia looked like she was doing math in her head. "The question is do we have enough support?"

Tamar knew her own cabal was down to five others. The war with Fudgie Whaloosie last year had killed off many of her friends and Rehab rules forbade turning any unwilling people. Maisie, Horton, and some other VampAmp people would show up, but if they were facing an army of the dead, they'd need more help. "Will any other cabal join in?"

Sophia listed all the other cabals in her head. She said, "The Black and Whites won't." That group of former actors wanted to pretend they were still '40s tough guys and gals. "Their part in the Fudgie battle soured them for any other struggles."

Tamar thought for a second. "The Glamazons don't care. They only want to party to their weird dance music. Plus, they don't like not being able to hunt."

Sophia snickered. "Sandy's O.C. bunch would probably complain about the drive."

Tamar laughed at those yuppies commuting for a rumble. It was ridiculous. "That leaves the Bomb Squad." Tamar's ex was the head of the cabal, but he also died fighting Fudgie.

"I haven't talked to them in forever."

"I think they still blame me for Alpha's death, but they're the ones I want next to me in a fight."

"Okay, we'll go see them. But first things first. Let's go knock on the witches' door."

"Should we bring Jeremiah?"

"No. Just us. Let's take care of business."

They took to the air in bat form, better than driving Sophia thought because she didn't have to talk anymore. Sophia felt simultaneously like a dam wanting to burst and someone who wanted a great deal of silent alone time. She had put up a good front with Tamar and Jeremiah, but now the aches settled in. Still, ending the war took precedent on the trip to Aida's apartment.

They landed at the corner, transformed back to human form, and went to the building's entrance. The front door had a buzzer system and they called for Aida.

"Hello?"

Tamar held the phone attached to the buzzer box. "Look out your window." Tamar turned, watching Sophia wave up at the window.

"You here to kill us?"

"Not yet. Come down for a talk. No violence."

Aida hung up without saying goodbye, so Tamar retreated to where Sophia stood. After a few minutes, Aida came down with Spex and Mina in tow. All three witches brandished silver daggers.

Tamar laughed. "I said no violence."

Her chuckling seemed to infuriate Aida even more, "Like I can fucking trust you."

"Word. I'd do the same." Tamar paused. "Look, we know what you want and we're here to offer it to you."

"The fuck does that mean?"

"This is a formal challenge. You want war, so let's get it on." Tamar looked at Sophia who nodded. "Name your time and place."

The three women pulled back. The black one seemed to be arguing with them, but the other two had made the decision. "Fine. One week. Forest Lawn Cemetery in Glendale."

Tamar looked at Sophia. The older vamp said, "Agreed. But we know why you're choosing that place. And we aren't scared."

"You will be." But Tamar could see the cracks in Aida's facade. The little witch was unsure if she had the power to win.

With the challenge accepted, Tamar and Sophia took back to the sky as was their plan. No need to taunt the coven lest they get some advantage. But Tamar worried as they flew back to the bar. Sophia had showed them an ace. Aida knew she was vulnerable and would be desperate to fix her faults. And desperate people often overcorrect. She hoped they were strong enough to resist.

After the vampires left, Aida felt worried for the first time since she'd awoken to her magic. The necromancy experiment scared her, making her unsure if they could pull off using the dead as an army. If they took on the vamps just with magic, she was sure they'd lose. Probably die in the attempt, also.

So she felt she needed to conquer the death magic, or at least get good enough at it that she could use it like she needed it.

The trio were humming with energy now that a battle date had been set. The next day, Spex decided to head down to Compton and see Ibrahim. They all definitely needed him preparing. Exactly what they didn't know, but they thought he would have some ideas, hopefully good ones.

Mina's recent breakthrough with fire magic had been good, but she was still having trouble retaining access to her source.

"I can only do it when I'm enraged. Not, like, angry, but full on crazy mad."

Aida knew words wouldn't help, but she had to try. "You know that isn't sustainable. This might be one for books. Do you think you could find some new research?"

"I joined a magic Reddit. I'm totally anonymous, but they help with spells and the like. They don't have the connection we have, but they have good tips for living. Maybe somewhere in there I can find something that works for me."

While Mina retreated to her room to the warm glow of her computer, Aida felt the need to get outside. Since moving into the apartment, she'd missed the one thing she like about homeless life: the wandering. She'd gotten to know so many weird crannies of downtown, but this neighborhood was a mystery. She laced up her boots, filled her backpack with magical gear, and went out into the streets.

Even during the day, she could feel the tension of the changing neighborhood. The mostly Mexican bar across the street—although they still wouldn't sell her liquor—had the feel of the old way: grungy, neon lit, catering to those with only a few bucks but a big thirst. But up the way was a new bar draped in the millennial outfit: multiple microbrews on tap in styles Aida had never heard of, cocktails starting at fifteen bucks, and a food menu featuring five different versions of tater tots.

In her mind, she called it the Columbus bar because it definitely catered to those who wanted a funky, offbeat experience without having to actually interact with the locals. But soon wouldn't they be the locals and the Mexicans would once again have to relocate to another watering hole? Aida wasn't sure, but it did seem like Los Angeles was becoming a giant country club and no poor people were allowed to join.

Aida had no idea where she was headed, so she decided to touch some nature. The park at the corner of Adams and Hoover would be empty right now as school was in and lunch was still a few hours away. She thought she might see some young mothers or such hanging out with toddlers, but she would have a little place to meditate in the grass.

Though mostly filled with children's areas where swings, slides, jungle gyms, and twirling rides predominated, Aida found a small concrete table underneath a craggy, leafless tree which looked right out of a witchy fairy tale. She went up and touched it, seeing if some of the wood magic pulsed through the branches. While she couldn't access it for spells, the old trunk still pulsed with a faint aura, ready to return when the rare rain would fall.

Aida knew she would find some key to why she was here but didn't think it would be in the trash. Nevertheless, the spark brought her over to a can filled with fast food wrappers and empty beer bottles. On the far side where she hadn't seen before lay a squirrel corpse, stiff with dried blood along its mouth.

Since this part of town had a big rat problem, Aida assumed this poor creature ate what was meant for its rodent cousin. Still, this was her chance to see if Quetzalcoatl's magic was a blessing or a curse.

She reached into her backpack. She used the knife to create a power circle, mindful to make sure it was complete. She still had a small amount of masa, but she had sealed the cut in her palm with Krazy Glue. She felt she didn't need much, so she pricked the tip of her index finger for a few drops of the necessary blood. She put the corpse into the middle of the circle and started praying, looking around first to make sure no one was looking at her.

Because she had direct access to the skin and bones, the spell worked a lot faster. Within thirty seconds, she had the corpse up and bounding around within the circle. But the same disappointment was there. She tried contacting the animal's mind but couldn't penetrate the screeching spiritual noise. But she knew, just knew, deep within herself that there must be some sort of control she could exert over these undead. She went deeper into her meditations, trying to reach deep into the earth to find a way to communicate with these zombies.

As her consciousness went deep into the earth, past the grass roots system, into the dirt, deep within to the sedimentary rock that still had memory of the shifting plates and other earthquakes, something opened up and she fell into a psychic chasm.

When she hit the ground, she looked up. She was outside Tonantzin's pyramid. The Mother had summoned her.

Aida picked herself up then entered the doorway. The usual feelings of peace and love had been replaced by something cold and unwelcoming. The pyramid felt hollow and vacant as if Aida were a stranger and an unwelcome one at that. She looked to the statue but felt the simmering rage emanating from it like a boiling mist.

"Mother?" Aida's voice sounded so small.

"You cannot call me by that name anymore. You have forsaken me."

"No! I still hold you above all. You are the light of the world. Of my world!"

"You have chosen to use others' magic instead of mine. You take what should be a boon to humanity and use it for devious purposes. The magic you use is profane and you will no longer use me to access it."

"But you gave me my mission."

"No, I gave you my magic. You are the one who wants to destroy the nightwalkers. While they are not my children, I never commanded you to be their undoing."

"But I need you. I need to feel the world through you."

"You may think yourself old, but you are a child. And children need to learn that actions take precedence over words and those actions have consequences."

"What does that mean?" Aida sounded desperate, but her mind was slowly coming around to what the goddess meant. The open door was closing.

"It means you must return to the beginning. You are not banned from my garden, but you are expelled. You will have to work hard and realign yourself with my power."

"How long will that take?"

"Even I don't know that. But the chance remains it may be never."

Aida felt something detach within her. She felt like she was at the bottom of the pool and had to get to the surface before drowning. Her consciousness floated upwards, her soul screaming for one last word from Tonantzin, but none was forthcoming.

When she awoke, she sat straight up and gasped for breath. She looked to the squirrel corpse, now lifeless and dead again. She looked to her hands, but all she could see was flesh. She could detect no aura and she couldn't feel the pulsing surges of power which had been her constant companion over the time of her reawakening. The contact to the divine was severed. She had no magic. She was normal.

She cried all the way home. Not sobbing, but a constant trickle as if the tears were the last fragments of her spirituality. When she returned to the apartment, she found Spex and Ibrahim had returned. When Mina came out of her room and looked into Aida's eyes, she paled. She could see the empty vessel in front of her.

Once they all heard the story, Ibrahim stood and took Aida's hands.

"They've been doing this your way for a long time. But now we see it hasn't worked. So we need a new plan, but I'm here to tell you I know what's what. What works. We're gonna take out them vamps and we're gonna do it my way."

He circled around and looked all three in the eyes.

"Come tomorrow, I'll initiate you all into Voudon and we'll let the power of the *loa* fill you. We'll set the zombies against the vampires. Hell, maybe we'll send the zombies after the whole damn city. But when this is all over, we'll have the power. And Hell will come to those who want to take it away."

Three months had passed since Tamar had seen Tamika, the head of the Bomb Squad, the African American cabal headquartered in South L.A. They had been hanging out regularly after Sophia took care of the Fudgie problem. Since The Bomb Squad had been led by men since their founding and Tamika was having a hard time keeping control as a woman, Tamar had been there to help show how it's done.

But as time wore on, everything L.A. led to their friendship drifting: the distance, the limited hours, the work of keeping a cabal running. They had a long running text chain, but that wasn't enough for a friendship. And Tamar needed her and her crew badly.

So she called and gave her the outline of what was going on. Tamika said their next meeting was in one day, so Tamar could come then and make her case. But Tamika warned her, "I ain't sure my people are gonna hear you."

Tamar took Sophia along, hoping her status in the vampire community would give their arguments weight, but when they walked into the headquarters, the one down Vermont that looked abandoned, she saw that the sheriff's presence might have made things worse as the attitude of the room cooled as soon as the two outsiders walked in.

Tamika gave Tamar a hug which helped break a little of the tension. Tamika addressed the room. "Some of y'all don't know Tamar, but she was Alpha's old lady when he died. She's all good here." Tamika then pointed to Sophia. "And Miss Sophia here took down Fudgie personally which was some bad ass shit."

Tamar wondered why she needed introducing, but then she took a good look around the room. Last time they'd talked, the Squad was five members, but nine sat in this room. She turned to Tamika.

"You been recruiting?"

"Had to, girl. Once you get below five, shit just gets weak." Tamika turned to Sophia. Tamar could hear her voice change, a code switch when talking to the white woman. "We followed all the guidelines to the letter. Everyone is here voluntarily, and they know we don't hunt humans for food."

"I would never doubt you." Sophia was always so smooth. Tamar liked how she fit herself into every situation. But still, her status might work against her tonight.

Tamar looked around the room at the newest members. This was a completely different scene than the original Squad. They'd been turned *en masse* from a '90s gang. These newest ones didn't have that same gangsta hardness. No, these looked like outcasts and weirdos. Nerds for lack of a better word.

She thought about her own cabal. They were also down to six, but if she went recruiting, she probably wouldn't get volunteers from the *cholo* sectors. They all wanted money and violence. If she were to find new Muertos, it would probably be those emo kids who got beat up for wearing mascara and all black. Kids like Aida. Her suppressed guilt rose to the surface for a second, but she let it sink back down. She had business.

Tamika called the meeting to order, then let Tamar speak. Tamar was nervous, more so than usual, because she knew how important this was. Her strength was action not words, but she needed to put her heart into it. She started with the facts.

"A little while back, I got into it with one of my neighbors, a human. She was this little girl, y'know, just out of high school and all. I didn't really know her, but some things went down. Some of you guys remember the brawl at my house when we learned Fudgie was gunning for all of us. She was there and got attacked and ended up in coma.

"Her brother, another kid, thought he was tough enough to defend her. He came to my house ready to fight—"

"You beat his ass?" This came from a recruit Tamar didn't know.

"Hell, yeah." Tamar smiled but then realized this wasn't what she wanted to say. "But that was a mistake. 'Cause now the girl showed up later wanting to kill me. My brother caught her breaking into our house, so he did what he thought was necessary. He told me he buried her in the desert and that was supposed to be that.

"But what we didn't know was she was into magic. Into it strong. She came back way more powerful and with a beef. Not just with me but with all vamps. She's gotten so powerful that she's gonna sick zombies on us."

The group couldn't help but laugh. Tamika even smiled, though she tried to hide it. "Get the fuck outta here. Zombies? What, y'all ran into some voodoo shit?"

"I've seen it." Sophia jumped in. "And yes, they have a Voudon helping them. But we have two advantages. One, they don't know how to control the zombies. And two, they don't have any idea how many we are."

Tamika bit her lip, looking like she had something to say but didn't want to. She let another longtime Bomber Queen Cee speak for her. "Shit, here we go again."

"What do you mean?" Sophia looked genuinely confused, but Tamar could sense what was coming.

"I know who y'all got. You got the Muertos ready to fight and now you want us. How we always on the front line in these supposed wars? How come we gotta put our asses on the line while all y'all O.C. people drive your Beemers around?"

"That's not true," Tamar said. "The VampAmp people are with us."

Queen laughed. "The ones who look funny at us when we go to their club?"

Tamar turned to Tamika. "Is that true?"

Tamika shrugged. "Not everyone. Jeremiah cool. But there's some deep racial shit there that ain't going away."

Sophia put her hand over her face. "We're always in bubbles, aren't we?" She looked to the cabal. "I've done my best here, but I know it's not good enough. We got you in the microloan system, we try and help out, but... damn, if it don't die hard."

Sophia looked overwhelmed, so Tamar put her hand on her shoulder then whispered, "You gotta let me do this." Sophia nodded, so Tamar stood tall.

"Sophia's good people. When Fudgie was around, we all know that the criminal element infected the Bomb Squad. Not once but twice did this cabal stab her in the back. But she never gave up. Tamika, you feel heard at the meetings when Sophia is around?"

Tamika nodded. It wasn't fierce agreement as Tamar could see Tamika wasn't sure where she was going.

"She's the best of us. Has been since she got here. But that's the real problem, ain't it? She ain't from here. She didn't grow up in South Central or Boyle Heights or Compton. She didn't have the white cops all up in her face just for standing on a corner. And she sure as hell didn't feel the rage that made us burn down our own neighborhood 'cause we never really felt like it was ours to begin with.

"And now the real funny thing is happening, right? All the people from Hollywood and the Valley, they're looking at our homes and going, damn! That's what I want. Ready to take it all away once again 'cause we don't have the money to stop them. And it was only ours when they didn't want it.

"So listen to me. These witches, they look like us. And they're trying to tell us the same thing: you don't belong. You don't deserve what you have. You're parasites on our earth. I'm not telling you to fight because the white vamps don't want to. I'm telling you that what we have is ours. I got mine. You got yours. And this is the one time I'm gonna keep what's mine. I'm gonna fight because my life is on the line. And nobody gets to make that choice but me."

As Tamar finished, she saw it had worked. She turned to Tamika. "You with me?"

"Damn straight!" The spiritual fire filled the room and soon Tamar and Tamika were discussing strategy. Tamar saw Sophia backing away and went over to her.

"Don't you want in on this?"

"You're in charge here. I think my fight my be different."

After all that fire, Tamar was ready to pull Sophia's head off. She whispered to keep the camaraderie together. "You ain't fighting?"

"Remember the Solstice? How I tapped into the voodoo within me? I have a feeling my struggle will be there. In the spirit world." Sophia looked her dead in the eye. "I will never abandon you. I will be putting body and soul on the line. Please don't doubt me now. Too much is riding on this."

Tamar nodded. Sophia had never run, not even when that would have been smart. But now Tamar was left with a real challenge. The one with the most power might be off the board. Did she have enough for this or was she fooling herself? She needed to see everybody in one room. Then she could know how this would end. She hoped she saw victory, but it was all too unclear right now.

Chapter Nineteen

They were each given a task. Ibrahim knew that Spex already had a connection to Shango, so they would spend the day going to botanicas to make sure they had the correct supplies for the ritual. Aida and Mina had their own items to collect, but they were also tasked with research. If they were to become *chevals* like Spex had temporarily been with Shango, they would have to know exactly who they would be connecting with.

Aida didn't take long to find her *loa*. Even the most cursory search would have led her to Erzuli Dantor, especially after seeing her picture. She was almost exactly like Tonantzin, so Aida thought she'd found her connection. Reading deeper, Aida found she was a mother character, a fierce agent of protection who would do anything in a fight to save those on her side. The picture showed her looking like the Lady of Guadeloupe but with two parallel scars on her right cheek. She held a girl baby, so not the baby Jesus. The little one was Anais and was integral for communication with Dantor: the *loa* had had her tongue severed and was therefore mute, so Anais had to do the talking.

After she made sure she had the right tools for her initiation, she took the Metro into downtown to get to Santee Alley where she and Spex had made their first purchases together. But instead of raw materials, she was looking for just the right doll to be Anais' avatar. In a small little toy store, not much bigger than her parents' closet, stuffed to the brim with knockoff faces from famous cartoons, she landed on a fake Dora the Explorer. Aida was sent back to childhood when that little face was the only Hispanic one she could relate to. She had spent so many afternoons with Dora and Diego that, even though it may not be culturally correct, Aida bought the doll. Hopefully, Erzuli Dantor was feeling ecumenical tonight.

She arrived back at the apartment at the same time as Mina. Her usually pouty face was gone, replaced with a sly smile. Aida wanted to ask her if she'd been with a boy but saw the bags full of clothes

Mina carried. No, she had something planned for tonight and it made the young woman happy. Aida was glad just for that.

Finally, the sun went down and they were ready for the ceremony. Ibrahim had brought his conga drums, which would power the ceremony, and many different accoutrements. He set up the circle with a small altar in the middle. There he placed a bottle of rum, another of Florida water, a sand-filled bowl for the incense sticks, a cigar, and five candles of differing colors. He prayed softly, whispering to himself as he lit everything including the cigar. He'd chosen a cheap one and the musky scent quickly filled the closed room alongside the perfumey nag champa incense. Aida placed her ceremonial dagger on the altar as he said she would need it.

Spex gave Aida a red bandanna. "Ibrahim said for you to dress in white and wrap this on your head."

Aida went and changed into her only white clothes, a linen dress like the kind she used to wear to church when she did that sort of thing. She bought it for nostalgia purposes but hadn't worn it since. With the head scarf, she thought she looked like some kind of Latin revolutionary, ready to storm the capitol. She thought it made a certain amount of sense for what was to come.

As she came out of her room holding the Dora doll, she saw Spex holding her Shango mask and the ax. Ibrahim took their hands individually and rubbed the Florida water underneath their wrists right where veins met skin. Aida had never used this stuff before, the cooling feeling of the evaporating alcohol pleasant. It smelled citrusy, with some flowery and spicy notes. Both of them sniffed at it, smiling at the pleasant feelings.

They both looked as Mina's door slowly opened. The smile on her face was huge as she finally seemed to be outwardly expressing her inner feelings. Her eyes had been blackened in ovals past her eyebrows. Her clothes included a top hat and a full tuxedo jacket which hung to the back of her knees. Her belt was plastic skulls—maybe she got them from a Halloween store or something—while she carried an oversize fork and knife. Ibrahim applauded the outfit.

"Yes! Baron Kriminel, the leader of the zombies. You chose well, kid." Ibrahim took his seat behind the congas. "Let's get started."

He began the invocation slowly, his hands softly tapping the drumheads. After about thirty seconds, he sped up, slapping harder and creating a ringing rhythm. Aida could feel herself swaying. How much was her grooving and how much was the spirits surrounding her she couldn't tell, but the smoke and the beat and perfume were all intoxicating.

Ibrahim let out a yell, then sang out, "I call upon the *loa* to feast on our sacrifice. Be pleased with our offerings as we open up to your visitation."

He pointed to Aida, having her move forward and into the circle. He continued, "I call upon Erzuli Dantor, our mother, she of the red eyes, protector of our children, the spirit of vengeance. Come join us."

The hip swaying became more rocking. Aida hadn't felt anything like this, not even when The Mother was initiating her way back when. She trembled as waves of passion rocked through her. She felt so many emotions simultaneously: anger, obstinacy, compassion, and hatred all flooded through her. Her shoulders spasmed as she tried to contain it all.

Ibrahim chanted as she felt the spirit descend upon her. "Seven stabs of the knife! Seven stabs of the sword!"

She felt compelled to pick up the knife, unsheathe it, and jab it into herself. She cut her right thigh, just above her left knee, the back of her left hand, and into her chest right on the sternum. The last two swipes were to her face, slicing twice in the same spot on her cheek as the Dantor picture she'd looked up.

She felt the pain but didn't feel bothered. In fact, it strengthened her, the adrenaline flowing as each wound throbbed. She found herself dancing wildly as Ibrahim's beat matched her every step.

She looked at the doll and felt a psychic connection. She could barely hold the doll aloft from fear, but the voice, not the one from television but a newer one with a French accent, calmed her. "Child, you have been hurt. You sought protection from the wrong mother. You should have come to me first."

"Tonantzin called out to me."

"She spoke first, but I shall speak loudest, even though I am mute. You desire vengeance, so you shall have it. I will guide your hand." The doll hadn't changed at all, but Aida could feel the *loa's* energy pulsing within it.

"What do I need to do?"

"Just open yourself to me, body and soul, and Mother Dantor will do the rest. Just remember to bring your knife and a bowl to the fight."

With that, Aida felt the spirit rise and leave her. She collapsed in the circle, but she knew how to get back to Dantor when the time came.

Aida left the circle, placing the doll down as she got to the end of the room. She wouldn't need to talk to Dantor anymore tonight. She looked to her arms and legs—the wounds were gone! She wanted to rub all the spots, but she needed to pay attention to the next ride.

Mina's turn was next. Ibrahim changed the beat. Somehow, darkness filled his hands even without the obvious change of a guitar or piano. This beat hit at odd points and the timbre was deeper, threatening. His chant changed also.

"Kill the pig! Eat the pig!"

The most dancing Aida had seen out of Mina was some twisting to electronic beats, but now she moved like a tribal warrior. Up on her toes, she jumped from one foot to the next, springing with each movement. She swung the eating utensils in broad backs and forth as if she wanted to carve the air for her dinner. Aida could sense her aura deepening. The *loa* was within her and he was dark. The deepest black Aida had ever seen surrounded her friend, even to the point of covering her skin. Finally, she saw only a living shadow, its maw open and ready to swallow everything. It felt similar to the hunger of the zombies but infinitely deeper. The baron was a hole that never could be filled. Aida was glad to have him on her side because this was fear incarnate.

Now it was Spex's turn. Aida could see fear in her face. She knew Spex had been wavering. Was all this too much for her? She hoped not because Shango had almost done what they needed. If he—and Spex—weren't at the fight, she wasn't sure they could win.

Spex was flat out terrified. Her initial possession by Shango had been empowering, but these new spirits looked so dangerous. Aida's was scary enough with the stabbing and the doll, but Mina's was another level of horror. Spex worried this would complete Mina's trip from depressed Goth to full-on psycho.

But the drums rang out, Ibrahim mimicking thunder very well, she entered the circle. She pulled the mask down over her face and drew the ax. Ibrahim chanted for her now. But she couldn't hear any

English words. She wasn't sure if he was speaking Creole or Yoruba or what. Nevertheless, she still felt herself moving with the beat.

Whereas before she had lost consciousness while being ridden, she now felt herself transported. All vision of the apartment was gone. She found herself sailing in a deep blue sky, flying as easily as a bird and drawn to a looming cloud formation, dark and pregnant with storm waters. She crested the edge, seeing a large man sitting on a throne. His proud face seethed with rage.

"You took so long to return to me, daughter. But you come back with this insult!"

"What're you talking about?"

Shango's laugh was brimming with contempt. "You are so untrained, you don't even know how you err. You ask me for assistance at the same time as one of the Ghede! They aren't worthy to occupy the same space as me."

"Who are you talking about?"

"The baron. Captain Zombi."

"You mean Kriminel?" Spex was struggling to remember all the names.

"Mark my words. Mingling with such filth will only bring you regret. And your first regret will be on my behalf. You aren't worthy to call upon me."

Spex felt an invisible force strike her in the chest. She was pushed over the cloud's edge into the open sky. But her flight was gone, replaced with falling. She lost all control as she plummeted.

She awoke when she hit the ground. She had fallen on her shoulder, the pain shooting all through her left side. But what shocked her the most was the split in her mask, broken in two right down the middle.

Aida's jaw hung low and she pointed at the ax. "Are you...?" She couldn't even finish the sentence.

Ibrahim hovered over her in the next second. "You aren't hurt?"

"Just my shoulder."

Aida looked concerned. "You swung the ax into your face. I don't know how, but the mask offered protection. Still, what did you see?"

"Shango rejected me. He said I wasn't worthy follower."

Ibrahim smiled cautiously. "Ah, I thought this might happen. We'll have to find someone else. Maybe Brigette or Brave—"

"No! No more!" Spex stood, holding her shoulder. "We've already gone too far. Look at us. We were supposed to be doing magic. Now we're a bunch of killers and zombie captains and all sorts of shit I can't fathom. I can't do this. I just fucking can't."

She saw Aida reach out to her, but Ibrahim inserted himself between them. "If you can't believe, then go. We're going to the crossroads here, not some picnic. To beat death, you must become death. And if you can't do it, then walk away."

She turned and looked at Mina who wore a thick frown. She had already kicked Spex out. She looked at Aida, the one who started all this. She couldn't look Spex in the eyes.

Spex walked out the door with no hesitation.

Spex felt bad about abandoning her friends and her uncle like that, but this had gone far enough. The gods, specifically Shango, were telling them this was a bad idea, but those three back there would only listen to those who agreed with them. The time for debate was over and Spex had lost.

She ran multiple blocks before she was convinced they weren't following her. She crossed over the interstate to Figueroa Street, the commercial strip right alongside USC, where she could be seen and not attacked. She called Rosalinda to see if they could meet, the older woman saying to go to her shop. Spex asked if Sophia could join and Rosalinda said she would call but could not make guarantees.

"I need to speak with her quick, but at the very least, I need to get away from the coven."

She called a rideshare which brought her to Eagle Rock but had to wait twenty minutes until Rosalinda showed up.

"I'm sorry, *miha*, but I don't move as fast as I used to." As Rosalinda put the kettle on, she addressed Spex's biggest worry. "Sophia will be here soon. But in the meantime, relax and tell me the whole story."

After listening to what Spex said, Rosalinda chuckled softly. "So they are *chevals* now, huh? After all this time with The Mother, she jumps to the next god who will give her power?"

"Aida hasn't been able to hear no for a very long time."

Rosalinda nodded. "She must learn, as you are presently, that sometimes no is the most important word we can hear."

Spex felt relieved that Rosalinda sided with her instead of her niece, but slowly it dawned on her that most of her own actions have been suspect. She turned to Rosalinda. "Why do you trust me now?"

"I have a certain level of empathy. I knew when Aida was lying to herself. And your own delusions, yes. But I can see you believe what you are doing is right." Another sly smile creeped out. "Just like when you said all vampires must die."

Spex felt that sting but kept her mouth shut. Nothing she said would change the situation. Any explanations were obvious.

Spex heard a knock on the door and Rosalinda brought Sophia in to join them. After the vampire heard Spex's tale, she looked nervous.

Sophia said, "That means when they bring forth the zombies, they'll be able to control them. At least somewhat."

"Probably." Spex looked lost.

"This takes away our main advantage. Now they'll be more powerful than all of the vampires in the Southland."

Rosalinda cleared her throat. "May I?"

Sophia nodded.

Rosalinda continued, "The connection between Dantor and Aida is tenuous at best. The connection my niece had to The Mother was built on a foundation of trust, rebirth, dedication, and prayer. All the *loa* have are convenience. They seek their perceived vengeance, but they won't consider these two to be important avatars."

Sophia nodded. "So you're saying if we can gain access to the spirit world and cut off the power there...?"

"That the rope will snap easily." Rosalinda's smile was sarcastic once again. "Why? Do you have access to the beyond?"

"A little. But not enough. I have yet another tough phone call to make. I'll let you know how it goes."

With that, Sophia left, leaving the two of them unsure of what was to come. But Spex had more pressing needs.

"Rosalinda, I can't go back there. And I can't go to Moms 'cause Ibrahim is there, too." Spex, realizing her living situation had once again been swept away, felt crushed with emotions. "I don't wanna go back to the shelters."

"What's the plan?"

"I didn't have time for a plan. I just got up outta there."

Rosalinda nodded as if something had been decided. "You'll stay here until after the battle. After that, you'll have to either make amends with your mother or go back to the streets."

"It's funny how easily you get comfortable. If we had been day-walking like when we first met, I never would've put up with Aida's bullshit. But then she became the boss and Mina provided the ride. I still want to do magic. Maybe even be someone like you. But I can't keep trucking down the left-hand path. It's too damn hard."

"If Aida survives this, it will probably be up to me to put her back together again." Rosalinda smiled. "But I can do the same for you. You have the talent—that initial summoning of Shango tells me so. But you need focus and, *dios mio*, you need a purpose. Together, we'll help you find that."

They spent a few minutes setting up Rosalinda's comfy chair as a sleeping place. Spex was small enough to crawl into cushions and speed off into the dreamland. When she woke up, she saw a note and a teabag on the table.

The note said, "Drink some tea and go here." A nearby address was written. After that, "I've paid for some breakfast there. You'll need to be out of the shop today as I have some appointments, but I'll see you when I'm ready to lock up at 5."

And so here she was again, having to fill her days and wait for shelter to open up at night. Maybe she'd head to USC and see if she could find Lisette and Gilly. They needed to hear her apology. Or maybe she'd head to the main library, back to the books where she first found magic to see if she could help in the fight. Or maybe she'd hoof it up to that mall at the end of Eagle Rock Blvd and see if she could get a job. All she knew was that a door had closed and now was the time to find the open window.

The time wasn't that late in Los Angeles, but Sophia remembered the two-hour difference in New Orleans. Although it was 3am down South, she still needed to talk to Lastie. She knew he was kind of a night owl, but this might be ridiculous.

Regardless, when she got back to the ZLVG Center, she pulled out her phone and called him.

"Lastie." He didn't sound like she had woken him up, so she relaxed.

"Lastie, this is Sophia." She heard a pause as if he wasn't sure who he was talking to. She jumped in. "Your vampire... friend."

"That might not be the right word for it. You still on the wagon?"

"Most definitely."

"Okay." He let out a breath. "I'm gonna assume you're not calling to see how mama and them is doing."

Sophia gave him the broad strokes of the situation but keeping out the voodoo angle at the beginning. But as she described the battle coming up, she finally dropped her name. "So do you know this guy Ibrahim?"

"Dammit. I thought we were done with this shit." He told Sophia about his run in with Israel and the zombie powder. "But you're saying they ain't using the powder?"

"No. They're going straight to the source. And since the youngsters got cut off from Tonantzin, they went to the *loa* for help."

"Ibrahim was initiating them?" Lastie's laugh was rueful. "I don't know him well, but he sure as shit ain't on that level."

"You'd know more than me. But you're getting me thinking. Our local psychic says that their connection is weak. That it could be broken. What do you think?"

"I'm gonna have to go talk to someone. I'll call you back."

Lastie hung up, so Sophia sat behind the front desk to see if she had any busy work. She knew they were meeting in the conference room, but she was surprised when Jeremiah walked out. When the rest of the group saw them in the same room, they quickly filed outside. Sophia could see Jeremiah was uncomfortable, but dammit, so was she. But she had to talk to him.

Sophia spoke first. "Why did you come here? I thought you were doing meetings at VampAmp."

"It was the only meeting on the schedule tonight. Well, in L.A. County. Plus all this fighting talk kinda got me riled. I needed to talk myself back down."

"What kind of blood did they have tonight?" Sophia wasn't really interested, but small talk was all she had available.

"Gopher. It was weird. Woody, I guess." He went to a corner and picked up a canvas bag. "This here's the last of my stuff. Okay?"

"Yeah. That's fine. You'll be at the club, right?"

"Yup." He turned to walk out, but she called out his name.

"Look. This is your first major fight as a vampire. You're going to feel way stronger than when you were a..."

"A possum?"

"Yeah. You might think no one can beat you. Not even these zombies because they're slow and they don't have minds. But right when you start feeling unbeatable is when you're the most vulnerable." She paused to find the right words but could only come up with, "I don't want you to die."

"Glad to hear that." His smirk reminded her of the hayseed she'd met last year.

"Kiss my ass. You know what I mean." She got serious again. "Tamar's already lost somebody. She needs you to be there once it's all over. So… yeah."

"Gotcha, boss. Head on a swivel. Don't get cocky." He gave her a genuine smile. "Thanks. I—"

But the phone rang then with Lastie's number and she picked it up. After she said hello, she looked up to see Jeremiah gone. Lastie had news.

"Legba showed me their connections. Ibrahim definitely didn't know what he was doing. The way they connected themselves to the *loa*, they could actually end up sacrificing themselves."

"You mean, these women could die?"

"Yep. So we'll be doing them a favor by severing the connections. It would take some work, but it's gonna take a team effort."

"So about that—"

"Oh, I know now. Were you gonna tell me you been using me to get to the spiritland?"

"I was. This isn't exactly a comfortable conversation. 'Oh, yeah, remember that time I almost killed you? Well, it helped me steal your power also. Isn't that great?'"

Lastie laughed. For real, not just a small chuckle. "You alright, vamp. I been backwards in my thinking about you. Anyway, whatever spark you have will be necessary. So when they're actually fighting, I'm gonna need you at the crossroads. *Comprendez?*"

"I haven't done that yet."

"I'll tell you all about it once I get some sleep. Talk to you later."

She hung up and looked at the schedule. Another meeting was starting in fifteen minutes and a few faces were standing around looking at their phones. The new vamp meeting leader, Timothy, a recent transplant from O.C. who wanted to be a part of VampAmp, was inside the boardroom. Sophia told him she wanted to run the meeting tonight and he deferred, although he would present the blood since he'd acquired it.

As they all settled in, she called for order. She stood, ready to testify.

"We don't talk about this enough, the fact about our long un-death. Most of you know how old I am, but sometimes even I can't comprehend it. Like anyone, I get into ruts and routines. You do things to get by and then, whoosh, 50 years are gone. All of a sudden, jazz is old people music and all of society's rules have been upended. But L.A. hasn't been like that. Oh, no."

After the knowing the chuckles, she looked around. "Most of you don't look your age. We all know that. We got a few of you pushing 70, 75 in here. And, with luck, you'll be able to double or triple that. But my question for you tonight is what are you doing with that time?

"There's gonna be a big fight this weekend. Some of you will help and some of you won't. I'm not here to say that every vampire has to jump on this cause. Some of Tamar's actions are coming home to roost. But I know why she's fighting. She and the Muertos and the Bomb Squad feel like time is leaving them behind. Some of us don't see that. We think we're all cool now and we can live and let live.

"But we have to go back to human time for a second. While 50 years could be a blur, the next ten are going to change this city. Do we let it or do we try and nudge that progress so everyone is happy? Because we have the privilege of time, why not stop and think about the future? What world do we want to have when the babies all across this city are running things?

"Some friends of mine are going to be gone in three days. Poof. Dust. They thought they'd get to see, what? Flying cars? Mars colonies? Who knows. But they won't be part of the future. We will do our best to remember them, but slowly, inexorably, memory will fade. We all lost someone in the last war with Fudgie. I'm asking you to remember them now and think what they would have wanted for the future and do right by them. Because while we have more time than the normals, we still only really have today."

As Sophia brought them together for convergence, she could see her words hit home. Now she would have to do right by herself and make sure to complete the task in front of her.

Chapter Twenty

Spex was gone. Aida would just have to deal with it. It seemed such a waste to go through so many life changes with someone, to get so close she thought Spex was a part of her. Being abandoned hurt all the more.

Could Aida blame her though? She'd also just been rejected by the very *loa* who first gave her magic. Aida did pause to think about it, but she had a new power in her life. Maybe after this war the two could reconcile, but the conflict was on the horizon. She had to put her mind to the bigger task.

More to the point, Aida saw the excitement brimming within Mina and Ibrahim. Those two had done the work and were ready to fight. She couldn't put them aside for doubts and speculations. The time had come for action, to exact revenge on that vampire and work toward ridding the world of their plague. This would be the first of many triumphs as they fought back against the darkness.

They took the day off to scout the cemetery. The sprawling grounds would be good as Mina, through her connection to Kriminel, could sense so many bodies ready to help them out. The control ability, which had slipped through Aida's fingers before, came naturally to Mina. She had a better vision of battle plans, strategy, and attack points that the old her would never have known.

The three had dinner at a small diner in Glendale right across from the yards. From there, they hoped it would be easy to sneak in. They talked while the sun set.

"I wish this burger were more rare." Mina tore into her dinner like a dog at a bowl. Aida remembered how little meat she used to eat. Kriminel was filling her every action.

"I'll be ready with the magic," Ibrahim said. "I can raise the army if you two direct it."

Aida thought that attitude was cowardly, but then realized how old Ibrahim was. He may have looked younger, but he was in his 70s. Standing up to a vampire would be tough for a *cheval*. As long as he could keep the waves of dead rolling, he would contribute.

Finally, the sun went down. Ibrahim raised himself up from the seat.

"Let's get there first. We'll want every advantage."

They went to the gate. It was higher than they had imagined, a brick wall with wrought iron spikes on top.

"How are we ...?" Ibrahim seemed deflated. Aida guessed the climb would seem impossible to someone older.

"Hold on." Aida may not have had contact with Tonantzin anymore, but she still knew the air spells. With a big push, she created a jet plume that threw all three of them into the air and over the fence. The landing was a bit rough on Ibrahim.

"Damn ankle," he said, but he could still limp through it.

They found a spot, a crossroads between three different grave developments. From there, they could work through each layer of the dead and bring about a few different patterns. Just as they were ready to begin casting, Aida felt a tingle.

"They're here." She didn't know how she knew, but Dantor was warning her. The spirit within was ready to fight.

Tamar knew this group was the LAPD's nightmare come to life. One-third black, another third brown, and all decked in leathers and other fighting gear. Because she knew they would be dealing with monsters, they brought weapons other than their own claws: baseball bats, billy clubs, and such.

Horton even brought a samurai sword. "Doesn't do me any good just hanging on the wall, right?"

Tamar couldn't argue with his logic.

They all gathered near the gate: the VampAmp crowd pulling up in electric cars, some of the O.C. crowd in gleaming new BMWs, the Bomb Squad all piled into their Escalade. Tamar and her crowd had been dropped off in the old Chevys by her brother and a friend. She felt outclassed, but still she was in charge.

Jeremiah stood next to her with his arms crossed. She thought, *This is the weirdest rap video ever.* As they gathered around her, she told them all to get over the gate.

Each found their own way, either as bat, mist, or plain-old hops. Tamar wasn't exactly sure where the battle would go down, so she let Jeremiah do the scouting. He used his nose to pick them out.

The cemetery itself was huge. It only took up a few blocks on Glendale Avenue but stretched far into the hills. Tamar had initially decided they should walk in, but she soon changed her mind. They all took to the air in bat form, dropping to the ground right before changing. This had the desired effect as the three waiting for them looked surprised as the dozens of vampires appeared from no-where.

As soon as their feet hit grass, the older man raised his staff and starting chanting. In only a few seconds, the grounds exploded as bodies popped up, all ready to fight. The vampires numbered doz-ens, but the zombies were easily a hundred.

They set their plan in motion. The main fighting force, led by Horton, would try to stave off the zombies while Tamar and Jere-miah would attack the leaders. Jeremiah sped toward the Asian one who looked like she was doing some weird Voodoo cosplay. Tamar would head straight for Aida, hoping to maybe cut the head off quickly and end the fight.

As Tamar got close, she felt the revulsion pointed at her. The hatred coming off the young woman was beyond what Tamar had experienced before. As she got within a ten yards, Tamar could see Aida was no longer herself. She had been possessed, probably willingly.

Aida dropped to her knees before a giant serving bowl. In hic-cupping spasms, she looked like she was choking until she vomited blood into the bowl. The crimson smile on her face chilled Tamar. Aida picked up the bowl and held it out.

"Isn't this what you want? To drink of my blood and drain me dry?"

"Who are you?"

"That is not your concern. Just know that when I spill blood, I exact it in equal measure."

With that, Aida sprung at Tamar, fighting with a knife in her right hand and a wooden cane in the other. The blows came quickly and Tamar defended. She could see Aida's strategy: contain with the stick to slash with the knife. Aida moved much more quickly than any human could, so Tamar was unable to both stave off the blows and slash out herself.

A cane blow connected to the ribs, surprising Tamar. Her leather jacket kept the bones from breaking, but more connections like that would be painful and maybe paralyzing. Tamar felt a slash on her sleeve and felt the leather tear. She realized she had to throw everything she had at this girl right now.

Scratching at Aida's face with both claws drove the younger woman back. Tamar got enough of a push with multiple swipes to throw Aida back six feet, breaking up the close combat. Aida's breath was now labored, but her nerve was intact.

The girl spoke, "I see your fear, abomination. If you think your strength is enough, you are mistaken."

Tamar hoped Sophia was on her way to sever these bonds. She could see this battle ending with her getting ashed if she didn't get some help.

Sophia waited in the car outside the gate. While part of her wanted to be there in the cemetery throwing punches and directly affecting the fight, she knew that her greater purpose lay elsewhere. She texted Lastie who returned with a thumbs up. She then chanted the words he'd sent to her earlier, taking sips of rum and puffs on a cigar to heighten the effects. After about a minute, her consciousness faded from Los Angeles and she found herself elsewhere.

When she got to the crossroads, she immediately felt home. The dirt paths, about twenty feet wide, intersected at a diagonal, so if she had looked at them from the air, they would be an x instead of a t. The rest of the area was grasslands, but near the cross was an ancient cypress, bald of leaves but a tangle of branches stretching high, maybe thirty, forty feet. This looked like the flatlands just outside the swamp on the road to New Orleans from about 1880 or so.

Standing under the tree was an older black man wearing an intricately woven robe and a rope belt which held a few old-fashioned skeleton keys, each about the size of her forearm. She knew this must be Legba. As she approached, Lastie shimmered in next to her, looking like he did those few years ago: dashiki and jeans, round hat on his head, thick beard. But his feet were bare, probably from the dancing ceremony he used to reach the spirit world.

Lastie didn't say anything to Sophia, instead bowing to the old man. "I honor you, grandfather, keeper of the keys and minder of the spirit world." Lastie looked at Sophia, waving his arms at her to do something similar.

She bowed. "I honor you, Legba."

Legba gave a churlish grin to Sophia. "Ah, as usual the white people get the power without knowing the proper way. I shall accept your honor, both of you." He bowed in return. "Has the battle begun?"

Sophia nodded. "It should have started by now."

"Then follow me." He lifted the key ring and a door appeared, a simple oaken flat front with an old brass lock within it. Legba turned a key in the lock and all three were swept within. They seemed to be walking in space, literally darkness and star points surrounding them. A few giant globes glowed white, each sending out beams which connected to smaller globes. Those connections looked powerful and set, blazing without heat. Legba walked easily here, but Sophia looked at Lastie.

"Have you ever been here before?"

He looked nervous. "No."

If this was his first time, Sophia knew this was something extraordinary. She felt her stomach drop with each step forward.

After who knows how long a walk, they came upon two globes hovering near each other. The tendrils of light were much more shaky, snaky and wobbly as they connected to the smaller orbs.

Legba looked concerned. "These may look weak—and they are—but that doesn't mean it will be easy to separate them. It will take a great deal of your power, grandson." He turned to Sophia. "And it will sever our connection. Your unearned power will be lost today. Will you accept these terms?"

"Yes, I will." Sophia didn't know how this would affect her in the long run. She didn't have time to consider it. She wanted the fight back on Earth over and done with.

"Fine." Legba turned to Lastie. "Begin the spell."

Lastie began his dance and Sophia chanted. They built up a harmony, Sophia using the same method as the convergence to find the powerful spots and expand them.

"It's working," Legba said as he worked keys into the streams of light, trying to snuff them. They flickered like a shorting light bulb, but before he could sever the connection, Legba was pushed back.

A tall black man wearing a top hat, his face colored to look like a skull, stepped out of a tear in the spatial fabric. He stood between Legba and the smaller globes. "Who dares interfere with my son's affairs?"

Sophia, the chant ceased, turned to Lastie. "Who's that?"

Lastie looked genuinely scared. "Papa Ghede."

Jeremiah felt troubled. This woman—he'd have called her a girl—was such a little thing, but the fierceness she was throwing at him was overwhelming. She fought with wooden stakes which frightened him even more. One slip up and his undeath, which had only started a little while ago, would be gone.

He was supposed to take her on directly but decided to ditch the plan. He fell back to where the others were fighting, right there in the middle of the zombies, which felt safer to him. But Mina followed, pushing through the dead bodies and them giving way.

Quickly, two battle lines were formed. Jeremiah collected the vamps, moving to the point. Horton stood next to him, a weird smile on his face.

"What's up?"

"Nothing. Just that I saw Sammy Davis, Jr's grave."

"No shit?"

Here's where Jeremiah realized how transformed Mina was. She ordered the zombies into their own formations, flanking the vamps and in perfect position to pincer. Jeremiah scanned his ranks.

"We lose anybody yet?"

Horton looked over his shoulder. "I thought I saw one of the newbie Bomb Squaders dust out."

"Buddy, we're in trouble."

Mina stood back, her wicked grin turning into a joyful dance. The zombies moved in on the vamps, slowly but inexorably. Jeremiah could feel the panic running through the line.

Jeremiah yelled, "Hold on, everybody! We've got to give Sophia a chance."

Horton called over his shoulder. "Dude, I don't know—"

"Just one more minute, I think—"

Maisie called back. "We gotta get that brat. Who can do mist form?"

Jeremiah knew he was the only one who'd learned the right way. He reached out a hand to Horton. "Gimme the sword."

He felt the hilt in his hand and went to mist. He felt himself barrel through the zombies and over the top of Mina, trying to get a back strike. He formed again, but right as he was about to become solid, she pivoted back, stabbing out with the stake. He swung the sword with all his might, not knowing what the outcome would be.

Legba had looked calm—if not cheerful—during most of the journey, but now he looked angry. Sophia and Lastie backed away, although Sophia wasn't sure any distance between her and the two *loa* would make a difference if a fight broke out. But Legba leaned back into his argument.

"Ghede, I am interfering, but your son's *cheval* is improper. She's not deserving."

"Who are you to question the rites? Who are you to judge what is deserving and what isn't?"

"Who am I? The gatekeeper!"

As the two argued without getting violent—yet. Sophia whispered to Lastie, "Who's going to win here?"

"Ghede takes the souls to the afterlife, but only if Legba allows them. It's usually a matter of course, but who knows." Lastie looked on as the two got even more heated. "If it's political, it falls to Legba. But this is family. And in times like these, any worship is good."

Sophia felt desperate, in so over her head that drowning felt like the best option. But even though Lastie tried to hold her back, she pushed her way into the argument.

"Papa Ghede, you need to know what's going on down there."

She could see Ghede's anger towards Legba now boiled over onto her. "Impudent whelp! How could your words have any meaning?" He turned to Legba. "This one? This is your notion of propriety?"

Legba's smile returned. "No, she's an interloper. But if you listen, just for a few moments, then I will defer to your will. But you must act honestly. Agreed?"

Ghede crossed his arms. "Fine."

The roiling globes out beyond them still made Sophia nervous, but the tension had calmed. She had the floor.

Sophia summoned all the grace she'd learned in deferring to powerful men. They needed kid-glove handling and she honeyed her voice for the right tone to her message. "Great Papa, Mr. Lastie tells me you guide the souls to their proper place in the spiritland. Is that correct?"

"Some of them, yes."

"The young woman who calls upon your son takes advantage of

his rage. She brings the dead bodies from the ground to fight a war. A war with my kind."

Ghede nodded. "There's no fondness for nightwalkers around here. But when Kriminel calls forth the zombies, it's always for a good cause."

"This isn't a good cause. It's revenge."

"Revenge can be worth it."

She was losing him, so she turned to Legba for a second. "I know I dishonor a lot of things by being here." She turned back to Ghede. "But look into my heart. I bring honor to my world. Ask your-self—how many souls have you had to ferry from my people killing humans lately?"

"The number seems down."

"I and my friends are trying to redeem ourselves. To rise up from beasthood in order to change the way things are done. We don't need war. We need understanding. Don't let your son be a pawn in a human battle."

As she said that, one of the connections, the thinner one, popped and fizzled away like a broken balloon. Ghede, who had swung around to see it, turned back to Sophia.

"You argued your case well, vampire, but it seems our discussion is moot. The connection is gone."

Legba looked at the bigger globes. "And of that one?"

Ghede laughed. "Dantor can speak for herself." And he disap-peared into the starry background.

Chapter Twenty-One

Tamar turned when she heard the collective scream. The main battle was only twenty yards away, so she could see the mist behind Mina forming into Jeremiah. The woman stabbed with her stake, landing her shot right in Jeremiah's chest. But as his body was crumbling, the sword continued its arc. As soon as the ash hit the ground, Mina's head rolled in it.

Tamar lost all feeling in her body. For the second time, she saw the vampire she loved fall in battle. But unlike last time, this was all unnecessary, all because of the temper tantrum of the brat next to her. Tamar found herself screaming wordlessly as she swiveled to face down Aida.

But she saw a miniature version of herself staring back at her. Aida's face was also violently contorted, screaming in agony. Tamar could feel no compassion for the young woman. Yes, she'd seen the death of her friend, but Tamar had lost so much so quickly. Neither of them hesitated anymore, falling into each other so they could eliminate the source of their pain.

Tamar couldn't get past the first strikes, a flurry of punches with the knife and staff, so she fell back. She popped her jacket's collar and zipped up all the way. Her neck now protected from cutting, she charged right at Aida.

She felt all the blows coming, but even Aida's unnatural strength had no effect. Tamar kept pushing through until her hands grasped Aida's throat. Using her claws to latch on, Tamar kicked out, tripping the Aida and landing on top of her. Up on her knees, Tamar pressed harder and harder as Aida made cracking noises as she attempted to breath.

Aida stabbed one of Tamar's hands and the vampire released her grip. Feeling a great gust of wind, Tamar was blown back ten feet until her momentum gave up. Getting up on one knee, she could see Aida standing up. But as Tamar's opponent was doing so, her knees buckled like a newborn horse. She stumbled, trying to stay upright, but soon Aida was on the ground.

Tamar was unsure what happened, but she hoped Sophia was the cause of that. Time had come to finish the job.

One connection remained. Legba turned his full attention to it, asking the two of them to restart the rites. Lastie pointed toward the glowing tether.

"The energy is reversing, Papa."

"It has. Now we are working for the child's life."

Sophia needed to know. "What's going on?"

Lastie started his dance. "Dantor has become a parasite, stealing the energy instead of giving it. It's what happens when the ceremonies are incomplete."

Sophia could now see the energy river churning with most of the flow going back toward the larger globe. She started her singing and, with the confluence of Lastie's dance, she could see the connection thinning. Into that point, Legba inserted one of the keys. But he pulled back when they all heard a screeching.

A face appeared in the bigger bubble, a black woman with two scars on her left cheek. But she could form no words, only guttural cries. Another smaller face appeared in the globe, a baby who could speak.

"Papa Legba, we are here to help our child. She needs our protection. She needs our strength."

"Anais, tell your mother she who would protect now does harm. The connection is false. You know it."

"She feeds us, Papa. Aida gives, so we give back."

"You have let yourself be blinded by admiration. You have done your part, but it's over."

"We can do more. We can destroy them all!"

Legba turned to Sophia and Lastie. "She can't see reason. Push now and push hard!"

Sophia gripped Lastie's hand and the two of them created a new glow, this one red in color. Sophia sang, feeling her voice find the spots where the connection was stressed. Legba reached out to them, absorbing the new aura and infusing one of his keys with the crimson light. Dantor cried out again, but it was no use. Lastie pushed the key into the connection, turned quickly to gather the material around the key, then pulled. The flow shredded and withered. Dantor disappeared within the bubble, no longer a threat to the material world.

And then they were back at the crossroads, Legba closing the door and it disappearing into the air.

Sophia turned to Lastie. She said, "If you ever see me again, I hope you will call me friend."

"I'll do that."

Legba approached her. "I need what's mine." He placed his hand on the top of her head. "Goodbye, daughter. Stay on the righteous path."

Her vision blurred, descending into white noise like an old television on no channel. Then she blinked and she was in the car outside the cemetery.

Ibrahim went running past her. He didn't pause, just hoofing into the night. Sophia guessed the worst was over, so she went into the grounds. The place was a mess with hundreds of graves overturned and piles of desiccated bones everywhere. No zombie was left standing, just her group of vamps looking exhausted. As she approached, she saw Tamar on top of Aida, choking the young woman in a fury. Sophia turned to Horton.

"Why is no one stopping her?"

Horton's face was so angry it scared Sophia. "Because they killed Jeremiah. She's getting what she deserves."

Sophia charged up, hoping she wasn't too late. There had been enough death and killing for one day.

Aida couldn't breathe. The vampire's grip was too strong. But the power Dantor had given her was still alive. A stab to the hand and a wind spell cleared away her opponent.

But Aida's body failed her. She hadn't seen it, but her power and her soul had been sapped by the *loa*. She could see Dantor had been doing everything she could for the vengeance, but that didn't extend to keeping Aida living. As Aida tried to stand, she found nothing left to keep her conscious.

She felt herself floating away from the body, nothing but a piece of soon-to-be rotting meat. She saw the golden tether, still connected to Dantor, pumping energy into the spiritland. She could feel the tugging even outside her body, a vacuum drawing her in. She tried to hold on, to not be swept away, but she didn't have the skills to do it. But right as she felt she could no longer resist, the connection snapped. Dantor no longer demanded her sacrifice.

But her soul still couldn't find her way back into her body. Aida realized it quickly: she was dead. Gone. This fleeting moment would be her last. As she contemplated the great void about to open up and take her in, another being entered her vision, standing over her body.

It was the deer, the one she had rejected at the beginning of her journey. It looked meek but also nurturing, smiling somehow on its non-human face.

"You can make that choice again. The Mother will forgive you."

"I... I don't know if she could ever take me back."

"She will. But the path ahead will be much harder. She won't grant much magic until you've earned it. And you will have to pray for great forgiveness to be able to do so."

"I want to live. I want another chance."

"Then you shall forgive your enemies, ask forgiveness from your friends, and start anew along the path."

"I will."

"Then go and renew your soul. Cleanse yourself in the fountain and prepare a new way."

With that, she felt the tug and soon found herself opening her eyes. She lay staring at the stars, feeling the cleansing breaths enter her lungs and the blood pumping through her system again.

But as she went to sit up, something flashed before her eyes and she felt choked once again. Tamar was on top of her again, trying to take away her recently renewed life.

"Die, die, die, dammit!" Her former neighbor was beyond talking, beyond negotiation.

As she struggled more, stars coming at the edge of her vision as the air was pressed out of her body, she heard a voice crying out to Tamar. Over and over, that voice called out the vampire's name, but the pain didn't stop.

But the grip was released and the air flowed again. She sat up to see Sophia had pulled Tamar up and was holding her above her head like a wrestler ready to bodyslam an opponent.

"It's over," cried Sophia. She looked to Aida. "It's over. Right?"

Aida nodded.

Sophia cried out again. "If any of us ever see you again, you're dead. Now leave here knowing that our fight has ended."

Aida stood up and ran. Out onto the street, down San Fernando Road, never stopping despite her exhaustion. She had one spot in mind and wouldn't stop until she made it there: Rosalinda's house.

Sophia could feel Tamar wriggling as she held the younger vamp aloft. She put her down, but Tamar's anger hadn't subsided.

Yelling "No! No! No!" in a high-pitched voice, Tamar swung at Sophia who felt she could do nothing but take the blows. Two, three, four punches to the face and the sound of her nose cracking didn't stop the attack, but when Tamar's extended claw dug into Sophia's neck, as close to a kill shot as there could be, Sophia reached up and grabbed Tamar's wrist. She bent it backwards until Tamar screamed and fell to her knees.

Sophia hugged Tamar, grasping her so close it would have squeezed the air out of a human. She kissed her cheek, letting Tamar know their friendship was still strong. Tamar hiccuped with tearless misery.

"Jeremiah's gone. Another one gone."

"I know. I know." Sophia released Tamar and they sat on the grass staring at each other.

Tamar, mental exhaustion evident, whispered, "Why did you let her go?"

"She doesn't have any more magic. For right now, she can't hurt us."

"What if she tries again?"

"We kill her." Sophia reached out and caressed Tamar's cheek. "But she won't. I know she won't."

They stood and walked back to the group, assessing the final damage. Two Bomb Squaders, a VampAmp employee, and one Muerto had passed. Sophia walked away and knelt by Jeremiah's ashes.

She wanted to keep her body up, but she couldn't. She collapsed in the grass. Memories of David and Chip flowed past, but then Jeremiah filled her brain. The possum changing, her saving him in Griffith Park, his goofy smile and stupid jokes. All of this overwhelmed her until she felt arms drawing her in. She opened her eyes.

It wasn't just Tamar. It was Maisie and Horton. It was everyone.

She could see how many lives Jeremiah had touched, maybe not hundreds or thousands, but it was more than enough to show how great he had been. They spontaneously formed a circle, Sophia leading a convergence that rang into the night.

They went to the bar after, drinking blood to replenish their power and telling stories. Every fallen vampire got their due, but the final tales were of Jeremiah. With the imminent sun, they all repaired to the coffins. Tamar touched Sophia's shoulder.

"Will you share a coffin with me?"

Sophia's maternal instincts kicked in as they climbed into the box. She took the big spoon, holding Tamar by the waist. Before they blacked out, Sophia closed her eyes and said, "I think things have to change."

"I think you're right. What do you want to do?"

"I'll tell you about it tomorrow."

And the darkness descended.

Even though it was a long walk, Aida made it to Eagle Rock within an hour. The sun was peeking over the mountains, turning the valley below purple and orange. Her aunt's little shop was closed, but she looked through the window on the off chance the older woman was around. She saw the room to the back door open, someone's foot on the recliner. She guessed by the skin tone it was Spex. She knocked loudly and soon she was let in.

"You gonna kill me?" Spex looked groggy but wary.

"No. Mina's dead. Ibrahim is gone. I got nothing left within me."

"You want some tea? That aunt of yours been pouring it down my throat."

"Yeah. Let's do it."

Over three pots of the various flavors, Aida told the final story. Spex looked sorry about Mina but said, "Something evil has been boiling in her a long time. I wish she was here to go back to who she was. It's all too sad."

Aida slumped over as she sipped her hot brew. "Gilly and Lisette were right. All of this could've be done better."

"Listen to me. You were right about that vamp. She needed to learn you can't just stomp normal people. But we can see what magic wants us to do. To move slowly, to influence, to guide. All these lightning strikes are full of energy at the levels that we can't do."

Spex finished her cup and refilled. "Look at Rosalinda. She's seen some powerful stuff. But she lets the cards guide her hand. And so far, she ain't been wrong once."

They had chosen herbal teas, so they soon curled up together and went back to sleep. At 10 am, Rosalinda came in and found the two of them still out. She puttered around, trying to be quiet, but soon they were awake. Aida stood and enveloped her aunt in a huge hug.

"I'm happy to see you alive, mi amor," Rosalinda said. "Part of me was sure you'd be destroyed, either by the vampires or Dantor."

"She tried. I guess I shouldn't mess with forces I don't understand."

Rosalinda sat in her chair while they stayed on the floor. "The true lesson is this. Knowledge isn't given. It's earned. We must work at our faith, not try and get results immediately. Dantor is powerful and she deserves praise. You only wanted a car to drive. That's not worship. You'll never grow if that's your attitude." But then she winked at her young niece. "But I hear The Mother will take you back."

"How...?"

"Don't question. It's my place to know things." Rosalinda stood. "Anyway, I'm thinking our wonderful city is no longer an option for you."

"We could go back on the streets." But Aida knew that even though Spex said it, she really didn't mean it.

"What would we get? Those days were important, but we have to move on."

Rosalinda smiled. "I have a short-term destination for you. Someplace that will open your eyes and possibly your soul." They leaned forward in anticipation. "The pyramid at Chichen Itza."

Aida smiled but immediately dismissed the thought. "We can't go there. I'm dead."

"Hold on." Spex considered the whole idea. "We know a few people who are good at being dead. Maybe they could help."

Rosalinda waited for the night to come and contacted Sophia. One of VampAmp's specialties was creating identities for the undead. She agreed to help Aida.

After a few hours, they set up a drop point in San Diego. That way, Aida and Spex were out of town and wouldn't run into any hostile vamps. Rosalinda pulled them all together after she returned from errands.

"Here." She gave them a thousand dollars, enough for the train ticket and a little spending money. "You'll have to earn for yourself after that, but this is your chance to reconnect with The Mother directly. This is your true spiritual journey, one without selfish motivations. Be open to what comes and you will be rewarded. Both of you. But this is for you alone, Aida." Rosalinda removed the necklace she always wore with the icon of The Mother dangling from the end. "Your great-great grandmother gave this to me when I started my journey. My time with it is through. It's now yours to carry, to continue the family traditions. As long as you keep it close, I and your other ancestors will never be far."

Aida took it, pulling the wooden beads over her head. As soon as the mini statue pressed to her chest, she could feel the spark once more. The energy pulsed from her heart to the tips of fingers and toes, spreading the light back into her body and purging the remaining dark. Spex saw the change flash through her.

"Wow." Spex paused, but then said, "We're taking the right-hand path, correct? No more of this fucking around."

"Yes. But we starting at the beginning."

"It's worth it. Let's go."

They gave Rosalinda big hugs and she disappeared into the shop. Aida had to go back to the apartment and grab some things, but they wouldn't delay. By nightfall, they'd be out of Los Angeles. By tomorrow, they'd be in Mexico. And by the time they reached Chichen Itza, they would be ready to shed their skin and begin anew in the light of faith.

Epilogue

The news went from a local sensation all over the television to a nationwide obsession. The final title that journalists settled on was the Forest Lawn Fiasco. Nobody could understand how so much damage could be done without any witnesses. In the end, Ibrahim was arrested for Mina's murder, but even the most aggressive cable station couldn't get completely behind it.

Everyone was still laughing at the "new developments," horseshit theories thrown around by attention-seeking "experts," when Sophia came into the VampAmp offices for the last time.

With Sandy and Pamela's help, she had transferred the ZLVG name and company to VampAmp and sold the Silver Lake building which netted far above her asking price of $1 million. All that remained were a few signatures.

Pamela looked sad, but Sandy remained her salty self.

"This ain't it, babe. We got video phones now even for our cold asses. We'll keep in touch."

As they all walked out, Sophia saw Tamar hugging Maisie and Horton. Sandy tapped Sophia on the shoulder.

"She's really coming with?"

"Yeah. She needs to see something other than L.A. for a while."

They had made the plan. Sophia felt she had done what she needed to do and it was time to go back. She would find a way back to New Orleans. But Tamar kept hounding her.

All the hows and whats finally built up until Sophia said, "Just come with me." It had been an atom bomb to Tamar's brain. After some cajoling and a long, sad session with Papi, she agreed.

So as they stood around, Pamela spoke up. "Okay, girl. You've been cagey about this. What are you going to do?"

Sophia looked around and saw everyone needed to know this. "I thought about this for weeks. Back home, we've got the old way, the council way. After being out here, I see the time has come for me to end that. I'm going back to free New Orleans and then any other city that needs it. I'll need your help. I'll need the chats and comments and the social media all saying that it's good what we do.

We'll have resistance and we'll probably have another big fight, but it's the right thing to do."

The excitement was palpable and within seconds all the techie vamps were typing furiously. But Sophia called out, "Whoa! Whoa! Let me get back home first."

"Yeah," Pamela said. "One month moratorium." She turned to Sophia. "Yes?"

"Yes."

And with hugs and near tears, Sophia and Tamar headed out the door. Tamar's cousin had given her a chopped '69 Camaro all set up for emergency nights if necessary. The blue and white stripes were sharp and Sophia looked pleased that this was her ride.

As they sat in the car, Tamar said, "Okay. Now what?"

Sophia smiled as the joy finally burst out of her. "Go to I-10 and take a right."

C.D. Brown is a writer, filmmaker, and educator from New Orleans, La. His books include *Vamp City* and *Fate's Stiletto*, and he edits and publishes *Dirty Magick Magazine*. He has written and directed two feature films, including *Angels Die Slowly* (a gothic neo-noir available on Tubi). His short fiction has been included in many recent anthologies, including *Unicorns vs Clowns In Hell*, *Gen X-ed*, and *Strange Aeon 2020*. He teaches first-year writing at Tulane and Loyola University New Orleans.

Go to dirtymagickmagazine.com/about for more info.

Message from the author:

"If you enjoyed this book or any of my others, please subscribe to *Dirty Magick Magazine.* I work very hard to publish great new stories from pros and early career writers in genres some other pubs won't touch."

www.dirtymagickmagazine.com/subscribe or go to weightlessbooks.com